BLACK DARKNESS ENVELOPED THEM. . . .

Then, just as unexpectedly, the too-bright green light returned, and by its light Bass could see a tall, slender figure standing on the silvery disc.

Slowly, the figure turned toward Bass and his men, stood for a moment staring at them while its lips moved soundlessly, then, raising and pointing a slightly belled length of metal ahead, it stepped off the disc and strode toward Bass.

He cursed himself for not bringing a pistol with him. His men might not recognize the thing being pointed as a deadly weapon, but he certainly did. It was probably one of those things called a heat-stunner, and here he was with only a sword and a couple of daggers. Nonetheless, he drew his Tara-steel sword and stepped out to meet this dangerous stranger with his weapon at low-guard.

As he began to move, the stranger called out: "Drop that sword, man, or I'll kill you!"

CASTAWAYS IN TIME #2

THE SEVEN MAGICAL JEWELS OF IRELAND

ROBERT ADAMS

A SIGNET BOOK

NEW AMERICAN LIBRARY

NAL BOOKS ARE AVAILABLE AT QUANTITY DISCOUNTS WHEN USED
TO PROMOTE PRODUCTS OR SERVICES. FOR INFORMATION PLEASE
WRITE TO PREMIUM MARKETING DIVISION, NEW AMERICAN LIBRARY,
1633 BROADWAY, NEW YORK, NEW YORK 10019.

SIGNET TRADEMARK REG. U.S. PAT. OFF. AND FOREIGN COUNTRIES
REGISTERED TRADEMARK—MARCA REGISTRADA
HECHO EN CHICAGO, U.S.A.

SIGNET, SIGNET CLASSIC, MENTOR, PLUME, MERIDIAN AND NAL BOOKS
are published by New American Library,
1633 Broadway, New York, New York 10019

First Printing, January, 1985

1 2 3 4 5 6 7 8 9

PRINTED IN THE UNITED STATES OF AMERICA

To the memory of Tim Daniels,
1955–1984

PROLOGUE

Whyffler Hall, it had once been called, the stark, rectangular tower built of big blocks of gray native stone, in centuries long past—motte, stronghold, residence of the generations who had held this stretch of the blood-soaked Scottish Marches for king after king of England and Wales. But when first Bass Foster saw that tower, it had become only a rear wing of the enlarged Whyffler Hall, a rambling, gracious Renaissance residence, its wide windows glazed with diamond-shaped panes set in lead, its inner bailey transformed into a formal garden.

From the first moment he set eyes upon it, Bass Foster had felt a strange compulsion to approach, to enter that ancient tower, that brooding stone edifice, but it was not until some years later that he was made privy to the knowledge that the very instrument which had drawn him and all the other people and objects* from twentieth-century North America to England of the seventeenth century (though an England of a much-altered history from his own world of that period) was immured within the dank cellar of the tower.

It was a savage, primitive world of war and death and seemingly senseless brutalities into which Bass and the nine other moderns were plunged, but he and most of the others were able to adapt. A woman died, one man was killed, another went mad, and a third was maimed in battle, but the

*See *Castaways in Time* by Robert Adams (Signet Books, 1982).

other six men and women managed to carve new lives and careers for themselves out of this very strange world into which they had been inextricably cast.

The arcane device spawned of far-future technology still squatted in the cellar of that ancient tower, its greenish glow providing the only light that had penetrated the chamber for the two and more generations since its single entry had been finally walled up and sealed by the authority of the then-reigning king.

Only a bare handful of living men and a single woman knew the truth of what lay beyond those mortared stones impressed with the royal seal of the House of Tudor . . . they, and uncountable generations of scuttling vermin to which the cellar had been home.

Although they welcomed the dim light cast by the chunky, rectangular, silver-gray device in what otherwise would have been utter, stygian darkness, the vermin otherwise tended to avoid it, for it often emitted sounds which hurt their sensitive ears.

But of a day, a wild stoat came from out the park and over the wall surrounding the outer bailey of Whyffler Hall. The slender, supple, gray-brown beast had no slightest trouble in moving unseen by man up through the formal gardens to the environs of the Hall itself, for he was a hunter, an ambusher, a born killer, and had ingested the arts of stealth with his mother's milk.

Near to the Hall, his keen nose detected the scent of rat, and he doggedly followed that scent a roundabout course to a burrow entry dug hard against a mossy, cyclopean stone. In a fraction of an eyeblink, the furry, snaky body had plunged into the earth in pursuit of his chosen prey.

After exploring numerous chambers—all, alas, empty of rodents—and equally numerous intersecting tunnels, the stoat found that the larger, older, most heavily traveled main burrow, which had descended to some depth, began to incline upward once more, and was soon filled with the strong scent of many rodents ahead and a wan, strange light.

The questing head the big hob stoat thrust out of the

burrow hole in the packed-earth floor of the tower cellar chanced to come nose to quivering nose with a rat that had been on the very point of entering that hole. The rat leaped a full body length backward and shrilled a terrified scream. That scream and the sudden stench of the stoat's musk initiated a few chaotic moments of rodent pandemonium, with rats of all sizes and ages and of both sexes streaking in all directions and shrieking a chorus of terror.

But fast as were the rats, the stoat hob was faster, and he had emerged into the midst of the panic and slain several smaller ones before most of the rest had found and fled down other holes. Now the only full-grown rats left in all the huge, open cellar were three which had taken sanctuary atop the glowing device, crouching and panting amongst the dust-coated knobs and levers and calibrated dial faces.

No stoat ever had really good eyesight, but their other keen senses more than compensated for this lack, so this particular mustelid knew just where those rats were, how many they numbered, their sizes, ages, sex, and degree of terror. He also knew, after a hurried circuit of the base of their glowing aerie, that there was no way he could get to and at them whilst they remained up there. Four feet straight up was simply beyond his somewhat limited jumping abilities, and the unrelievedly smooth, hard surfaces would prevent him from climbing up to his prey.

Frustrated and furious, the stoat chattered briefly to himself, then futilely jumped the less than a foot he could manage, vainly trying to get his stubby claws into the steel sides as he slid back down to thump onto the silvery disk on which the device reposed.

Feeble as had been the attempt, nonetheless, it and the sounds of it had further terrified the three rats, driving them into a frenzy which suddenly erupted into a three-way battle to the death amongst them. The squealing, biting, clawing, furry ball rolled hither and yon amongst the control switches and buttons and levers and knobs thickly scattered over the top of the device. Scaly tails lashed as the three big rats fought on, heedless of what they struck or moved, heedless now, too, of the facts that the ear-hurting noises were become suddenly constant and louder, that the greenish glow was become much brighter.

Below, the hob stoat waited, hoping that in their fury the rats would roll off to fall down within reach of his teeth.

Far and far to the south of Whyffler Hall, within the long-besieged City of London, one of those three sleek rats would have brought a full onza of gold in almost any quarter in which it chanced to be hawked, for the siegelines had been drawn tightly about that city and its starvling, frantic, and embattled inhabitants. Nor did there appear to be any hope of succor now, for the last remnants of last year's Crusading hosts were being relentlessly hunted down, while every attempt by the Papal forces to resupply the beleaguered city had been foiled, all ending in resupplying King Arthur's army instead.

In the most recent incursion of a Papal supply fleet up the Thames, young Admiral Bigod's English fleet had lurked out of sight until the leased merchanters and their heavily armed escorts were well up the river. Then, while his line-of-battle ships and armed merchant vessels trailed the foreign ships just out of the range of the long guns, a dozen small, speedy galleys issued from out certain creekmouths and immediately engaged two of the four-masted galleons that composed the van of the fleet.

Each of these galleys was equipped with but a single cannon, but these cannon were all of the superior sort manufactured at York by the redoubtable Master Fairley. The guns were breech-loaded and fired pointed, cylindrical projectiles—both solid and explosive-shell.

The well-drilled crews handled the galleys with aplomb, scooting around the huge, high-sided, cumbersome galleons like so many waterbugs, discharging their breechloaders again and again to fearsome effect into their unmissable targets, while the return fire howled and hummed uselessly high over their heads.

After watching his companion galleon shot almost to

splinters, before either a lucky shell or one of the several blazing fires reached her magazine and she first exploded, then sank like a stone, Walid Dahub Pasha saw his own galleon's rudder blown away by one of the devilish shells. At that point, he ordered most of his men up from the gundecks, to be put to better use in fighting fires, manning the pumps, and tending the many wounded; there was no way of which he knew to fight with a ship you could not steer. He also had a sounding made, and, pale with the thought of less than a full fathom of water beneath his keel, with the flowing tide pushing him farther and farther up the unfamiliar river, he had the fore anchor dropped.

As the anchor chain rattled out into the river, Walid Dahub Pasha saw the dozen galleys back off from his now helpless ship, hold a brief, shouted, council of war, then set off toward the knot of merchanters and the remaining galleons. After that, he and those of his men still hale were all too busy saving their ship and stores and comrades to pay any attention to aught that befell the rest of the Papal fleet.

While he hacked at a tangle of rigging and splintered yards—for Walid prided himself on never forgetting his antecedents nor asking his seamen to do aught that he would not himself do—he reflected that only the worst possible string of ill luck had gotten him and his fine ship involved in this Roman mess to begin. The Bishop of the East at Constantinople had nothing to do with the Roman Crusade, though he had given leave for any of his as had the desire to join in it. Walid certainly had never for a minute entertained any such desire, yet now he would in all likelihood lose his ship if not his life through being caught up in the Roman stupidity. The sultan in Anghara would be in no way pleased, either, when and if Walid returned to report the loss of ship, guns and all. A chill coursed through Walid's powerful body despite the heat engendered by his exertions, for he had seen strong men live for long hours after being impaled—screaming, pleading, babbling, dying by bare inches, while the remorseless wooden stake tore up through their bodies. He shuddered. That was no way for a decent Tripolitan seaman to die!

Much later, he was on the main gundeck, supervising the drawing of the charges from several of his battery of bronze culverins, when Fahrooq al-Ahmar, a captain and the sole remaining officer of Walid's contingent of fighting men, found him with a message.

Arrived on his quarterdeck, one look through his long-glass was enough to tell the tale. The remainder of the Papal fleet was once more sailing upriver, but no longer under Papal ensigns; each and every one of the ships and galleons now bore the personal banner of Arthur III Tudor, King of England and Wales. The fleet was being shepherded by some English galleons and frigates, while the squadron of galleys seemed to be beating in the general direction of Walid's crippled galleon. The thought flitted through his mind that perhaps they meant to give him and his no quarter, in which case he had unloaded those culverins too soon.

He turned to a quartermaster. "Haul down that Roman rag and hoist Sultan Omar's banner in its proper place." Then, "Fahrooq, send a man down to tell them to get those culverins reloaded immediately, load the swivels, get yourself and your men armed for close combat, open the main arms chests for the seamen, and send a man to my cabin to help me get into my armor. They may kill us all in the end, but this particular batch of Franks will know they've come up against real men, by the beard of the Prophet and the tail of Christ's holy ass!"

As the seamen and soldiers set to their tasks aboard the immobilized galleon, the row galleys crept across the intervening water. Closer they came, ever closer. When they were just beyond the effective range of a long eighteen-pounder culverin shot, they divided, half of them passing across the galleon's stern quarter to form a line on her port side, the others similarly positioned to menace her starboard side.

Watching the deadly vessels through his fine long-glass, Walid could discern the raised platforms for the single gun that each galley mounted. Absently, he noted that they looked to be nine- or maybe twelve-pounders.

With both his sides menaced properly, eleven of the galleys held their places, using their oars only enough to keep them in those places, while a single galley began to stroke slowly toward the galleon. No gunners stood on the platform; there was but a single man—helmetless, but wearing half-armor, sword, dagger, and pistols and holding the haft of a bladeless boarding pike to which a grayish-white square of cloth had been affixed.

"Looks to be a herald of some kind," remarked Walid, then he ordered, "No one's to fire on them until and unless I say to do so. But keep your eyes on the other galleys, most especially on those off the port bow. We can lose nothing by hearing what this Frank bastard has to say to us."

As the small galley neared, Walid thought to himself that some of the oarmen were easily the most villainous-looking humans he had ever set eyes to in a lifetime spent at sea and in some of the roughest ports in all the wide world. The herald, on the other hand, though his face was well scarred and his nose was canted and a bit crooked and though he might have looked fearsome if viewed alone, seemed to represent an uncommon degree of gentility when compared to the satanic-looking crew whose efforts propelled the galley.

Then the rowcraft turned to starboard and came directly toward the galleon, and all that Walid could see were the backs of the rowers, the supposed herald, the steersman, and another he assumed to be the master on the minuscule steering deck at the stern.

And on that small steering deck, Squire John Stakeley felt far more exposed to imminent death or maiming than ever he had even when spurring on at the very forefront of a cavalry charge. Though he was no true seaman and made no such pretensions, he well knew just how frail was this galley and her crew when one contemplated a hit by even a single ball from an eighteen-pounder culverin, and they were now within perfect range if that Roman bastard elected to pull his broadside or any part thereof.

Of course, if he did that—fired on a herald—the rest of the squadron would proceed to pound the galleon to pieces, before boarding the hulk and butchering every man aboard

her. But that would be of no help to Squire John and the
noble herald and the gallowglasses who were rowing closer to
the anchored warship with every stroke of the long, heavy
sweeps.

Hailing from an inland county and being thus conversant
with damn-all of ships in general, Squire John failed to
recognize the new, gaudy standard that had been run up to
replace the even gaudier Papal one. But the herald saw it for
what it was, and, as the galley came alongside the galleon,
with a brace of brawny Irishmen contriving to keep her there
against the tug of the current with boathooks and main strength,
the herald shouted up at a swarthy, bearded man who stood
by the rail with a glowing length of matchcord in one tar-
stained hand and the other grasping the aiming rod of a
swivel gun—a three-inch drake, mounted in the rail specifically to repel boarders.

In purest Arabic, he demanded and threatened and insulted
so meticulously that Walid and every man of his within the
hearing immediately recognized a kindred ethnic spirit.

"Throw me down a ladder at once, you sorry by-blow
outcome of a diseased sow and a spavined camel's perversions,
else I'll see you given that swivel gun and all within it as the
hottest clyster that your foul fundament ever has known!"

At Walid's curt nod of approval, the gunner laid aside his
slow-match and, grinning his own appreciation of the herald's
admirably couched words, heaved down a rope ladder from
the galleon's waist rail to the bobbing galley below.

Leaving the white flag leaning against the gun carriage, the
herald stepped onto the gunwale of the galley and ascended
the swaying, jerking ladder as nimbly as any barefoot seaman,
despite his heavy boots, armor, long-skirted buffcoat, and
dangling weapons.

As Fahrooq ushered the newcomer up onto the quarterdeck,
Walid noted that the herald moved with a pantherish grace
and so was most likely an exceeding deadly swordsman.
Otherwise, he looked to be much akin to Walid himself.

Both were of average height—some five and one-half feet
from soles to pate—with black hair and eyes, swart skin, and

fine, prominent noses, heads, hands, and feet a bit on the small side, fingers long and slender. Both men were possessed of slim waists and thick shoulders, but the herald also showed the flat thighs of a horseman and considerable facial scarring, more than Walid had managed to collect in his own lifetime.

"*Sahlahmoo aleikoom, Òhbtáhn.* I am Sir Ali ibn Hussain."

"*Aleikoomah sahlahm.*" Walid intoned the ritual greeting, but then demanded, "By the flames of Gehenna, now, how is it that an Arabian knight is serving an excommunicated Frankish king who is making war—rather successful war, but still war—upon the Holy Apostolic Church? Man, you risk your soul in the hereafter, not to contemplate what will be done to your body if you find yourself taken and brought before an ecclesiastical court."

"Oh, I serve not King Arthur," was the reply. "At least, not directly. No, I have the great honor to be the herald of his grace, Sir Sebastian, Duke of Norfolk, Earl of Rutland, Markgraf von Velegrad, Baron of Strathtyne, Knight of the Garter of the Kingdom of England and Wales, Noble Fellow of the Order of the Red Eagle of the Holy Roman Empire, and Lord Commander of Horse in the Armies of Arthur III Tudor, King of England and Wales."

Walid shook his head. "How do you manage to remember all of that Frankish gibberish in its proper order, Sir Ali? Never mind, here's the *kahvay*—let's have a cup so we can at least trust each other here, on board my ship."

When one seaman had set up the elaborately chased silver tray-table on its carven ebony legs, when another had set it with a a trio of tiny gold-washed and bejeweled silver cups, then a brass brazier full of glowing coals was passed up from the firebox in the waist and a hideously scarred and pock-marked man of late middle years set about the preparation of the ceremonial food and drink.

In the center of the table was set a smaller silver tray on which rested a few soaked and softened ship's biscuits and a bowl of coarse, brownish salt. First Walid, then Fahrooq took up a bit of biscuit between the fore and middle fingers of their right hands, dipped them in the salt, and proffered them to Sir Ali. The herald, for his part, accepted and slowly ate the offerings, then did the same to Walid and Fahrooq, in turn.

Meantime, the man at the brazier had dropped a generous handful of dried coffee beans into a small, preheated iron skillet, wherein he had thoroughly roasted them, then dumped the almost scorched beans into a marble mortar and rapidly reduced them to coarse powder. The powder he had poured into a brass pot with a long wooden handle, adding some pint or so of water and a piece of a sugarloaf. When he had nestled the pot into an iron trivet above the bed of coals, he began to alternately blow upon the coals and carefully watch the contents of the pot.

As the coffee came to its initial boil, the man adroitly took it from the heat, added three cardamom pods, then replaced it over the coals. As the mixture boiled up the second time, he again took it up and this time spooned a generous measure of the rich brown froth into each of the three waiting silver cups.

On the third boiling, the man removed the pot from the heat, dashed into it a large spoonful of unheated water, then filled the three cups with the fragrantly steaming, thick, syrupy, stygian-black brew.

"It is many years since I have savored *áhwah* in the Turkic style," the herald commented politely, still speaking Arabic.

Walid shrugged. "Thank you for the compliment, Sir Ali, but I understand, *believe me*, I more than understand. You will have noticed that I did not dignify it by calling it *áhwah*. I shipped this sorry Turk aboard in Izmir, after my own cook was killed in a dockside brawl. And *áhwah* or even a simple *kuskus* simply baffles him.

"But now, I am a blunt seaman, Sir Ali, so let us get down to business, eh? For what purpose did this Bey Sebastian send you to me? This galleon is his for the taking, already; even a landsman could see that she cannot be steered. The bread of slavery is bitter at best, but forced to it, I imagine that the most of my crew would prefer becoming slaves to becoming corpses, today. As for me, after the loss of this vessel and the guns, I'd as lief remain as far as possible from Sultan Omar's domains . . . for reasons of bodily health, you understand.''

Sir Ali grinned briefly. "Yes, I've heard that he's possessed of a foul temper, though exceeding generous to those who can please him. But tell me this—how is it that one of Sultan Omar's fine war galleons is escorting ships sent by the Pope of the West? Is all the Church allied against England, then?''

Walid snorted scornfully. "Not hardly, Sir Ali! Our Pope's last word on the matter was that anyone simpleminded enough to go west and risk his fortune and/or neck to try to help put a bastard-spawn usurper onto the throne of England at the behest of old Pope Abdul would probably have been killed by his own stupidity sooner or later anyhow, wherever he chanced to be.

"No, bad luck and illegal coercion brought me and mine here to this sorry pass. Nor have that Moorish dog who styles himself Pope of the West and his criminal Roman cohorts heard the end of the coercion business, either, not if I ever get the ship back to Turkey, they haven't.

"The Turkish ambassador to the court of King Giovanni, in Napoli, having died—he and all his family, of a summer pestilence—I had conveyed the new ambassador and his household to Napoli and was asea enroute to the Port of Marsala to take aboard certain cargo consigned to Sultan Omar's chamberlain when, of a late, dark night, a freak, unseasonal tempest all but swamped the galleon, killed or injured several of my crewmen, and seriously damaged my rigging. When all was done, I found my position to be far nor'-nor'west of where I'd been at the start, and somehow I managed to get the vessel into the Port of Gaeta, a small port on the mainland . . . and squarely into the claws of Pope Abdul, the blackhearted bastard sibling of those noisome canine creatures that subsist on thrice-vomited camels' dung.

"Now understand, Sir Ali, all that I required was a few score fathoms of decent rope, some small items of hardware, some good, seasoned hardwood lumber, and a few pinewood spars, for all of which I was prepared to pay fair value in new, unclipped golden omars. And for all of my first day in that port it seemed that I would soon be accommodated at a better than good price; indeed, I was received and feted in the manner of some visiting bey. But one 'unavoidable' delay followed on the heels of another for more than a week. Finally, I was informed that materials of the quality and in the quantity I required simply were not available anywhere in the environs of Gaeta-port.

"At that juncture, I offered to hire a few of the larger coasters and crews to tow my galleon south to Napoli, which port I knew was well enough stocked to effect my repairs and which lay less than sixty sea miles distant. But, Sir Ali, not one coaster captain or fishing-boat master would look at my gold, though I offered enough to all but buy their wallowing little tubs outright.

"Then, when I was making ready to sail out under a juryrig and follow the coastline down to Napoli as best I could, the damned two-faced Dago harbormaster, claiming most piously to be in fear for the safety of me, my crew, and the sultan's ship, sealed my moorings with armed guards on the dock, and most sadly informed me that if I should try to leave the port without his say-so, the fort gunners had orders to hull me with their demicannon! Can you credit it?"

"It sounds not like a friendly act," Sir Ali commented dryly. "So, what happened then?"

With a strong tinge of sarcasm, Walid said, "Lo and behold, two days later, a Roman Papal galleon—that same one that your galleys blew up and sank earlier today, for which may God always love you all!—came bowling into Gaeta-port and I was shortly given to understand that the only way I would get out of that overgrown fishing hamlet with my ship and crew intact and before we all grew long, white beards was to allow the Roman to take us under tow and convey us thus to the Port of Livorno, some days' sailing to the north."

The Arabian knight nodded, brusquely. "And you agreed."

"What else could I do?" Walid shrugged and shook his head. "On the way north, I must admit, I toyed with the thought of possibly contriving a broken tow cable, then maneuvering my 'benefactor' into position to hull him with my main-deck battery. Then I could cripple his rigging and sweep his decks with my nines and swivels, and possibly serve him up a few red-hot shot for good measure, before I tried to make it down to Napoli alone. But then, the second day out of Gaeta, a brace of big galleases beat down from the north and I realized that at these new odds, resistance would be suicidal.''

The seaman padded over on his bare, dirty feet and refilled the tiny cups with more of the strong Turkish *kahvay*, while another man removed the ceremonial tray of bread and salt to replace it with another small tray of black, wrinkled, sundried olives, dried Izmir figs, raisins, and similar oddments.

Walid sipped delicately at the boiling-hot liquid, then went on with his tale. "The harbor basin at Livorno was packed with vessels like stockfish in a cask, Sir Ali. There was at least one vessel moored at every slip, with others moored to the starboard of those, where there was room. Every type and size of vessel in all the Middle Sea was there to be seen— cogs, caravels, carracks, galleys and galleases, coasters of every conceivable shape and rig, all engaged in lading, preparing, arming, victualing, and manning yonder fleet your arms have just captured. They—''

"Pardon,'' interjected the herald, his eyebrows raised quizzically, "how many principalities would you say were there represented in the preparation of that fleet? Which ones were they, do you recall?''

Ticking off his fingers, Walid answered slowly, jogging his memory. "Well, let's see, Sir Ali. The Papal State, of course, and Genoa—Livorno's owned by Genoa, though it's been on long-term lease to the Roman See for as long as I can recall—both the North and the South Franks had ships there, as did the Spanish, the Aragonese, the Emirate of Granada, the Sultan of Morocco, the Hafsid caliph, the Grand Duchy of Sardinia, the King of Sicily, the Prince of Serbia, the Archcount of Corfu, and the King of Hungary. I was told, but did not myself see, that supplies had arrived from Iskanderia;

if true, they must have been private merchants, though, for I cannot imagine Sultan Mehemet getting any of his fleet involved in a clearly Roman dispute, not with the bulk of his army away down south fighting the Aethiops and their allies.''

"No Portugees?'' probed the herald. "No Germans, Venetians, or Neapolitans? No Greeks or Levantines?''

"No!'' Walid attested emphatically. "Not one Portugee there, nor when this fleet called at Lisboa on the voyage northward would the Portugee king contribute anything save a few score pipes of wine, rather a poor vintage, too, I was later told. While there were a few German ships in Livorno, they took pains to keep a distance from the Papal fleet and its suppliers. As for Greeks, Levantines, and Venetians, though there had been more than a few of them all in the harbor at Napoli, not a one was to be seen in the basin of Livorno.

"There was, however, a coaster flying the Neapolitan ensign. Fahrooq here was able to get to her captain and entrust to him a message to be delivered to Sultan Omar's ambassador at the court of King Giovanni, at Napoli, telling of the virtual armed impressment of my ship and crew by the minions of Pope Abdul.''

"So, it was either sail in company with the fleet or die, eh?'' asked Sir Ali, with a note of sympathy.

But Walid shook his head slowly. "Not exactly, my friend, not exactly. You think like the warrior you are, with all things in pure black or pure white, but statesmen and, especially, churchmen never deal in such purities, trafficking rather in innumerable shadings of gray. So did they deal with me.

"Upon arrival in Livorno, my vessel was anchored in the basin until a slip could be cleared in the navy yard, then we were warped in and moored fast. Immediately we were fast, an arrogant Roman officer and his well-armed escort boarded my ship and I was ordered to collect my ship's papers and accompany him to his superiors. I did. I could just then do no other, like it or not. With my damages, the oldest and most ill-kept cog could have sailed rings around me, not to even think of what the full cannon mounted by that fortress at Livorno could have done to me.

"But we had not proceeded far through the navy yard when an older man, most distinguished of appearance, with the walk of a seaman and the honorable scars of a veteran warrior—neither of which had been evidenced by the supercilious, peacock-pretty, Roman puppy!—confronted us and announced that as senior captain of the navy yard, he had first claim on my person and time. The Roman first spluttered, then argued, then made to bluster, laying hand to hilt and calling up his pikemen. But when the older man whistled once and a double squad of matchlock-armed marines, the matches smoking-ready in the cocks, came trotting into view, the Roman backed off with the whinings of a kicked cur, whilst his own pikemen laughed behind their hands at his cowardice and discomfiture.

"And so it was that on that auspicious day, I made the acquaintance first of the renowned Conde Evaldo di Monteorso."

CHAPTER ——————
THE FIRST

With his crippled galleon under tow toward a destination known to none aboard save the herald, Sir Ali ibn Hussein, Walid Dahub Pasha stood his quarterdeck at the side of the enemy's emissary. Walid still wore his best armor and bore cursive sword, big battle dagger, and slimmer boot dagger as well as several well-hidden edge weapons of varying sizes, shapes, and purposes.

Below, in the waist, Walid's one-eyed boatswain, Turgüt al-Ayn, and his mates closely supervised the repair and/or replacement of both classes of rigging, now and again lowering to the deck a shot-shredded remnant of canvas or a splintered spar.

Still lower, out of Walid's sight on the gundecks, Captain Fahrooq had seen the last of the broadside guns unloaded, powder and shot and wads stowed in their respective places. The gunpowder was stowed back into copper-hooped casks. The casks then were carefully laid back in the security of the thick-walled, felt-lined magazine; the wads were, one by one, washed, squeezed dry, then stacked back in the wad chests; shot went into ready racks affixed to the hull above each gunport.

While a carpenter and his single surviving mate went about the patching of battle damage on the main gundeck, Fahrooq ordered the gun captains to set their crews to cleaning and polishing the secured guns and the mounts and ancillary equipment before once more shrouding them from damp and dust.

His immediate orders fully discharged, the officer made his way abaft to the spot whereon the surgeon and his mates had established themselves and their apparatus at the commencement of this most costly conflict. Despite the long hours which had passed since cessation of hostilities, the sweating, blood-soaked practitioners still were hard at work with knives, saws, pincers, probes, and needles upon the latest occupant of their makeshift table, which dripped clotting gore at all four corners and all along each edge.

As he waited for the senior surgeon, Master Jibral, to finish his current undertaking, Fahrooq took down one of the lanterns and began to carefully pick his way among the recumbent forms lying close-packed on the blotched and shadowy deck. His bootsoles grated on the sand which had been liberally scattered over blood pools to provide secure footing to Master Jibral and the rest.

He found two of his soldiers almost at once. One lay dead, cold, beginning to stiffen already. The other lay equally still, but he still lived . . . most of him, at least. His left leg now ended just a bit below the knee, but the stump was neatly done up in almost-clean bandages. Although the man's eyes were open, they did not focus; Fahrooq correctly surmised that the cripple had been well dosed with poppy, probably before they took off his foot and leg.

Further search revealed yet another wounded soldier, also poppy-drugged and bandaged, but no trace of the young officer he sought, his nephew, Suliman ibn Zemal.

While his assistants manhandled the last patient off the gory table to a place on the deck, Master Jibral wiped his red-dripping hands on his blood-soggy kaftan. Taking a waterskin down from a peg, he played the thin stream into his open mouth for a moment, swished the lukewarm liquid about tongue and teeth, then leaned and spat it into a half-barrel filled with severed limbs before again throwing back his head and swallowing a pint or so of the tepid water. When he had rehung the waterskin, he sighed once, then turned toward Fahrooq, smiling tiredly.

The waiting captain shuddered involuntarily, for in the dim

and flaring lantern light, in the close, noisome atmosphere of this place of stinks and blood and death, the surgeon's face—with precious little skin visible under the layers of old and new blood, spade beard and mustaches stiff with clotted gore, the just-rinsed teeth shining startlingly white—bore an uncanny resemblance to how Fahrooq assumed a man-eating Mareed from out the very depths of Gehenna must look.

But Captain Fahrooq was basically a rational man, nor did he lack of courage. Firmly setting aside his fleeting, superstitious fancy, he spoke formally. "Good Master Jibral, I seek young Lieutenant Suliman. His sergeant informed me that he was brought to you, wounded, early on in the battle. Where will he be found?"

The surgeon raised one bushy, clot-matted eyebrow. "Lieutenant Suliman . . . ? Oh, that must've been the one in the fancy lamellar djawshan, heh? In that pile of corpses in the outer space, there, probably on the bottom of the pile, or near to it."

Fahrooq sighed. "You . . . you did your best for him, Master?"

The surgeon shook his head. "I had another feed him poppy paste, Captain. Aside from that, there was naught any man could have done save to have given him a faster death, perhaps. When that ball hit this ship, it drove a sharp oaken splinter more than a cubit long and near a handsbreadth wide into the space between the lower edge of his djawshan and his private parts. Men with punctured bowels don't live, Captain, no matter what is done to or for them. His bowels assuredly were punctured several times over, and I would have been remiss in my responsibility to other men whose wounds were less grave had I wasted time on a man who could not be saved in any case.

"I tell you, his uncle, this, just as I would say it to Walid Pasha . . . or to the dead man's father himself, should I be called upon to so do."

"You then are acquainted with the father of the late Lieutenant Suliman, Master?" The captain's tone was relaxed, conversational, but a barely perceptible aura of tenseness surrounded him, radiated from him, and his right hand hovered near the access slit to a well-hidden envenomed dagger.

His answer was a tired smile. "Captain, that secret was ill kept. I know who the young man was, and so too do the most of the original crewmen of this ship, though no one of the Westerners ever learned aught of it, you may be sure. I know just who and what you truly are, too, Captain, but that secret is no less safe than was the other. Why you are aboard in such guise I have no idea, but then the doings and schemings of such persons as yourself are not and should not be and have never been the affair of this lowly one.

"You have my sworn word that I will never betray you. If that is not sufficient to you, use that weapon beneath your hand. Otherwise, please grant me your leave to get back to my patients yonder."

"We're at least as safe here as we could be at Rutland or anywhere else, Bass," began the third page of Krystal Foster's letter. "Both King Arthur and King James are maintaining garrisons round about Whyffler Hall while the negotiations drag on, some of Hal's episcopal guards are usually in residence, Geoff has somehow raised and armed and mounted and is now training (he claims) a ragtag bunch of rogues from both sides of the border. *He* seems almighty proud of them, though they look to me to be just another pack of savage, deadly border bandits. But both Sir Liam and dear Uri assure me that Geoff's vaunted 'Whyffler Launces' are brave, stout, reliable, first-class troops, and as they both and Melchoro, too, often ride out with them, they're probably right about them.

"I don't blame you about that Rutland business, Bass. You only saw it briefly and in good, warm weather. Honey, believe me, winter residence was just impossible. We could have burned every tree for miles around in those fireplaces (and some of them looked as if they could have easily accommodated whole trees, too) without getting much of the bone-deep chill out of those high, drafty rooms. Most of that pile was built in the thirteenth century, Bass, for easy defense, not for comfort.

"When I found chilblains on little Joe's hands and feet, I talked it over with Melchoro and Uri, then with Sir Liam, and we decided to come back up here to Whyffler Hall as soon as we could. If, as you indicated, Rutland seemed to offer more in the way of creature comforts than does your residence in Norfolk, then I can only pity you, poor dear, and hope that you soon will be free to join me, your son, and your friends here, in the north.

"I love you, Bass Foster, so take good care of yourself. No excuses, you are now a very important man to the kingdom, so let someone else take the chances and run the deadly risks; just recall what old Earl Howell told you—'The Lord Commander of the Horse is not expected to lead cavalry charges any more than is the king; both are too important to the army and the kingdom to risk in open battle.'

"I so wish that dear, jolly Barón Melchoro would stay up here with us, but he is insistent on joining you down there in the south, so he and his retinue and some score and a half of now recuperated gallowglasses will ride out in the morning and bear this letter to you from your loving wife. (Sounds corny, huh? But it's true.)"

The Duke of Norfolk's "River Cavalry"—the fleetlet of small galleys, each mounting one of Pete Fairley's new, powerful, fast-firing ten-pounder rifled cannon—had been the idea born of a weekend of drinking and scheming among Bass, Pete, Nugai, Sir Ali, Sir Calum MacLeòid, Captain Sir Lùcais MacantSaoir, and Dave Atkins, who had ridden down from York with Pete.

Dave's first few months in this new, strange, primitive world had been unremittingly hard on him and his companion, Susan Sunshine, mostly because they had been suddenly and irreversibly cut off from the plethora of drugs that had sustained them in twentieth-century America. But they had survived the ordeal, and Dave now was one of Pete's assistants in the huge Royal Manufactory at York, which turned out new and innovative firearms and stronger blends of gunpowder for the Royal Army, delighting King Arthur and utterly confounding the machinations of his enemies.

"The bottoms are available, y'r grace," Sir Calum had said. "There be more than a score of them, mostly of a size. Fitted for twelve oars, a steering sweep, and a small lugsail, they are. Small labor would it be to add thole pins along the gunwales, rework the footings for quick stepping or unstepping of the mast, then lighten them a bit to give more speed and ease of handling.

"Y'r grace, it ain't but the one way the thrice-damned Papal forces can resupply the City of Lunnun, invested and all like she be, and that be by the river up from the sea. Yes, they've tried it before and failed, but sure as St. Peter's holy balls, they must try again, and with a stronger force.

"Thick as the mist lies on that river of times, a score or so of low, mastless row vessels could right easy come up so close 'neath the hulks that precious few of their guns could avail them aught. And before they hardly knew, y'r grace's fine, fierce *galloglaiches* would be swarming over the ship like so many rats, would have prized her to y'r glory and renown."

Bass had shaken his head. "A brave, daring plan, Sir Calum, but far and away too risky. Why, man, you'd all be sitting ducks out there on that river, hostage to the slightest breeze that might whisk the fog away and expose you to the sharp-eyed gunners. King Arthur and I prize you and the gallowglasses far too much to take such a chance for so little gain. Bigod and his fleet have done good work in halting the Papal fleets thus far; no doubt they'll do equally well when called upon again. I know that you and the men are bored. So am I, but there's naught that can be done for it. Aside from the few remaining brigands scattered hither and yon, there's just no one left in England for cavalry to fight. But . . . perhaps I could prevail upon his majesty to loan you gallowglasses to King James for a while, eh? His Scotch majesty is still having trouble with certain of his Lowlander lairds, they say. . . ."

Sir Calum sighed. "Unless y'r Grace go tae Scotland, his Royal Gallowglasses go not tae Scotland."

Bass sighed. They had been over this ground before, many times.

But then Pete spoke up. "Bass, Sir Calum, he had him a good ideer, far as it went, but I think I can take it further. Lissen, I got me up to York some ten- and twelve-pounder rifles, breechloaders all of 'em and fitted with the friction-spring primers that Carey and Dan Smith dreamed up, too. They ain't heavy, Bass, not put up 'gainst reg'lar guns they ain't, and they got real *range*—more range than any gun any ship'll be likely to be mounting, and better accuracy than these folks has ever seen afore, I betcha.

"Bass, boy, you mount one of thesehere rifles in the middle of ever one of your rowboats, run in close to them big sailboats, see. You've seed the kinda guns boats use—cain't hardly none of the big guns be traversed none, and if they tries to depress 'em too much, the friggin' charges come a-rollin' out the muzzles, most times.

"So if yawl get too close for their big guns to bear on you, but too far for the slingpieces and such like, you can perlitely shoot them muthas to pieces with my ten- and twelve-pounder rifles, then close with 'em when they got more to worry 'bout than boarders."

Admiral Bigod had not been receptive in the least to the idea or the diversion of the breech-loading rifles—originally intended as chasers for his small but pugnacious fleet—until Bass had managed to persuade the seaman to observe the flotilla of galleys on maneuvers on the river. Then the admiral's support became more than enthusiastic, and he had ridden roughshod over the objections of the more conservative-minded of his captains.

Now of one mind in the matter, neither the Lord Admiral nor the Lord Commander of the Royal Horse could see any reason to broach the plan to the king, so they concentrated on preparations and practice and maneuvers up to the very day that a coaster spotted the Papal fleet beating for Thames-mouth.

*   *   *

Bass, when finally the news caught up to him, was non-plused by Sir Ali's accomplishment and acquisition in his—Bass's—name. He had assumed when he sailed off with Bigod and the main fleet that the crippled and clearly *hors de combat* Papal galleon would be towed to Bigod's fleet anchorage if her master chose to strike or cheerfully pounded to pieces if he did not so choose.

"Sir Ali, why in God's name did you see fit to tow a king's prize into one of my ports? Bigod will be most wroth, and I'll not blame him one bit. You surely had to pass by his Essex base to get to your present anchorage."

Barón Melchoró looked up from the chair in which he had sprawled his rotund body. "Sebastián, old friend, cool you down. In this instance your fine knight, Sir Ali, is of a much rightness. Think you, now, 'twas *your* condotta first fought and crippled, then prized that ship, not the Royal English Fleet nor eke the Royal English Horse. D'you follow? You are a cavalry commander and yon was a purely naval action, which you and yours fought as free swords without your king's orders or, likely, knowledge; therefore, any proceeds of such action are and should rightly be yours to disperse to your officers, gentlemen, and other ranks as you and you alone see fit."

"But his majesty—" Bass began, only to be politely interrupted by his Portugese friend.

"—has the rest of the Papal fleet and cargoes, my ducal companion, which is rich enough of a prize, or so one hears about the camps and court. It would appear that his supposed holiness, old Abdul, packed all that he could beg, borrow, impress, or outright steal into this single effort . . . and now King Arthur has it all. Not one crust of bread, one grain of powder got through to London. That city cannot last long, after this."

"And just what am I supposed to do with a huge, ocean-going warship, manned by a crew of Turks, Egyptians, Moors, and God alone knows what others? I'm no seaman, God knows."

Melchoro smiled languidly and shrugged. "And no need

for you to be, *meu amigo*. Seamen and sailing masters can be hired on, just like soldiers, and most I have encountered hold gold in much higher esteem than the land of their birth. Certain this one is that the music of a few golden onzas would speedily convert the most of that ship's crew to the loyalty you might expect from most condottas."

"But to what possible purpose, Melchoro?" demanded Bass, a bit exasperatedly now. "There'll be damn-all trade until this business of interdictions and excommunications and Crusadings is over and done for good and all. And that ship is just too big, draws too much water, to use her as a coaster. How big is she, Sir Ali?"

"Some one thousand tons burthen . . . or so states her present master, Walid Pasha, your grace," the slim Arab replied.

"How many guns is her broadside, Sir Ali?" questioned Barón Melchoro. "What other armaments has she?"

The knight began to tick off his calloused fingers. "Eight demicannon, four cannon-perriers, twenty fine bronze culverins, these being arranged on the lower gundecks. Above, twelve brass demiculverins, ten sakers, one minion, four portpieces, five fowlers, eight basies on the forecastle, six falcons, and nine falconets. Not all of these smaller ordnance are presently mounted, you understand, my lords; some were damaged in the action and some others were dismounted that other damages might be easier repaired."

The *barón* turned toward his host, smiling. "So, *meu amigo*, you have here a sailing ship of some thousand tons burthen, mounting a broadside of at least sixteen heavy guns. You have an experienced crew whom you could probably hire for shares alone, not to mention an unemployed condotta who would probably make the finest sea-soldiers this side of the Gates of Hell.

"Now, true, you might have trouble in some ports, some places, under an English ensign, but as Markgraf von Velegrad, you can legally sail under the ensign of the Empire, and that's respected, honored everywhere, these days.

"Man, your fortune is made! Can't you see it? Within five

years, with any kind of luck, you'll be plating your solid-gold pisspots with tin and brass to discourage burglars!"

"I'm certain that you think you know just what you're talking about, Melchoro," said Bass gently, "but I assuredly do not."

The *barón* vented another jolly laugh. "*Amigo, amigo*, I am but suggesting that you and your condotta take out this fine, strong, well-armed ship and somewhat disrupt the merchant trade of your sovereign's multitudinous enemies, while at one and the same time lining your own purse a bit. Large as is your ship and the complement she is capable of carrying, you might even raid a few coastal towns for variety. I, personally, can think of at least two ill-defended places on the northern coast of Spain that would be well worth the intaking. . . ."

Suddenly, it all came clear to Bass. "*Piracy*? You're suggesting that I take this ship and turn pirate, Melchoro?"

"It's an old and most honorable profession," the *barón* said, adding, "I might even ship along with you for a while . . . just until you get the hang of things, *amigo*. I have had some small experience in the field."

Feeling himself in poor position to offend these men who were by now become his closest friends and trustiest advisers in this new, strange, savage world into which he had been thrown, Bass nonetheless refused to answer directly yes or no, saying only that he would consider and muse upon the possible uses of the warship. But secretly, within himself, he was shocked that his boon companions—Barón Melchoro, Sir Ali, Sir Calum, Captain Sir Lùcais, Sir Richard Cromwell, Reichsherzog Wolfgang, even his bodyguard-servant, Nugai the Kalmyk, and Pete Fairley—all seemed so pleased and downright enthusiastic about shoving him into, of joining him in, a life of high-seas piracy and coastal raiding.

He waited until affairs again called him to the vicinity of Sir Paul Bigod's headquarters, then arranged a dinner invitation. When at long last he was able to get a few words alone with the Lord Admiral, he touched first upon the matter of the ship seized by Sir Ali and the rest.

Bigod beamed over the rim of his gilded-silver wine goblet. "A rare stroke of luck for you, that one, your grace. According to Papal fleet records, she's an impressed Turkish vessel. Sultan Omar might well be willing to pay a most handsome sum to the English nobleman who . . . shall we say, freed her from her odious bondage to Rome.

"But negotiations with Anqahra will surely take a good bit of time, what with the distances involved and the still-unsettled conditions hereabouts. Your grace should have plenty of time for some profitable voyages out against the merchant shipping of the damned Frenchies, Spanishers, and suchlike."

He lowered his tone and leaned forward conspiratorily. "I can loan you a few small support bottoms and crews, your grace, can we two come to a reasonable agreement on shares. And should land operations be contemplated, I might even take a few ships out in company with yours . . . under my private ensign, of course."

"But, Sir Paul . . . the king, won't he object to his ships being used for acts of piracy and personal gain?"

"Why no, your grace. With the exceptions of those three Spanishers your brigade of horse prized, none of the ships belong to his majesty. All are either commandeered or on long-term lease to the Crown."

"And what of the ships of this fleet and the earlier Papal fleets you and your force captured—are none of them the king's either?" demanded Bass puzzledly.

"Why no, your grace," Bigod replied. "I had thought that your grace understood these matters. They all belong to whatever knight or nobleman first raised his ensign over them after their capitulation, just as you came into ownership of your Turkic galleon, your grace.

"Speaking of which, that galleon probably should be careened, cleaned off, recaulked, and, after the action, repaired in sundry ways before she sets out against targets of opportunity. The basin here is adequate to any and all of those uses, your grace, and we will be more than pleased and honored to accommodate that fine prize whenever your grace finds the time fitting."

*   *   *

Master Walid Dahub Pasha, it developed, possessed a fair, if very heavily accented, amount of English, but Captain Fahrooq's few utterances required translation by Sir Ali or Barón Melchoro.

The two had been surprised when allowed to walk, face forward, into the presence of their captor. Before him, however, they both fell to their knees and thumped their foreheads on the carpet and stayed thus until Sir Ali commanded them to arise.

From his canopied armchair, Bass studied his captives. Walid Pasha looked more Greek than Arab or Moor; his skin tones were dark enough, almost as dark as Sir Ali's, but his eyes were a dark green, and a bit of chestnut hue tinged his beard; he walked with the rolling gait of a seaman, and what Bass could see of his body and limbs denoted big bones, rolling muscles, and hirsute skin.

The other man was much younger, no more than twenty-five, Bass thought, and no Arab, either. Indeed, he was racially dissimilar from every other man in the room. His spike beard and pencil-thin, drooping mustachios were as black as sin, but where not weathered his skin was fair and the corners of his blue eyes had a slight epicanthic fold. He was as tall as Walid Pasha or Sir Ali—about five feet seven—and his movements were catlike, graceful. Like Sir Ali, he had a small head and flat ears, but he lacked the huge, beaklike nose of the Arab.

Moreover, both men looked and smelled clean, and that raised their personal stocks appreciably in the reckoning of their captor.

"Walid Pasha," began Bass, "I am informed that you and your ship were forced to sail against England by the minions of Pope Abdul, that you consider yourself to be a neutral and most ill used by Rome. However that may be, you and your ship were fought by and captured by my galleys whilst you sailed in company with the sworn enemies of his majesty, Arthur III Tudor, King of England and Wales.

"I already have been approached by a Burgundian dealer in

slaves who has made an offer for the lot of you—you and all your crew. Also, I am reliably informed that Sultan Omar will likely ransom the ship and guns most handsomely, given time."

The older man gulped once and set his jaw. The expression of the younger, however, did not change.

"But I do not believe in slavery. None of you will be sold into bondage," Bass reassured the two. "At the very most, those of your crew who are amenable may be signed on by various of the ships now comprising the Royal Fleet for the duration of this war. At its conclusion, they can likely work their passages back to the Eastern Mediterranean on board merchanters."

"What of those, Sebastián Bey, who for reasons of health might decide a return to Turkish dominions unwise? Will they, too, be sent away?" Walid Pasha asked diffidently.

Bass smiled. "Sir Ali has explained something of your deadly difficulty to me, Walid Pasha. No, you are more than welcome to remain in England, if you wish. Perhaps I can find a place for you in my household, but we'll cross that bridge when we come to it. Just now, I have an alternate plan to broach, one which may well be of immense benefit to all in this room and many another as well."

The dusty messenger found the famous (some said infamous) Duce di Bolgia in a shady spot on a hillside just beyond the shattered town his condotta had just conquered and were now despoiling in the savage, time-honored fashion known as intaking. Shouts, the ring of steel, screams of every description and intensity, thuds and crashes and the crackling of new-set fires served as dinner music for the big, beefy captain and certain of his officers as they broke bread on the stony sward beneath the trees.

The messenger himself was not allowed to approach the great captain, of course. He and his escort perforce waited under heavy guard at the foot of the hill while the beribboned, wax-sealed vellum roll was carried up to its intended recipient by a squat, hideously scarred, and fully armed heavy horseman.

Those soldiers set to guard the messenger and his escort eyed the fine, if dusty and travel-stained, clothing and effects of their charges with unconcealed avarice, all the while fingering the well-honed blades of their battle-axes or hefting the short-hafted weapons where they lay, ready to hand, across their saddle pommels, sniggering and exchanging glances and terse comments in Umbrian or some such uncultured dialect.

The messenger reflected silently that sworn service to the household of a Papal legate could take an unsuspecting gentleman to some strange and exceedingly dangerous places. After another wary look around at the murderous pack surrounding him and his escort, he silently consigned his soul to heaven, although he kept his face totally blank lest the ill-born peasant dogs derive pleasure from the belief that they had frightened a Roman nobleman.

"Hmmph!" the messenger thought to himself as he watched the condottiere on the hillside. "He can read. Maybe there's something to those tales of him being gentleborn after all. Although I for one have never considered it all that heinous that he might have hacked out his patents of nobility by the strength of his arm and the weight of his steel—hell, put to it, it's probable that every noble house in the known world began just that way, a strong, ruthless man with a sharp sword and enough followers to consolidate his victories. Perhaps his own house . . ."

But the burly figure of Duce Timoteo had arisen. One big hand still clutching the message, he waved the other imperiously. "Ho, *sergente*, escort the *signore* up here to me. And the rest of you, those peacocks and their horses belong to him who may be our next employer; be ye all warned."

The messenger dismounted, threw his travel cloak over his sweaty saddle, and followed it with his dust veil. With some slow deliberation, he took his sword from the travel scabbard buckled to the saddle skirt and inserted the sheathed weapon snugly into his baldric. Only then did he turn and set his feet to the pathway that led up the hillside to the knot of men who sat or squatted under the silver-leaved olive trees.

When a few feet separated them, the *duce* growled in a

tone that could have been friendly or not, "And who might you be, boy? You're no clerk, by the cut of you, no damned Moor, either. You seem to have a measure of guts. Can't you find a better employer than a pack of accursed Africans? Or do you simply like old Abdul's brand of sodomy? Eh?"

Gritting his teeth against an intemperate reply—after all, his battle rapier would avail him little against these mostly armored professional soldiers and their broadswords, wheellock pistols, and other weapons—the messenger swept off his sweat-soggy hat and thrust a leg forward in a bow.

"Your grace, I have the honor to be Sir Ugo D'Orsini, a knight of the household of his eminence, Cardinal Bartolomeo D'Este, Archbishop of Palermo."

Before any more words might be exchanged, there came the clatter of hooves on cobblestones and a chorus of deep-voiced shouts from within the town. Then, from out the shattered gate, burst a big white mule at a full, jarring gallop. Bestriding his saddleless back, bare thighs and knees gripping the muscular barrel while small, unshod heels kicked at the flanks to encourage greater speed, was a naked red-haired woman. Waist-length hair billowed out behind her, and this hair was her undoing.

The bareheaded, half-armored horseman pursuing her spurred his warhorse close enough behind to grasp a big handful of that billowing hair and dragged her from her insecure seat. Then, while still she was a bit stunned, he secured her wrists with a length of thong and deposited his catch, belly down, across the neck of his mount. Laughing, that black-bearded man reined about and headed back toward the town at a fast walk, handling his reins high while the busy fingers of his free hand explored the juncture of the woman's now-thrashing legs and his ears were assailed by her screams of outrage and the vile curses she gasped up at him.

"Better not try to kiss her, Gilberto," shouted one of the officers on the hillside. "A woman like that bit my cousin's tongue off!"

"With Gilberto's luck," put in another. "it'll be something far more important than a tongue the strumpet's teeth meet in!''

"Be sure to keep the baggage's hands tied tight," yet another officer advised. "She strikes me as the stripe of an eye-gouger with those claws she has on the ends of her fingers.''

"I just hope he's careful in there," still another of the gathered officers muttered to no one in particular. "Spanish bugger owes me eleven ducats.''

"Never you fear about our Gilberto, Andrea," chuckled a nearby man. "I've soldiered with him for many a year and I'm here to tell you that he can gentle any doxy, highborn or low, and in damn-all time, too. They soon learn just who their master is! Why, I recall this woman in—"

But just then the *duce* cleared his throat and silence fell.

"Gentlemen, here's the chance we've all been champing at our bits to see." He flourished the beribboned parchment once and continued, "With any sort of luck, we have sacked our last, piss-poor Sicilian town for his parsimonious highness of Naples. This hints at an offer of employment somewhere outside Italy. Now, while it's signed by the Archbishop of Palermo, we all know that he alone could never afford my hire or yours, so without doubt bigger fish are involved covertly, and no thinking man would need to overly tax his brain to determine one powerful enough to use a cardinal, a noble-born prince of the church, for his stalking-horse.

"My brother, Roberto, will be in command of the company in my absence. Give the men no more than two more days in that town, then drag every swinging dick back into camp and take as much as another day to straighten them up, but I want you and them under the walls of Palermo in eight days' time.

"Giovanni, if any damage comes to these damned olive trees or to those vineyards, it will be on your head. They're the reason for this so-called campaign, after all.

"Arpad, any decent riding or draft animals that fall to hand are the property of my company. Let the men keep whatever other portable loot they find in there. No prisoners, though; I prefer ransoms in something more substantial than olive oil and casks of sour wine. And you know what to do if any of them try to drag any women along.

"Ottorino, in addition to my axmen, I'll be wanting twenty dragoons. Lieutenant Pandolfo will command them, the sumpters, and the remounts. Take my smaller tent, and food and grain for all the men and beasts for four days. See my man, Pietro, back at camp for my chest of better clothing. He'll be coming, too; see to it."

Roberto di Bolgia, thought the messenger, might have been almost a twin of his famous brother, so similar were their faces, the set of their blue eyes, the wavy ripples of their dark-brown hair, their bristling mustaches and straight-bridged noses, and the dark blueness of their shaven cheeks and chins. But the younger was a couple of fingers shorter than the elder, owned a physique not quite as massive, and lacked the upper half of his left ear.

As the *duce* finished his instructions to Ottorino, Roberto asked, "But what of the royal garrison, lord brother? If we leave the town unoccupied, they might have to retake it whenever they get here."

Duce Timoteo laughed coldly. "Do the bastards good to do a bit of real fighting for a change. They were supposed to have been here two weeks agone, weren't they? Well, then, we've done the job for which we supposedly are going to be paid . . . someday, in some coin or other. If they drag their oversized feet for so long a time that these feisty Sicilians have time to repair their walls and gates and rearm sufficiently to stand them off, then so be it!

"No, you all adhere to the schedule I've here outlined. Let his Neapolitan majesty overtax some folk somewhere who aren't as good at defending themselves, say I."

Taking a brass ewer and an empty cup from the ground near his feet, the duce filled the one from the other and thrust the measure of wine toward the messenger. "Best drink whilst you can, Sir Ugo. Four days hence, I mean to be in Palermo, which is going to mean hard riding for us all, with precious few stops and damned short ones, even then. We'll see if your horsemanship and endurance matches your courage, sirrah."

The Swedish caravel *Sjöhäst*, Master Lars von Asnen commanding, heavy-laden with a hold full of pig iron, copper ingots, casks of stockfish, and a few casks of priests' powder and a deck cargo of timber and resin, chanced across the strange ship only a day's easy sailing out of the Seine's mouth.

Whilst the master, hastily summoned onto the quarterdeck from an inspection of the hold below, was carefully uncasing his own, personal, high-quality long-glass, his first officer filled him in on what little informtion had been so far ascertained in regard to the strange vessel.

"She's a four-masted galleon, pierced for about thirty guns, though all her ports are just now closed. She looks to be carvel-built, which could mean she hails from the Middle Sea . . . the south, anyway."

"What's her ensign?" asked von Asnen brusquely.

"The topmost is Papal . . . Roman Papal, that is. The lower is one I don't recognize."

"Papal, hey? Well, that would tally. Old Abdul has been shipping Crusaders and supplies into England, fleets of 'em. Likely this is some straggler. I've no time for crusades, but the king did allow this one be proclaimed throughout the land, so let's see if we can be of assistance to them."

As the *Revenge* towed the battered, blood-soaked *Sjöhäst* into port, Bass still felt sick over what had occurred at sea. A lucky shot had brought down the mainmast, and another from the very next broadside had brought down most of the foremast, whereupon, Walid Pasha had brought the *Revenge* into grapnel range, closed, and boarded the stricken vessel. By the time Bass had been able to rein in the gallowglasses, Turks, Moors, Arabs, and assorted Englishmen, every last Swede had been shot or hacked down; not even those poor wights injured or wounded in the cannonade had been spared.

Nor were his companions understanding of his qualms.

Sir Calum laughed merrily. "The lads had been penned up too lang is all, y'r grace. They just needed a taste of hot blood."

Walid Pasha shrugged. "Yes, we could have gotten good prices for such big, strong, fair men in Fez or farther east. But think, Sebastian Bey, of what it would have cost to feed them while shipping them there. And at least a third always die of the gelding process, anyway."

Sir Ali sighed. "It was a little akin to butchering goats in a pen. None of them were trained warriors, just simple seamen. And the battery on that ship is laughable—she's pierced for twenty and only mounts fourteen and I would wager my good sword that not a few of those guns are a hundred or more years old. A miracle it is that only one of them exploded when fired . . . but Allah looks after fools and lunatics, 'tis said."

Dave Atkins, who had sailed along on the voyage to report back to Pete regarding the new guns mounted here and there on the *Revenge*, was blunt. "Bass, this here ain't no Boy Scout war these people are fighting. There's no Geneva Convention in this world. The things done to prisoners by both sides is plumb awful, by how you and me was raised on our world, but they're SOP, here, and the sooner you realize and accept that, the better for you and everybody else. Could I choose, I'd a lot sooner check out the way them Swedes did than some ways I've seen and heard tell of here."

Sir Paul Bigod did not understand at all and put Bass's ill humor and senseless complaints down to overtiredness, fine-drawn nerves, and, like as not, sleeplessness, on the part of a commander after a successful voyage.

"It is a most auspicious maiden voyage, your grace. No gold or gems, aside from that box of raw amber, but then there is seldom suchlike in these latitudes. The naval basin here will take all of that timber, the resins, the iron, and the copper. I doubt your grace's agents will experience difficulty in selling the stockfish at a good price; it's all prime stuff.

"As regards the ship herself, she looks sound, aside from the battle damage, of course. If you would like to lease her out to the Crown, she could be repaired here and fitted with decent, modern guns; her existing battery were best sold for scrap—I'd never take the risk of putting linstock to one of them. The bronze ones could be melted down and recast, of course. Perhaps your grace's friend at York would buy them for the Royal Foundry.

"I beg your grace's leave to speak bluntly. Command is never easy, naval command being especially harsh and heavy at most times. This night, your grace should dine well, drink deeply, and roll the night away in a feather bed with a brisk young doxy. On the morrow, the world will be a much brighter, more promising place in which to live. Your grace will see."

Bass only took a third of the well-meant advice, though, and even to the very moment he slipped from his chair in a drunken stupor, he still could see the glazing, terror-filled, accusing eyes of that butchered crew of dead Swedes.

CHAPTER ——————————
THE SECOND

It was not one, not two, but no less than three cardinals that Sir Timoteo, Duce di Bolgia, found awaiting him in the ornate archbishop's palace of Palermo when he was escorted there on the morning after his arrival in that ancient city.

He had made the time he had set himself for the journey, actually bettered it by a few hours and killed only four horses out of the party, although seven more had been foundered in the process. All of Timoteo's own men had kept pace with him, but a brace of young Sir Ugo's escorts—both older men—had fallen by the wayside; one had been found dead in his cloak, apparently having expired in his sleep, the other had fallen from off his horse unseen and been trampled to death in the darkness.

But the massive soldier was as pleased as punch with the slender, foppish-seeming Roman knight, although he would never have allowed the object of his pleasure to know it. Sir Ugo, never once complaining, had endured every mile and hour of the brutally hard trip in or close behind the van of the party.

Timoteo had spent a good portion of his life proving to an unbelieving world that Italians—scorned by a multitude of races as brutish peasants, impractical artisans, or spineless effetes—were the equal of any mercenaries in the world, if properly trained and led. This young Roman nobleman had proved himself to be a bit more proof of the di Bolgia pudding, as it were. If an untried member of the old nobility—many of whom were, if the truth be known, nothing less than effete—could will himself to keep pace on a ride that had left even Timoteo's strong body and hard muscles sore and aching with strain and exertion, then perhaps there might be still a measure of hope for the class. If a way could be arranged, he meant to keep this Sir Ugo by him for a few years and see just what he was made of. Mayhap . . . ? This one might be *the* one, the worthy heir of a hard-won duchy, a crack condotta, and a not inconsiderable fortune.

Timoteo had sired a daughter and two sons of his first wife and a daughter by his second, and at least a dozen by-blows were scattered in the wake of his campaignings, but none of his male offspring seemed to have inherited their father's own unique blend of talents and strengths and there would likely never be more, for he had not quickened any woman since that hellish day that the forsworn Sforzas and their torturers had kept him in torment before Roberto and the condotta had burst in and rescued him.

He smiled grimly to himself. Saints' swelling cocks, but it had been sweet to hear the screams and pleadings of those Sforza scum as all that they had planned for Timoteo was wreaked upon their own flesh and bones. That alone had been almost worth getting as good as gelded by them!

Sir Ugo did not dismount when he called at the inn which Timoteo and his soldiers had virtually taken over. The young man sat a richly caparisoned roan mule in the innyard until di Bolgia and his men were making ready to mount, then he kneed the hybrid closer and said, "Your grace, I will be escorting you to your initial meeting with his eminence. One or two of your own men will be allowed as far as the outer gates of the palace, but to bring more . . . well, his eminence might conclude that you distrust either the Archcount of Palermo or him."

Timoteo looked up at the young Roman and shrugged. "His eminence can think whatsoever he likes. Like any man successful in my business, I own a multitude of enemies, precious few proven friends, and I long ago learned that to stand an even chance of being alive tomorrow, it were wise to

guard one's back today. My dragoons and axmen ride with
me, excepting only a corporal's guard who remain here to
watch over our gear and beasts.

"If his eminence sees me, it will be my way, Sir Ugo.
Yes, the most of the guards will halt at the gates, but you, I,
and Lieutenant Pandolfo di Crespa will go on from there. If
you feel your employer will stick at one extra man, then I'll
not bother to put foot to stirrup. *He* can just come down here
to see *me*, by the well-worn cooze of Mary Magdalene!"

Di Bolgia noted with satisfaction that the young knight no
longer cringed or even paled at the sound of blasphemies.
Good, he was growing up, if somewhat hard and fast.

Sir Ugo detached one of his own attendants to ride ahead to
the palace and perhaps smooth the way for the unexpected
change of plans, but the column caught up to the man a little
over halfway to his assigned destination, his way and theirs
blocked solidly by a milling mass of people filling a piazza
through which they must pass. At a growled word from the
duce, the riders all backed their mounts some yards the way
they had come, then the dragoons took the forefront of the
column, drew their sabers, and put their big troop horses to
the trot.

Bellowing a deep-throated chorus of " 'Way for his grace,
the illustrious Captain Sir Timoteo, Duce di Bolgia! 'Way,
you scum!" and riding four abreast, they bore down upon the
shouting crowd in the piazza.

No one of the big, hard-faced, half-armored men used the
edge of his razor-sharp saber, depending rather upon the
weight and impetus of their horses to break up the crowd,
while encouraging speed of laggards by judicious use of the
blade flats. Some few deaths and injuries were, indeed, inflicted by horsehoof, mainly those too slow or feeble or
unlucky to avoid the progress of the column. But the vast
majority of those killed and hurt in that piazza were knocked
down and/or trampled by their fellow townsfolk as they
overenthusiastically "made way" for their betters.

Fortunately for the retention of his breakfast, Sir Ugo did

not get a glimpse of what that piazza looked like in the first moments after the column had trotted through it.

The second catch of the *Revenge* was a Gascon coaster running a cargo of raw wool, tallow, beeswax, and saffron from San Sebastián to St. Malo in Brittany. No tricks or false ensigns were used to draw the small, dumpy, two-masted, virtually unarmed carrack close, nor was one cannon shot needed. The *Revenge* very nearly collided with the little vessel in a fog bank. By the time the fog had somewhat cleared, the master and small crew of the Gascon carrack were become more than aware, most uncomfortably aware, that they were vastly outnumbered and tremendously outgunned, and all of them seemed overjoyed to clamber down into their trailing longboat and begin to pull with a true will toward the smudge on the horizon that was the French coast.

Bass did not get drunk on the night of return from that voyage. He was not aware that one of the small companion vessels Bigod had loaned had followed after and sunk that longboat with all hands almost within sight of land; no bloodthirstiness was involved, of course, only the need to conceal for as long as possible reports and accurate descriptions of the English raider operating in these waters. The officer who sent the pursuit vessel off assumed that in the press of affairs, his grace had simply neglected to order so obviously needful a thing.

Sir Paul Bigod was overjoyed, rubbing his palms rapidly together in an excess of visible glee. "Marvelous, your grace, simply marvelous! Again, no treasure ship, this, but still, a treasure of sorts, by the Rood. And taken without loss of a single man. Luck is assuredly sailing with your grace.

"Let's see to her lading, here. Hmm. Tallow and beeswax, capital; I'll take all of those off your grace's hands, along with any ships' stores or powder your grace doesn't want for his own fleet, as before. Wool? Your grace's agents will get better prices for it if they cart or pack it inland. Saffron? This bill doesn't state what grade it is. His majesty would no doubt be most appreciative of a few pounds; he's quite fond of fowl with saffron sauces. For the rest, I'd keep it, your grace—it stores well and, dear as it and all spices have become of late in our England, it should be as good a nest egg as minted gold onzas.

"Once your grace has taken all he wants out of the carrack, have her sailed up here. I'll have my men go over her, see that she's sound, determine just how much weight of gun she can carry without adversely affecting her balance or maneuverability—surely something more and heavier than those six pitiful little falcons!—then pierce her and mount such ordnance as is then available. God willing, your grace will soon have another ship for his private fleet."

Bundled tightly in his warm boatcloak against the cold mist as the barge conveyed him back out to where the *Revenge* lay moored in the channel, his grace, the Duke of Norfolk, Earl of Rutland, Markgraf von Velegrad, Baron of Strathtyne, and now red-handed sea robber, Sir Bass Foster thought furiously, "How in hell do I manage to keep getting myself into these bloody messes, time after time after time? All I want, all I've wanted for years, is simply to settle down somewhere and live a quiet, uncomplicated, nonviolent life with Krystal and little Joe, my son, maybe find the time and opportunity to give him a sibling or three before I get too old to cut the mustard.

"But no matter how hard I try, which way I turn, I find myself mired deeper and deeper in the savagery, the blood-lusting, the senseless violence on which people here and now seem to truly dote. Oh, yes, I did my full share of it for King Arthur, but with the last of the foreign Crusaders driven out or killed, with a friendly emperor on the throne of the Holy Roman Empire, with the Irish High King and the King of Scotland both suing not only for peace but for alliances against the Roman Papacy, with peace throughout most of England and Wales and London certain to fall to the king any day now, I'd been hoping that soon I could hang up this sword and the pistols and never have to so much as look at the damned deadly things again. Then I could get back to being the kind of a man I really am, not the killing machine I've had to become.

"When the king failed to formally muster the horse this past spring, didn't even visit the Essex cavalry camp to inspect such units as did arrive on time and intact, no one was more overjoyed than the Lord Commander of the Royal Horse. I figured this gory business was finally winding down, and my biggest worry was how to get that pack known as the Royal Tara Gallowglasses back to Ireland before they got bored enough with the lack of bloodshed to slip their leashes and get themselves and me into deep shit. Those men are frightening enough, God knows, on *our* side. I'd hate like hell to be the one who had to hunt them down on a royal writ for crimes against the populace.

"That galley thing, now, that seemed like the perfect plan to give the crazy Gaels exercise, if nothing else, since they can seldom be induced to take part in formal cavalry drill. How did Burns put it? 'The best-planned lays of mice and men . . .' or something similar. The galleys captured a ship and now the damned ship has captured me and I'm back on the same old treadmill I thought I'd escaped. How the hell do you get off? Or do you ever get off in this world and time?"

He continued to muse as the barge came alongside the *Revenge* and was still so lost in thought that he forgot his usual vertigo and clambered up the ladder hung over the rail of the galleon's waist as nimbly as any seaman might have done.

The rambling waterfront palazzo of the Archbishops of Palermo had been built by the Moors on a Roman foundation, heavily fortified by Normans, modernized—according to thirteenth-century standards—by Germans, refortified by Spaniards, remodernized by Neapolitans, and, most lately, made comfortable by current standards by its occupant of some years, his Eminence, Cardinal Bartolomeo D'Este, holder of the archdiocese.

The D'Estes were a very well-known noble family of Northern Italy. For generations the various branches of their

house had produced princes of both worlds, temporal and
ecclesiastical—dukes and cardinals, counts and archbishops,
barons and bishops and abbots, great captains and equally
great scholars. Almost every D'Este who had ever entered the
public eye had been in some manner remarkable, and
Bartolomeo was no exception.

Shrewd investment of the modest incomes from certain of
his patrimonial properties, and then reinvestment of accruing
proceeds, had in two decades made of Bartolomeo a rather
wealthy man. The original incomes from northern vineyards
and farms continued to trickle in, moreover, though now
virtually submerged in the floods of returns from his investments, which now included his outright if often covert ownership of trading ventures, warehouses and inns and stables, oil
presses and cooperages and foundries and mills. Through
other agents, the cardinal owned ships, dealt in maritime
insurance, and even practiced usury on occasion.

And Bartolomeo was gifted in other ways as well. Without
ceding any easily noticeable aspects of security, he had transformed a marginally habitable Neapolitan waterfront garrison
building into a palazzo in every sense of that word.

When the complex had been rendered as clean as the hand
of man could make it, from deepest subcellars to highest,
half-hidden garrets, the then-new Archbishop of Palermo had
had the living areas furnished with carpets and drapes and
wall hangings and tasteful, modern furniture before he moved
in his household. With his staff, his servants, his guards, his
women, and his children and their servants comfortably
ensconced, he had set to work on the exteriors of the residence.

The outer face of every stone was painstakingly cleansed of
centuries' worth of grime, birdlime, rust stains, and oxidation.
Then, while master stonemasons applied to some areas fa-
cades of costly marble, each and every other visible bit of
stonework was thickly coated with a long-wearing exterior
plaster composed of powdered marble. Roofings of slate and
tile were repaired where needed, then given a generous coat-
ing of the same expensive cement.

Dusty interior courts and wellyards, filled with the trash,

debris, and filth of half a millennium, were dug out, sodded, and transformed into tiny green oases, where flowers grew beneath the fruit trees and small, brilliantly colored birds hopped and twittered and sang, while fountains plashed their silvery water.

"Very nice, Bartolomeo, all very nice" had been the comment of old Cardinal Prospero Sicola when he and the younger Cardinal Murad Yakubian first came down from Rome. "Nonetheless, comfortable life or no comfortable life, I cannot imagine how so vibrant and astute a man as yourself can stand to not be more in Rome. You could rise far higher than a mere backwater archbishop, you know, but the opportunities are fleeting and they always lie in Rome.

"Oh, I'll never rise higher, not forceful enough, I suppose. But had I, at your age, been blessed with your undeniable talents and resources, I've no slightest doubt but what I'd be Pope Sicola, this day . . . if some Moor hadn't poisoned me already, of course."

"Speaking of Moors . . . ?" Bartolomeo paused, eyebrows raised.

Prospero sighed forcefully, his mouth twisting as if he had unexpectedly bitten into a piece of sour fruit. "His holiness grows more senile every day, more feeble physically, too. His physicians despair that he'll last another year. And when Abdul goes . . ." Prospero paused and stared hard into nothingness, loudly cracking all his knuckles at once.

"It's really that bad, is it, then?" probed Bartolomeo.

"Worse, my boy, ten times worse than anything you could have imagined. The African faction doesn't intend for its control of the Papacy to die with Abdul; its supporters— hellfire, let's call it a private army and have done with subterfuge!—are armed to the very teeth, but so too is the Spanish faction. Of course, Rome has had those two competing factions locked in a virtual death struggle for fifty years and more, but now, with the election of this intemperate young hothead as Holy Roman Emperor, the long-quiescent German faction is rapidly consolidating and openly recruiting support. Most of the Slavs are solidly on the German hip, now likewise the Savoyards, and not a few Northern Italians. You can be certain that the Swedes will not be long in joining, so too the Danes, likely even the damned Burgundians before it's done with.

"The French and the Portuguese are the wild cards, of course. They and the Scots and Irish, for you can bet that England will be kept powerless in Romish politics, no matter what may occur in worldly affairs, at least until Abdul's successor is installed."

Bartolomeo shrugged. "No, the English will likely hate Moors for many a year to come. And who can blame them, all things considered? Certain of my correspondents, among whom are many recognized authorities on the subject, maintain to this day that the original interdictions of England and Wales, the excommunication of Arthur Tudor and the preaching of the Crusade against England were none of them strictly legal according to Canon Law."

"All quite true, more's the pity," Prospero agreed sadly. "Nor, I fear, will a simple hatred of Moors alone be all of it or even the worst of it. So disillusioned are the English and the Welsh clergy and laity that they seem to be going very forcefully about the establishment of what may amount to a *fourth* Papacy! Their Archbishop Harold di York appears to be the prime mover in this, and he has attracted clerical interest from outside the Kingdom of England, too—parts of the Empire, Burgundy, Scotland, the Swiss Cantons, and Ireland."

"Whew!" exclaimed Bartolomeo, feelingly. "What a motley pack! Burgunds and Switzers? Irish and Scots *and* English? It's akin to persuading lynx and fox or owl and rat to unite in a common purpose. The mere thought of such is frightening in its implications. Wasn't this di York tried for witchcraft in his youth, or was that his father or uncle? Only a proven warlock could effect such irrational alliances."

Prospero snorted disdainfully. "Oh, come, come, Bartolomeo, act your age. Only the ignorant characterize things they don't or can't comprehend as witchcraft, and if there is one thing we all have abundant proof"—he waved at the sumptuous furnishings and works of art—"that you are not, it is ignorant!

"Yes, di York was long ago haled up before an ecclesiastical court on a charge of witchcraft, but that charge was proved groundless, laid in pure jealousy by some of his fellow medical practitioners when he cured the father of the present King of England of some wasting illness after their methods had all proved inefficacious. He was a physician to the royal family prior to becoming a priest, you see."

D'Este wrinkled his brow. "But I had heard that he was a goldsmith, at least a journeyman at the trade."

"And more recently," put in the normally silent Cardinal Murad Yakubian, "the English archbishop has been one of his monarch's leading captains and the prime negotiator of the incipient alliance with King James of Scotland. He is patron of the great new manufactory of arms and cannon and unhallowed gunpowder in York, and, when he chances to be in that city, it is said that he often takes active and constructive roles in the innovations there produced for the king's army and fleet. There are rumors about that he also is conducting experiments in the breeding of superior livestock on one of his estates. He has long been renowned as a most accomplished alchemist. He grinds better glass lenses than any Moor or Venetian, though in understandably small quantities for his own use or for a few gifts. He—"

"Suffice it to say," interrupted Prospero, "that this Harold di York is a multitalented man and should long since have been brought to Rome and elevated, afforded the due that such rare men as he deserve.

"Understand me, Bartolomeo, I have been laboring for nearly twenty years to get Harold di York brought to Rome and granted power and position with income and free time that his mind might be allowed to soar, as the Holy Church has done to her benefit with other geniuses in times past. But these foolish, hidebound, superstitious and vicious Moors and Spaniards have balked each time I broached the subject and effectively blocked my every move.

"Oh, they have always given an excuse of one kind or

another," Prospero added, seeing D'Este's look of disbelief. "One that they trot out from time to time is his supposed impossible age. If you'd care to believe they don't misread the few available records, he would indeed be impossibly ancient, over two hundred years old, give or take a few years.

"But you know how record-keeping goes. Even the best copyists make small errors, especially so if they happen to be translating or transliterating—say, from a Northern European version of ecclesiastical Latin into Roman ecclesiastical Latin rendered in Arabic characters, as too many records of the Holy See have been of late years.

"Anyhow, the records state that *a*"—he carefully emphasized the article—"Harold di York, Physicker, did save the life of Arthur, Prince of Wales—which is the title held by crown princes of England, for whatever reason. Now you know and I know the truth of this matter. This late-fifteenth-century Harold di York was possibly the father but more likely the grandfather of this present Archbishop Harold. What more normal and natural than that a son and/or grandson should follow the family trade or profession, especially if that position be practiced exclusively upon royalty and the higher echelons of nobility?

"I think that the thing that may truly have bewildered these overly pious Moorish ninnies is that there have been three Archbishops Harold di York, all long-lived and talented men, in the course of the last century and a half. But reflect you, is it unusual for monarchs to nurture men of promise, even to provide for their get if they too show promise?

"The sad excuse of the Moors and the Spaniards, that this current di York is a preternaturally old man, is based, I feel, on nothing more uncanny or unnatural than a family dynasty of brilliant, multitalented royal physicians and churchmen plus a few easily understandable errors on the parts of a few clerk-copyists.

"So, thanks to a sad compilation of years of church politics, superstitious fear mislabeled 'piety,' and a seldom-voiced but very real dislike of northern clergy, di York ended excommunicated and now all his vast compendium of abilities are turned against us at a most ticklish juncture in time. He is probably the most dangerous enemy that Rome has anywhere, just now."

"Well, surely," said D'Este, "there are clever assassins for the hire in England as in any other land? No, that might be a mistake; even if they did not take our hireling alive and wring the truth from him, everyone still would suspect Rome. He would become a martyr, a rallying point, overnight."

"Precisely!" said Prospero. "Did I not earlier allude to your quick and astute mind, Bartolomeo? The very last thing we can afford to give this cabal of would-be seccessionists is a nice, ready-made martyr. No, we dare not strike directly at di York. Nor, in the wake of last year's string of unmitigated military disasters, do I think that we'll be able to raise any meaningful numbers of Crusaders against England, not for years to come, not in the form of either true Crusaders or paid mercenaries."

"But is not the Grand Duke of Leon launching another invasion of England sometime next spring?" queried Bartolomeo. "Word of it was bandied about here in Palermo last autumn."

Prospero frowned and shook his bald head. "Yet another of the hotheaded Spanish sort who are too full of supercilious pride to see when they're beaten or admit to it if they could see. If the grand duke gets together enough ships and if the English fleet—which is becoming larger and more aggressive with every passing day, 'tis said—doesn't catch him at sea, and if he finds and secures a spot where at he can land and marshal his troops, then . . . ah, then, brothers in faith, I entertain not the slightest doubt but that King Arthur will march his redoubtable army out and drub the grand duke as thoroughly as he did no less than four other armies last year. Much as I like the idea of Spaniards being killed or captured, which humiliates the arrogant swine almost as much as they deserve, it is to be remembered that the more Spanish gold that goes to England to pay off ransoms, the less there will be in Spain for León to send to Rome. So let us heartily pray that his grace of León is unable to find enough ships for his venture into stupidity. And the last word that I had on the subject was that he was hard pressed in that regard, scraping the sides and bottom of the barrel, as it were.''

The second Swedish ship taken by Bass's squadron bore cargo of nothing save naval stores—cordages, assortments of hardware and tackle, spars and other items of preworked timber, sheets of copper, tallow, resin, sacks of oats—and papers giving her destination as the Port of Gijón. The vessel was put under a prize crew and sailed back directly to Sir Paul Bigod's naval basin, while the squadron sailed on in search of more prey.

It was a bad week for the Scandinavians. The very next ship prized by the *Revenge* and her escorts proved to be out of Copenhagen. The vessel was solidly packed with barrels of salt pork, stockfish, cheese, and pigs of lead, with a deck cargo of roughed-out spars. This cargo seriously hampered her crew's efforts to use the four demiculverins in her waist, and the ten culverins making up her main batteries were all thoroughly blocked off by barrels of salt pork.

A single deck-sweeping salvo from guns loaded with langrage-shot hurled by the upper batteries of the *Revenge* was enough to bring the ensign dipping down from its halyard at the stern of the merchanter.

The short, one-eyed, dirty-blond-haired man who surrendered his old, dull-bladed, ill-kept sword to Bass when haled before him was furious. In barely comprehensible English, he railed, "Well, murderous pig-dogs, you, when does Englaender schiffen to make wahr on Hanse? Or chust a dirty pirate is you den? Well, turd-mann, mein t'roat here iss." He ripped aside a grimy-gray neckcloth to expose an expanse of dirt-creased skin under a bristly chin. "Do you to cut it now or later? Velcome vill be even your coward's blade, for liefer I vould be dead than alife mitout mein schiffe."

More than a little conscience-stricken, Bass simply turned and walked away, pretending not to understand the pidgin spoken by the Dane or the words shouted after him as he strode away. It was not until he returned to England that he heard of how the Danish captain had hanged himself in the hold wherein he and his crew had been cast while the prize crew manhandled the cranky, overloaded, unfamiliarly rigged flute back to friendly waters.

Examination of the capture's papers revealed that, oddly enough, this one, too, was bound for the Port of Gijón.

Another French coaster, this one sailing out of Seine-mouth laden with sailcloth and cheap wine—and bearing for none other than Gijón-port—was easily overhauled and taken by two smaller escort vessels in waters too shallow for the draft of the *Revenge*.

But a three-masted galleon running in from the Atlantic before a stern wind first essayed to outrun the squadron, then, as the fickle winds shifted and slacked off abruptly, turned and fought furiously and tenaciously.

It was the first real toe-to-toe, broadside-for-broadside sea battle between equal or near-equal ships in which Bass had ever taken part, and after that one he never sought a part in any other.

Walid Pasha, clinging like an ape high in the standing rigging, studied the enemy galleon as the *Revenge* bore down on her, driving bows-under at a speed of at least eight knots and wetting every man forward of the mainmast on the upper decks with flung spray. Finally closing and casing his long-glass, the captain slid rapidly down to the rail and leaped lightly to the deck, where he disclosed the fruits of his reconnaissance to Bass, Fahrooq, Sir Ali, and the rest of the officers.

"Yon galleon was probably built nigh to a century agone, but she has been refurbished and refitted often and is generally well-found, to judge by her appearance and sailing qualities. She means to fight; the gunports were being opened even as I spied. And it will be a *fight*, if your grace choose to engage her. Her port side is pierced for fifteen guns, her stern for four chasers, which last were already run out and looked to be long fifteens or eighteens, bronze or brass. She has soldiers, or at least many men in armor, on board, too. Well, Sebastián Bey, do we accept or decline?"

"What would Walid Pasha advise?" Bass questioned. "My experience lies on land, on horseback, mostly."

Walid signaled his boatswain to slow the galleon's speed, lest they overhaul the pugnacious stranger before any decision or preparations had been made to fight, then turned back to Bass Foster.

"Your grace, were it this galleon alone, understrength as we are from losses to the prize crews, facing so strong-looking a ship, I would say to decline the offer of battle. But backed as we are by the caravel *Krystal* and the three sloops of Paul Pasha, I must say to accept, fight, and conquer her. She will make a splendid addition to the squadron of Sebastián Bey."

"Besides, y'r grace," added Sir Calum, "we must attack her, now she's seen us so close for so long, else we'll have every *bateau de guerre* from Brittany to Navarre out looking for us. And that right speedily."

Bass sighed and nodded. "And the squadron would be of scant value to his majesty on the bottom of the sea, and that's where we soon would be if we had to fight full-armed warships every day, for our every prize. Very well, Walid Pasha, engage them. Yours will be the overall command; you've done this before."

At a distance just beyond the range of smoothbore broadside cannon, *Revenge* and *Krystal*, one behind the other, sailed slowly in a great circle around the galleon, which now had run up a French battle ensign along with several other, unfamiliar colors.

Using the three new rifled cannon developed by Pete Fairley, which each of these larger ships now mounted on swivels at bow and stern, they pounded the target mercilessly, while return fire dropped into the sea or went skipping over the waves before sinking.

As Bass watched, Nugai and a Fairley-trained guncrew opened the breech, swabbed the bore from the chamber end, slipped a long, pointed, fused shell into the rifling grooves, following it with a waxed-linen cartridge, slammed the breech and gave the handle the half-turn that locked it, then pricked open the powder cartridge, filled the vent with priming, and carefully sighted the gun. Balancing easily on his short, bowed legs, the self-appointed Kalmyk guncaptain stood like a yellow-brown statue, awaiting the precise moment that the *Revenge* began her upswing before laying his smoking slow-match directly atop the filled vent.

Following the shot with his binoculars, Bass saw it crash through the upper level of the sterncastle, and a split second later, he saw what looked like a door blasted down into the crowded waist, while a sheet of fire and a hail of small debris burst out of the sterncastle's rear windows.

After a single broadside from each of their full batteries, the French wisely ceased use of the outranged guns, only essaying shots whenever the *Revenge* or the *Krystal* lay athwart bow or stern, where the longer-ranged chasers could be brought into play. And the French gunners quickly proved their expertise, scoring a total of five hits on the two ships, none of which, however, did any real damage or inflicted any injuries.

The same, unfortunately for the French, could not be said of what was being done by Pete Fairley's fearsome breech-loading rifled cannon. Binoculars and long-glasses showed not a few still or thrashing bodies on her decks, along with a couple of spars and a decent-sized jumble of rigging, tackle, and shredded sailcloth. There was at least one fire on her gundecks to judge by the amounts of smoke billowing out of the still-open gunports. Occasionally, the wind bore down to the attackers the rattle of a drum or a thin wail that might have been a scream of agony. Like so many ants at this distance, tiny figures scurried about, fighting the fires blazing in both fore- and sterncastles, apparently oblivious to the shells still bursting among them, up in the rigging or in the fabric of the ship herself.

Had there been sufficient supply of the cylindrical shells, they well might have continued to bleed the French galleon at a safe range until the ship was so crippled or her crew so reduced as to ensure a quick, easy victory on closing, but the numbers of the explosive shells had been limited at the very inception of the voyage and several had been used as chaser shots in earlier actions. So when the bottommost layer of the shell boxes was reached, Walid Pasha ordered the long-range shelling halted and the second, more normal and far more dangerous phase of his plan of battle commenced.

CHAPTER
THE THIRD

Abbot Fergus had been journeying back from Edinburgh when the great, fearsome thunderbolt had set the thatch roof of the abbey barn afire. The monks and the lay brothers, the few hale guests, as well as folk of all ages who'd run up from the village at sight of the flames, and even some of the patients—for this was a nursing order—had done all that was humanly possible to save the contents of the ancient stone buildings, while the whipping winds of the tempest had imparted murderous life to the flames.

The all-devouring conflagration had leapt from one building to another and another and yet another, while terrified kine bawled, while men and women shouted and howled and shrieked and screamed. Tonsured cleric and hairy smith risked their lives side by side to rip loose and throw down great armsful of the heavy, stinking, smoldering thatch. Others ran into buildings already afire to bear out the few poor treasures, furnishings, stores, and sufferers too ill to help themselves.

In the cold, misty forenoon that followed that hellish night, Abbot Fergus arrived at his journey's end and, in company with Brother Pàruig, his longtime secretary, walked the grounds and, amongst the still-smoking ruins, compiled mental evaluations of the losses and began to frame in his own mind the letter and detailed report of the calamity which he soon must dictate and send off to the parent house in the Western Isles. Such damages as he saw before him would cost far more to make right than he thought he could obtain locally.

". . . three cows, one of them big with calf, alas. The roof of the byre collapsed, flaming, ere the last two could be led out. As for the other, she was found dead where she had been tethered, and no burn or other mark upon her.

"The oxen all were saved, God be praised, likewise the asses and the small mule that was willed to the monastery last year. The fires never got to the cellars, so we'll not lack for food and drink, at least, nor the beasts for grain, though every one of the nearer haystacks burned and—"

"But the folk," broke in Abbot Fergus. "What of the folk, brother?"

Brother Pàruing sighed and signed himself, piously. "Two of our brothers we know are dead—Brothers Gilleasbuig and Donnochadh-ogh—one of a broken skull when he fell off a roof, the other burnt with the last brace of cows he had run in to lead out to safety. Father Mark the Sassenach is missing; so also are two of the lay brothers who were sharing the nightwatch in the main hospital."

"Their names, these lay brothers?" prodded Abbot Fergus.

"Gilliosa Hay. Brother Gilliosa Hay, he and that wild Highlander barbarian, Ian MacBean."

"And our charges, the sick and injured for whom we were caring in their need?" demanded Abbot Fergus. "Were all of them saved?"

Brother Pàruig wrung his hands and sighed. "No, not all were saved, I fear me. In the dark and the confusion there was . . . was a . . . a regrettable error made. It was no one's fault, really, but . . . but" A glimpse of familiar and feared fire in the abbot's steely eyes sent Brother Pàruig stuttering on with his tale.

"It was simply that . . . that the villagers all thought that we, the brothers, had fetched out the seriously ill patients. We all thought that they, the villagers, had done that deed of mercy. And by the time we—I—realized that . . . that . . ."

The younger monk began to tremble uncontrollably and whimper like a hurt child, while a great gush of tears bathed his stubbled cheeks. Patting the man's shoulder, the old abbot led Brother Pàruig to a jumbled pile of boxes and casks and sat him down, beckoning over another monk to care for him. Any man, the abbot well knew, could take but so much and no more; poor Pàruig had never been as strong as average, and the horrific events of last night and earlier this morning, whilst he was nominally in charge of monastery affairs, had simply pushed him temporarily beyond his limits of endurance.

The two missing lay brothers were found as soon as the monks and villagers got around to delving into the charred ruins of the main hospital building, but the corpse of the priest did not turn up until a trio of husky monks went to feed the three madmen lodged in a row of five low stone-built cells that composed the last remains of the very first monastery to stand upon this ground, possibly as much as ten centuries past.

Abbot Fergus was frantically summoned to the spot to find one of the three madmen gone. In his malodorous little cell lay the naked corpse of Father Mark. The priest's face was horribly contorted and discolored, his tongue protruding well beyond his jaws and lips. His eyes too were bulging from their sockets, and the thin cord which had been used to throttle him—it looked to be made of braided hair—was still knotted deadly tight about his neck and throat.

The priest's warm woolen habit was gone, as was the peculiar foreign footgear he affected—something on the order of Lowlander brogues, but finer and crafted of finished leather rather than rawhide.

Back at the ruins of the monastery, Abbot Fergus penned in his own hand an addendum to the letter to his parent house, noting that Father Mark had been found dead, murdered by a mad Sassenach, one Uilleam Kawlyer, who now was roaming at large in the habit and shoes of the murdered priest.

Sir Ugo led the Duce di Bolgia and the lieutenant along a well-lit interior corridor which debouched into a great hall boasting a high, vaulted ceiling, and with loggias on no less than three sides, one of these being faced with carven wood-and-ivory privacy screens in the Moorish manner and designed to prevent observers from being themselves observed.

From the lavishly decorated and furnished great hall, they entered another short corridor, then climbed a flight of stairs and passed along one of a pair of marble-arched loggias which faced one another over a long, narrow garden of tile walks, manicured greensward, carefully tended shrubs and small fruit trees, flowers, twittering, darting birds, and gurgling fountains.

The loggia they had traversed and now quitted extended on around to the right, and halfway down that stretch, two huge, towering, albeit a little pudgy men with shiny blue-black skins and shaven heads stood obvious guard before a pair of carven and inlaid doors. The ball-butts of a brace of wheellock pistols projected from under each blackamoor's saffron sash. Heavy and very cursive scimitars hung from their baldrics, and, in addition, one was armed with a two-barreled wheellock fowler with bores looking to be as wide as small cannon, while the other leaned on a six-foot pike.

Di Bolgia knew quite a bit about firearms, and he knew that even as big as that guard was, if ever he had to fire just one of those two-digit-wide barrels without a harquebus prop, he was going to find himself on his arse ten feet back from where he'd started, likely with a caved-in chest, to boot. The two men with their too-smooth faces were probably *castrati*, which meant that behind those doors lay the women's wing of the cardinal's palazzo. And the cardinal was deluding himself if he thought that that garish duo of Aethiop eunuchs provided any true protection of his hareem from invasion by any really determined body.

They were instructed to wait in a chamber whilst Sir Ugo went off somewhere alone. Silently, a servitor entered bearing a silver-gilt tray on which were a ewer and a pair of goblets—ruby-red glass bowls set in heavy, intricately carven silver. Wordlessly, the man poured wine into the goblets and would then have departed had di Bolgia not grasped an arm in one powerful hand.

Waving at the goblets, he growled, "You drink first, a

good healthy swallow out of each, or . . ." He laid his other hand to the jeweled hilt of his dagger.

With an indulgent smile, but still no words, the servitor padded back over to the table and obediently lifted first one goblet, then the other, taking a double swallow from each, then refilling them from the ewer. With another deep bow, the wordless man turned and left the way he had come.

Picking up one of the goblets, di Bolgia remarked to the lieutenant, "That little farce proves nothing, of course. He could have hurried back to a waiting emetic or antidote. His employers might have failed to inform him of the fact that he was to serve poisoned wine. He could even have been willing to sacrifice his own life in order to take mine . . . and yours, too, of course, my boy. But I've found it never hurts to take such rudimentary precautions.

"Ahhh, this is indeed a fine vintage. A hint of sweetness and an aftertaste of well-hung apples. This is a northern wine, my boy, none of this vinegar-sour Sicilian horsepiss. His eminence has a superb palate. My estimate of him has risen to new heights, and I've yet to even lay eyes to the man."

From somewhere nearby came a single, dry chuckle. As the two soldiers glanced all around the room, a section of the western wall swung silently open to reveal another, larger chamber wherein sat three men garbed as cardinals. Sir Ugo stood a bit off to one side of the trio.

"Come in, your grace of Bolgia, Lieutenant di Crespa. Bring the wine and we all will share it. It comes of one of my own vineyards located in one of the westerly electorates of the Empire. Viticulture has been practiced in the valley of the Moselle River, there, since the days of the Caesars."

Most of the westernmost wall of the larger chamber consisted of five pairs of doors with clear glass panels letting onto a wide, deep balcony. Silhouetted against the bright sunlight flooding in through these glass doors, no details could be seen of the faces of the three seated clergy.

But, once more, that resonant, well-modulated baritone voice invited, "I say, come in, gentlemen. We have been awaiting you."

Leaving Pandolfo to fetch the ewer, Timoteo strode through the concealed doorway . . . and nearly dropped his goblet. The cardinal in the center seat, he who had been speaking, was none other than the catfooted, wordless "servitor" he had intimidated into drinking of the wine when first it had been proffered. Setting down the goblet, he hurriedly swept off his cap, dropped to one knee, and kissed the ring on the extended hand. The nails were manicured and the hand soft, but with a perceptible hint of steely strength in the muscles and sinews underlying the flesh.

When he had been introduced and had made his obeisances to the other two prelates, Sir Ugo returned to the chamber followed by a column of servitors, who bore in a carven and upholstered chair with arms and back for di Bolgia, an armless chair for Sir Ugo, a backless arm stool for Lieutenant di Crespa, four more of the glass-and-silver goblets, and a second, larger ewer of wine.

When all were seated and the doors tightly closed behind the servitors, Cardinal D'Este began by asking, "Your grace, how much do you know of the English Problem?"

Shifting his baldric slightly, Timoteo crossed his booted legs and leaned forward. "Enough, your eminence, to stay as far away from that part of the world as is humanly possible. That kingdom is become of late a meatgrinder of armies, and not even the Holy See has enough money to hire me and mine to follow in the footsteps of old Conte Hreszko. Nor am I alone in this firm resolve, your eminence. The *conte* left Rome proud and confident, a living legend amongst professional captains. He came back a humbled and broken old dotard who, they say, will not live long because, disgraced, he no longer has the will to live.

"Therefore, I doubt me that any captain of note would hire either himself or his company out for a campaign in England or Wales. Or even in Scotland, for that matter.

"So, if that is the offer, your eminence, thank you, but no, not for one thousand ducats per day, per man!"

"Your bluntness verges close upon insult, di Bolgia,"

snapped Cardinal Sicola. The cardinal seemed upon the point of saying more when D'Este waved a placating hand.

"Your grace misunderstands. I have no intention of securing his services for England, for I can see no point in prolonging an affair that it may have been ill-advised to even commence. I feel that a few years of benign neglect by Rome may end in accomplishing far more in England than would the services of a score of armies. So rest your mind on that issue.

"But let us two touch now upon the subject of geography, eh? There is a largish island just to the west of England, is there not, your grace?"

Di Bolgia nodded curtly. "Yes, your eminence. It contains a number of tiny, so-called kingdoms, plus one leader who calls himself something equivalent to *regno grande* but usually has even less land than any of the others and no real power over them. The folk are called 'Irlandese,' and I've soldiered with many of them over the years. They are good fighters individually, but respond ill to any sort of discipline and seem to stay drunk most of the time.

"I know little of the internal politics of the land, save that I am led to believe that the various kingdoms have been warring amongst themselves constantly for generations at least, possibly for centuries. There seem to be three or more racial strains native to the island, and they make war along racial lines, too.

"It is rumored that one of these little kingdoms has implanted one or more colonies called in totality 'Great Irland' somewhere south of Vinland and north of Nueva España."

D'Este nodded, smiling. "You are well informed, your grace. Now, tell me, would you hire out yourself and your company for an initial contract of two years' service in Irland?"

Timoteo sipped delicately at his wine and dabbed at his full, sensual lips with a lace cuff before replying with a question of his own. "Under what circumstances of initial service, your eminence—aggressive or defensive? That is, will we be expected to quit our ships and make an opposed landing under fire from the Irlandese? Such tactics are always risky and could cost me a hefty percentum of my company in killed, drowned, and wounded.''

D'Este held up a hand and shook his head vigorously. "Oh, no, your grace, you are assured of a safe landing, offloaded from ship to quay directly, under the numerous guns of a fortified port city which will be your base of operations, thenceforth. The port city is one of the principal cities of Rome's firm and steady ally, King Tàmhas of Munster.

"Until very recently, King Tàmhas was being very hard pressed by the troops of the high king, Brian VIII, and he has lost more than a third of his realm to his enemy. But now the high king has withdrawn the bulk of his forces from the disputed lands and is devoting his far from inconsiderable talents to an attempt to do that which never has been done in all of known history. It is Brian's aim to unite all or at least the most of Irland under his leadership against Rome and Holy Mother the Church.

"This vital monarch has already won over some of the other kings, and he and they throughout all the lands they control have seized Church-owned properties and treasures, ships, gunpowder mills and supplies of gunpowder and priests' powder. Shocking to state, some Irland-born clergy have turned renegade and are now making powder for the high king, *unhallowed* powder."

Although he listened in respectful silence, this last did not impress di Bolgia. He knew how to make gunpowder himself, from scratch, and hallowed or unhallowed, it all did the same deadly work in pistol, arquebus, cannon, or petard. And he liked what he was hearing of this High King Brian. Small, relatively weak states lay constantly at the mercy of larger, stronger ones, and the only answer was to get out and conquer, consolidate lands, become a larger, stronger state oneself, a state to be feared and therefore respected by its peers-in-power.

Such a man as this King Brian, he thought, should make an interesting antagonist, and when once his two-year contract to Rome had been filled and he and his company would be in Irland anyway, he might explore the possibility of hiring on with the armies of the high king. After all, every legend he had heard over the long years had reputed Irland to be a land rich in gold, silver, and jewels.

"Sebastián Bey," said Walid Pasha solemnly, "it were wise now to arm. For after the close and exchange of broadside cannonades, to order grappling, I shall, and then we all must board and fight or die as God wills. The two larger sloops have orders to await the end of the cannonade, then to sail up and lock onto the enemy galleon at stem and at stern and board her from those directions; the plan will give us more men on board her and force her complement to fight foes at both front and rear, which should serve to disconcert them to a degree."

Bass had long since ceased being amazed at the overall competence of the master of the ship they had renamed the *Revenge*. He would find a way to accomplish virtually whatever task he was set, and he would accomplish it well, with his own special flourish.

Nor did the other officers and men of the warship seem to resent the fact that, for all their apparent freedom, they were little better than military slaves. There was no animosity—either overt or covert—toward the Englishmen, Welshmen, Irishmen, and Scots. The Mediterraneans deferred to officers and sergeants, of course, but seemed to accept the mass of other ranks as just another batch of landlubber soldiers shipped aboard to do the fighting and, they hoped, the dying while they the sailors handled the ship.

In the sterncastle cabin that he had insisted they share with him aboard the crowded ship, Sir Ali and Nugai assisted Bass to arm. After stripping down to his silken drawers and crotch-length linen undertunic, he first strapped on a horn-and-boiled-leather codpiece and made certain that his penis and scrotum were tucked well inside the protective device and were not in danger of being pinched by its edges. Then he pulled on a pair of tight-legged breeches which incorporated broad straps under the instep of each foot. Squatting, Nugai gartered these just below the knee to prevent them riding up the leg should the straps break.

While Sir Ali held it gaped for him, Bass slipped head and arms into a long-sleeved, hip-long quilted garment—soft finished leather outside, fine velvet inside, raw wool in between—and the nimble yellow-brown fingers of the waiting Nugai secured the dozen points that fastened upper and lower garments together.

Bass stepped into his cavalry boots, made to his exact specifications by a bemused and wondering bootier. Into stitched pockets spaced closely all around the leg of the boot and extending from just below the knee down to the ankle, Sir Ali and Nugai inserted splints of fine armor steel. The steel cop to guard the patella was built into the thigh-high boots, as too was the panel of ring mail that protected the tendons in the backs and sides of the knee. Additional stitched-pocket, steel-splint arrangements on the thigh leathers' fronts and exposed outer sides gave reasonable leg protection without the cumbersome leg armor still worn by many horsemen over their boots.

Bass had decided to do without a mail hauberk, but Sir Ali and Nugai would not hear of such insanity, and he grudgingly but obediently knelt and held up his arms that the two shorter men might fit the thirty-odd pounds of riveted-steel rings. It sagged to well below his crotch, but Sir Ali, searching out certain larger rings and threading through them a length of hide thong, gathered up several inches of length and belted the armor so that a portion of the weight was carried by his hips.

This armor was all of the best quality; it had been made for him, to his exact measurements, by King Arthur's own resident Milanese armorers. Due mostly to continual badgering on the parts of Sir Ali, Nugai, and certain other members of his well-meaning staff, Bass had spent many a long hour in this armor—afoot and ahorse, practicing with a plethora of weapons, tilting and riding cross-country in good weather and foul. But none of that meant that he had learned to like wearing the hot, heavy, confining, and basically uncomfortable collection of steel plates, mesh, bolts, rivets, and buckles.

Sir Ali held the backplate in place while Nugai strapped it on over the hauberk, then they reversed roles, with Nugai holding up the breastplate while Sir Ali inserted the hingepins on one side and did up the buckles on the other. The gorget was placed over a length of linen lapped around Bass's neck and throat before the two arming men added spauldrons on the shoulders, rerebrace plates over the long sleeves of the hauberk to guard the upper arms, and vambrace plates on the lower arms. Then they strapped couters and elbow cops between the two.

Around his hips, loins, and buttocks, they attached the taces. Tasset plates were buckled to the lower front edges of the taces to protect the upper thighs. The two were upon the very point of adding a plastron, or reinforcing plate, over the breast plate when Bass called a halt.

"Good Lord, Ali, any more weight and I won't be able to move, much less jump from one ship to another and then fight! As it is, I'll have to be very mindful of my footing, for if I hit water, it'll be goodbye Bass Foster; I'll sink like a stone and be long drowned before I can get a tenth of this scrap iron off me."

"Nonsense, your grace," the crooked-nosed Arabian knight reassured him. "A century ago, when armor was heavier and less easy to move in than this modern stuff is, one of the tests of a prospective knight was to swim a river or lake or bay fully armed. Be a man a good swimmer and uninjured, his armor alone won't drown him.

"But, your grace, you really should let us put on the plastron. Superb as is the quality of your breastplate, it simply lacks the thickness and strength to stop a harquebus ball at close range."

However, when his grace, Sir Sebastian Foster, Duke of Norfolk, strode out onto the deck of his flagship. it was without the plastron. His missed the familiar feel of scabbarded Tara steel slapping against his left leg, but he had deliberately left the blade ashore, correctly estimating the long cavalry broadsword to be ill suited to shipboard combats.

In the place of that priceless weapon, his baldric held a hybrid of his own design—an old *cinquedea* two-foot dagger blade rehilted with the quillions, pommel, and pierced-steel handguard from a Spanish broadsword captured at the Battle of Bloody Rye. In its present configuration, the century-old blade—some four inches wide just below the quillions, double-edged, and tapering to an acute point—had never been bloodied. This day would either prove or disprove its worth for the task it faced.

The broad belt cinched around Bass's waist over the armor was fitted with brass hooks along its lower edge. From four of these dangled wheellock pistols, two of them double-barreled weapons, all full-charged, primed and spanned, ready to fire. Two other hooks—one on each side—supported daggers, one a metal flask of charging powder, and one a stiff-leathern wallet containing cast-lead pistol balls, greased patches, a small flask of priming powder, and a spanner that would fit the wheels of all four pistols.

In the crook of his left arm, as he took his place beside Walid Pasha on the quarterdeck, was his choice of helmets for today—an old-fashioned burgonet covered in bright-green samite and fitted with a bar visor; bars and edges had been gilded.

As the *Revenge* inexorably bore down upon her quarry, Walid Pasha ordered all the remaining shells for the big rifles to be borne forward to the two bow-mounted guns, then ordered them to concentrate their fire on the fighting-tops of the two larger masts—main and fore.

"They are chancy targets at best, Sebastian Bey," he told Bass in explanation, "but even if God fails to smile upon our gunners in this, the shot still will do certain damage to the sails and rigging and thus render her more difficult to control with any certainty in the coming close battle."

But luck did grin. The second shot from the gun Nugai had taken over not only struck and exploded in the crowded and heavily armed maintop, but apparently also set off their own powder supply. A great flameshot flash and a billow of dense smoke was the first indication of this telling blow. As bodies, pieces of bodies, and debris of all sorts showered onto the waist below and the earsplitting roar of the two merged explosions reached the ears of those aboard the *Revenge*, the upper reaches of the mainmast—sails, yards, rigging, tackle, and all—tipped, tipped, tipped, then suddenly pitched forward onto the foremast, which also broke through under the excessive weight, smothering the foretop in canvas and cordage.

Walid Pasha smiled grimly as he lowered his glass. "It could hardly have chanced better for our arms, Sebastián Bey. Your Kalmyk is a rare gunner, and a rare naval gunner, which is even less common. But not even he could have told that mast which way to fall. That was God's holy doing.

"Waiting boarders and deck crews often suffer severely from swivels, arquesbuses, and pistols employed by the men stationed in those tops. Now the Frenchman's largest one has entirely ceased to be and the foretop is rendered completely useless until seamen can get up there and ax them free. For some odd reason, that ship lacks a fighting-top on the mizzenmast; a long, narrow platform, right enough, but no provision for swivels or men to serve them."

Revenge had been bearing down on the starboard side of the French galleon, but had drawn only sporadic fire from the big main guns, no concentrated fire from battery or even deck, and as they drew closer a possible reason for this became apparent.

Halfway between stern and mainmast, thick billows of smoke poured from one or more of the starboard gunports, obscuring at least half of the ports and probably making proper gunlaying an impossibility. After studying signal flags displayed by the caravel *Krystal*, Walid said, "That must be a big fire on those gundecks, for the port batteries are not offering much more gunnery than are these starboard ones, your grace. God has indeed smiled upon us thus far. Let us all pray that we retain His favor."

Slowly, the gap between the two ships narrowed. When

some bare hundred yards separated them, Walid sailed past the starboard of the French ship, coming up from the stern, his portside batteries firing on the virtually unmissable target as each gun came to bear. These culverins and demiculverins threw their balls at the gundecks of the Frenchman, while the waist guns, the stern- and forecastle guns, the rail swivels, and the top swivels, as well as the ship's complement of arquebusiers, sped their loads against rigging and exposed personnel.

Immediately Walid had completed his sail-by, *Krystal* began the same maneuver on the Frenchman's port side. Then Walid turned the ship about and, at a bit over fifty yards, came by from the opposite direction, bringing his starboard broadside into play. Again, as soon as he had finished, the caravel emulated his actions on the other side of the French galleon.

"Did we not desire to capture the ship in reasonably good condition, your grace," commented Walid Pasha, "now would be the time to come around once more, steer really close, and strive to hull her with the culverins, while pouring red-hot shot from the demiculverins and sakers into her stern- and forecastles and her 'tween decks. Another Turkish captain and I did just this to a Venetian galleon—but that one was a four-master—some years back. Would that we had Marwan Pasha and his great galleon over there in the place of the caravel *Krystal.*"

The return fire, though sporadic and not at all concerted, was not entirely inaccurate. The *Revenge* had suffered a number of round-shot damages to her fabric—more of them and more severe on her starboard than on her port, of course, due to the lessened range at which the starboard had been presented as target. There was fresh blood in more than one place on the decks visible from the bridge, and barefoot sailors were even as Bass watched shaking sand over the red blotches to improve footing. In his 'tween-decks cubby far below, Master Jibral and his mates already were hard at work with knives, saws, forceps, and needles.

Bass wondered how Captain Edwin Alfshott and Sir Liam

Kavanaugh were faring on board the *Krystal*. Despite the strengthenings and general repairs and renovations done by Sir Paul Bigod's men at the Royal Naval Basin and Yards, the caravel had not been either designed or built to be a warship and it was conceivable that hits that might not do any real or lasting harm to *Revenge* could irreparably damage the far more lightly built ship.

"Immediately the starboard guns are reloaded, we steer in to close quarters," said Walid Pasha, before beginning to bark orders in Turkish and Arabic to various of his officers. These officers in turn scattered to bark their own orders, and the already busy, crowded waist became a bustle of activity.

Some dozen big iron grapnels were brought out to have lengths of strong cordage rove to their shank eyes and their bits tested for sharpness and, where necessary, touched up with file and stone; then they were laid in convenient spots by the starboard rails.

The ship's carpenter and his mate supervised the bringing on deck of several long, thick planks varying in width from a foot to about eighteen inches, then set about driving iron spikes, two or three of them, through each end of the planks—boarding-bridges-to-be.

The boatswain and his mates began to pass among the common seamen, arming them with short, heavy swords, dirks, battleaxes, and boarding pikes. They also passed out plain, simple skullcaps of steel to go under turbans or *kafiyehs* and twine-tied bundles of foot-long fletched darts and a few longer javelins. Last of all, they brought up and carefully unwrapped a few short bows, which were delivered to certain older men, all of them Turks.

Bass noted that the bows must be extremely powerful, for two men's strength was required to string them. Strung, however, no one of them was more than a bare three feet in length, and the arrows, plucked out of lacquered leather cylinders and carefully examined, were short as well, two feet or less from nocks to points.

With bows and arrow cases hung down their backs, eight

Turks took to the rigging, climbing swiftly and surely up to spots that were obviously predetermined.

When but twenty yards separated the two ships, both of the French galleon's starboard-bow chasers fired loads of langrage at the packed forecastle deck of the *Revenge*, but with poor results. One piece was fired too soon and the antipersonnel charge was wasted against the bow timbers; the other was fired a split second too late, sending most of it aloft to pepper the sails and foremast.

Then they were gliding alongside the battered French galleon, with a bare three or four yards of water between the two hulls. Every other gun of the starboard batteries was fired, directly at the French gunports, then, while swivels, slingpieces, and other smaller ordnance swept the decks from rails to both castles and fighting-tops, with arquebusiers and archers adding their ounces of lead and feathered shafts to the deadly sleet, brawny arms whirled the grapnels about to gain momentum, then hurled them across the narrow space to thud onto decks and sink their points deeply into rails and coamings, ladders and woodwork. Seamen and soldiers alike heaved at the lines of well-imbedded hooks, slowly warping the ships even closer, as others stood ready with the spiked planks.

Ax-wielding men rushed to where the grapnels had imbedded themselves and some few were able to ax through the taut lines before being transfixed by short arrows from the small but powerful bows of the Turks aloft in *Revenge*'s rigging. They were, Bass noted with a part of his mind, far more valuable than would have been an equal number of arquesbusiers in that their "reloading" took split seconds, so that they could drop the original axman in one breath and the man who rushed to take up that ax in the very next.

One more salvo was fired from the sakers in the waist and the swivel guns, poured full into the mob in the waist of the enemy galleon—which rode some two feet lower than did the larger, four-masted *Revenge*—then the waiting planks were tipped over and thudded down to sink their spikes into the Frenchman's rails. At once, soldiers and seamen swarmed onto the narrow, springy footing, weapons out and ready.

The three cardinals, di Bolgia, Sir Ugo, and the lieutenant had arisen and now stood about a large table in a better-lit area nearer to the glass doors. With goblets and hands they were anchoring a huge parchment map D'Este had just unrolled.

Using an antique ballock dagger's slender blade as a pointer, D'Este explained, "Your grace and his company would board ship here, in Palermo harbor. There will be three large ships—two three-masted galleons and one four-masted—so there should not be overmuch crowding on the voyage. The two three-masters are really merchant ships owned by a man I know quite well, but still the both of them are well enough armed to hold their own against most marauders.

"The larger ship, on the other hand, is a line-of-battle ship, leased from the King of France and originally scheduled to take part in an attempt to revictual and resupply the besieged City of London. Unfortunately—or, possibly, very fortunately, since that entire fleet was sunk or captured by King Arthur's navy—this galleon was very late in arriving at Livorno and missed the sailing date of the supply fleet by over a month. She and her French captain and crew have been in Livorno since, but I have dispatched a message summoning them down here, to Palermo. After all, their rent is paid for a twelvemonth; no profit in letting them sit useless.

"Beyond the Pillars of Hercules, your ship captains will have orders to stand southwestward along the Afriquan coast to the port of Anfa Antiqua. There, additional persons, cargo, and ships will be added to the fleet, and all will, allowing God's grace of decent weather, proceed immediately due north to Irland and your landfall.

"Once landed, your grace should report at once to Archbishop Giosué di Rezzi. He will be our—your grace's employers'—voice in Irland, and though ostensibly you will be King Tàmhas's general, you will be answerable only to the archbishop. Understood?"

"Understood, your eminence," Timoteo said, then asked, "But this archbishop . . . there is a retired condottiere, a very great captain in his time . . . ?"

D'Este replied, "The archbishop is a younger brother of the still-esteemed Barone Mario di Rezzi, though it is my understanding that the two brothers differ in many ways.

"But back to our subject. In addition to the troops with which your grace lands in Irland, you will be expected to take in hand and reorganize some two thousands of Flemish mercenaries—both foot and horse—who were routed, badly battered, by a much smaller force of Irlandese under the King of Lagan, last year. Their captain was slain in that action, and they retreated behind the walls of Dublin City, from whence they were brought down south by ship by King Tàmhas at the instigation of Archbishop Giosué, subsequent to the departure of their erstwhile employer, Cardinal Mustapha il-Ganub.

"They are rather dispirited, I understand, but a captain of the well-earned reputation of your grace should be able to whip them back into shape. Your grace has *carta blanca* in this matter; flog, maim, or hang as many as necessary to make them reliable soldiers once more. You and those of your officers and sergeants involved in this task will, of course, receive additional recompense.

"The port fortifications and the principal citadel in King Tàmhas's capital city are commanded, officered, and partially manned by Venetian specialist-cannoneers serving long-term contracts to the king. The archbishop attests them to be a prickly lot and easily offended, but your grace can only do his best to remain on at least civil terms with them.

"The third and largest group of fighting men will be King

Tàmhas's Royal Munster Army. Being supposedly the king's hired general, a part of your job will be to see what can be done to make this army battle-ready.''

"Does his eminence know aught of the general makeup of the army of this pocket-king?'' asked di Bolgia slowly, keeping his gaze on the map and pulling absently at his lower lip.

D'Este shrugged. "Very little, really. Archbishop Giosué avers that while a large force for those climes, most of it is ill trained and not very reliable. The best, he says, of all the pack are a contingent—numbers unstated—of Irlandese noblemen who have all soldiered elsewhere than Irland and one or more units of a class of soldier called 'galhogleses' or some similar barbaric term.''

" 'Gallowglasses,' your eminence,'' corrected di Bolgia politely. "I, myself, have yet to see aught of them, but I have both heard and read reports concerning them and their origins, uses, strengths, and weaknesses. Originally, they were all footmen, employing as principal weapon-of-choice an early variety of poleax. But over the years they are become a type of dragoon, all mounted. They still carry an oversized ax and can wreak as bloodily afoot as ever they could, but now they wear half-armor and carry pistols, swords, fuzees, and, sometimes, even darts or throwing axes. There are not over many of them in any one generation, and they seem to fight noplace save in Irland, for all that the most of them come not from Irland but the western islands of the Kingdom of Scotland.''

"Your grace seems wondrous well versed in these matters,'' the youngest of the cardinals, Murad Yakubian, commented. "That is, for one who claims never to have soldiered in Irland or England.''

Timoteo picked up his goblet and sipped at the rare, no doubt expensive vintage. He kept his face blank, impassive. After all, the Armenian goat-fucker hadn't actually called him a liar, hadn't actually accused him of concealing portions of his past. He *had* concealed certain aspects of his experiences in the north, but nothing that had any bearing upon this current matter.

"I doubt not, your eminence di Yakubian, that you assiduously seek out those returned recently from distant lands that you may learn from them of those topics which most concern you. I do the same, ferreting out all that I may hear of a military nature. For ever do I try to think of new, untried, and better ways of waging war.

"Now if your eminence feels me to be deceitful, feels that I have withheld knowledge or personal experience that might have a bearing upon the enterprise at hand, perhaps it were better that I withdraw, thanking you all for your kind hospitality, and return to the service of his highness of Naples, leaving your eminences free to secure the services of a captain you can trust. For few are the mutually agreeable contracts entered into by signatories basically distrustful the one of the other."

Which was a mouthful of pious claptrap, thought Timoteo, and if you don't know it, my red-capped friend, you are far dumber than I think.

Yakubian smiled lazily. "What need of contracts at all, if all men in this world trusted one another? But you misunderstood, your grace. I was but commenting upon your rather surprising erudition—surprising, that is, for a professional warrior—not suggesting that you had misled us as to your campaigns and your other travels in foreign lands."

"King Tàmhas has a largish personal guard for so relatively unimportant a monarch," D'Este went on. "In addition to perhaps half a hundred Irlandese noblemen, he has for long employed a band of some twoscore Rus-Goths who call themselves something on the order of 'Ulfhednarren.' Does your grace possibly know aught of this rare type, also?"

Timoteo shook his head. "I've never been as far east as Rus, your eminence, nor conversed with many as have. Sweda-Goths all consider Rus-Goths to be a strange, barbaric folk with ancient, near-pagan customs and practices; some are no longer even pure Gothic, having intermarried with Finns and Kalmyks and other, singular, pagan peoples, over the centuries. Someone of the Order of Teutonic Knights could probably tell you much more of the Rus-Goths, since they have been fighting them for many a year.''

D'Este nodded. ''Well, then, your grace, how long will it require for your company to march to Palermo?''

Timoteo grinned. ''They will be under the city walls by the end of this week, your eminence. They are on the march, even as we converse. When will the ships be here for them to board?''

D'Este answered the grin with a pleased smile. ''It is most refreshing to deal again with a direct, honest man, your grace. As regards the ships: one is presently unloading here after a voyage from the Spanish Indies; after that, a few days should suffice for the crew to refit her to carry men rather than cargo. The second is due in port any day now from Joppa. As for the French warship, I should estimate a fortnight or something less.''

Timoteo gave a brusque nod of his head. ''Very well, your eminence. That will give me the time to sail over to Naples, collect the last of the monies due me from his majesty, and notify him at the same time that I am signing a contract with the Holy See for service outside Italy or Sicily. This last should somewhat ease his mind, for one reason he has for so long retained me was his fear that one of his many enemies would hire me to fight against him; the service he has had me and mine doing for the last year or more could have been accomplished much more cheaply by a far less expensive company or even by the Neapolitan Guards.

''When I come back from Naples, I'll expect the contracts to be ready for the signing and sealing. I'll also expect to be paid the initial third of the agreed-upon sum, in new-minted gold, please—Spanish onzas would be fine and should be easy to come by in a mercantile city such as Palermo.''

''Your grace, then, distrusts the coinage of his prospective employer, the Holy See?'' inquired old Cardinal Sicola, with an inscrutable demeanor.

''Your eminence,'' replied di Bolgia, ''a coin that contains less than nine of ten parts gold is not and should not be called a gold coin; and when put to the Archimedean water test, a

truly distressing number of Romish gold coins have proved to
be as little as three-quarters gold, worth their stated value
nowhere save in the states ruled directly from Rome . . . if
there.''

The condottiere braced himself for some sort of indignant
explosion, a burst of ecclesiastical wrath from old Sicola. But
it failed to materialize. The old man seemed almost to be
pleased by the blunt, if unpalatable, truth.

''Very well, your grace,'' D'Este agreed, smiling, ''the
contracts will be drawn and ready for the signing, sealing,
and witnessing immediately upon your return from Naples.
Your gold will be here too, in Spanish onzas, as you request.''

Bass Foster had but just placed foot to bridging board when
a culverin mounted immediately below that board in the
Frenchman's main starboard battery was loosed off, point-
blank into the very bowels of her attacker. Bass felt the
slippery, springy board rise and shift under his boot soles,
then he was falling and, terrified, he tried to brace himself for
impact with the cold water that he knew would so very
shortly envelop him. He seemed to fall forever, thinking with
one part of his mind that it would be suicidal, most likely, to
come up between the two ships and be ground between the
hulls; but with this much weight on, staying down until he
had swum around to the stern or portside of *Revenge* should
be no problem. The problem for him would be in swimming
at all, and then in the right direction, while underwater.

The impact of his body slamming full-length on its back on
the hard deck momentarily stunned him, sending a galaxy of
multicolored stars and suns and planets spinning before his
eyes. But then arms were under him and hands were pulling
him erect, giving him support until his legs again became a
true part of him and could assume their job.

''Luck mit you still iss, mein Herr von Norfolk,'' the
familiar voice of his ever-faithful bodyguard and servant,
Nugai, spoke from close beside him. ''One foot more on zee
plank out had you been, between zee ships fallen you vould!''

Then, with Nugai's aid, he was back upon the rail and out

on a plank for seeming eons—a plank which bucked and pitched and seemed determined to dump him off to be drowned or crushed. But then, in an eyeblink, he was across, a strangely carven ship's rail was underfoot, and a maelstrom of breast-to-breast combat lay just ahead and below him.

With other boarders pushing from behind, no more anxious than he had been to spend more time than absolutely necessary on that swaying, treacherous plank bridge, Bass eyed the seething boil of battle as well as he could through his somewhat restrictive visor, seeking a bare spot of decking on which he might light. The search seemed vain and he was deciding he would just have to jump onto one of the embattled men when a large number of the heavy belowdecks guns roared out almost simutaneously and the French galleon heeled over to port, tilting the entire ship enough to send a sizable proportion of the battlers slipping and sliding into a dense mass against the portside rails.

Making a four-point landing on hands and knees, Bass pushed himself almost up, then was smashed down flat as the Frenchman's portside battery suddenly fired off a salvo and the earlier heel and subsequent tilt was repeated in reverse. Before he could even think of again arising, the mob of fighting men were tumbling and staggering back over to the starboard side of the deck, trampling him underfoot, those who chanced to not trip over or fall onto his recumbent armored body.

He levered himself back onto hands and knees just in time for someone to fall directly onto his back, shrieking dementedly and finally sliding down to where Bass could see him—a stocky man with reddish-brown skin, still screaming, while making frantic efforts with blood-slimed hands to hold shut a gashed-open belly.

It was not until he had slid and rolled himself to the sheltering lee of the first level of the sterncastle that Bass was able to stand erect once more, look about, and try to sort out just what was going on in the battle royal that the Frenchman's waist and forecastle were become.

He decided that Walid Pasha must be right about this being

a true ship-of-war, rather than simply a well-armed merchant vessel; nothing else could possibly account for the large numbers of fighters in his sight on the upper decks while there still were obviously enough left belowdecks to serve and fire the heavy guns. He gulped at realization of the distinct possibility that he and his flotilla had, this time around, bitten off a mite more than they could easily chew.

The bulk of both boarding parties—from *Revenge* and *Krystal*—were now fighting on the decks of the French galleon, yet so many were the men opposing them that they looked to his eye to be close to evenly matched. The only edge he and they seemed to hold was that they were more fully armed than the most of the French. But he had seen too little of real sea combats to know for certain just how much that might or might not count in the scales of victory or defeat.

The tumult was indescribable, but he was surprised at the few gunshots—and most of them from overhead in the rigging, or from his own ships—until it came to him all at once that the boarders had probably fired their one or two pistols early on and had had neither the time nor the opportunity to recharge the pieces, even if they had managed to hold on to them.

With his mind running in such direction, he hastily drew and checked the priming in all of his own pistols, then drew his sword and hung it securely from his wrist by the knot. And then he took a closer look at the broil, seeking where he could be of best use just now.

There, stalking through the melee in almost full plate— very ornate, highly decorated plate, at that—strode a man about as tall as Bass Foster, roaring something that sounded a bit like a song and was certainly not in French, and swinging to deadly effect something that looked a good bit like a Lochaber ax.

Bass looked at that bloody axblade, looked at his makeshift shortsword, and shook his head. "No way!" He unslung one of the wheellock horsepistols, glanced to see that the pyrites were hard against the wheel, leveled the two-foot weapon, and squeezed the trigger.

The big pistol belched a yard of flame and a ten-gauge leaden ball, its recoil kicking its muzzle high in the air. When the smoke had cleared, the armored axman was on his back on the deck and other combats were raging over and around him.

Something clanged against Bass's breastplate, then fell at his feet. He looked down to see something that tugged at some part of his memory: a heavy, grooved, rounded stone with a curved hardwood handle shrunk around it and what looked like a single tine from a deer antler mounted on one side of the stone.

But he was granted no time to think where he might have seen the like of this outré weapon, for from out the mob, rushing hard at him, came another axman, armored similarly to the first, but with less complete and far less ornate armor. It was the same impressive, very frightening kind of ax, though, so Bass drew another pistol and shot down this man as well. He was hopeful that the French foe would run out of armored axmen before he ran out of loaded horsepistols.

"I was a goddamned fool to let them get me gussied up and come on this boarding party anyhow. This kind of warfare is a *young* man's game, and I'm over forty years old! How the hell did I wind up with the reputation of a diehard fire-eater in the first place? All I've done since we first arrived in this blood-soaked slice of universe was try to stay alive and in one piece. The last thing I wanted to do was to hurt anybody.

"So, what happened to old peace-loving Bass Foster? I had to start killing the very first day I got here and I've since found myself being shoved, willy-nilly, from one slaughtering place to another, year after year, expected to make killing and maiming and crippling men my life's work.

"And part of what scares me about it is that I do it so well, so naturally, that even career ruffians like de Burgh and the rest of the *galloglaiches* are sure that I'm one of *them*! In *my* world, in the world I came from, people like what I've become here are locked away for life in soft rooms, not cheered and honored and rewarded. . . ."

His momentary musing was interrupted by the onset of a fresh, though smaller, wave of boarders. They came pouring out of the stern- and forecastles, the men from the two Bigod sloops.

Bass halted the couple of dozen armed men before they could all exit the sterncastle and become lost in the madhouse in the waist. Raising his visor for recognition, he ordered, "Go below, to the gundecks, and kill every gunner you can catch. Two or three salvos at this range are about all that the caravel can tolerate, and they're not doing my flagship any good, either."

As the men disappeared into the bowels of the embattled ship, Bass peered again into the shifting, gory fracas in the waist, trying in vain to spot Sir Ali ibn Hussain or Nugai the Kalmyk. He could not see them anywhere on their feet . . . and most of the bodies on the decks could not be seen long enough between the legs and feet of the combatants to be identified.

Unbeknownst to Bass, the heel of the French galleon following the first salvo, that which had flung him face down onto the deck, had precipitated the Arabian knight into the water between the Frenchman and *Revenge*. But what had happened to Nugai had been of even more singular a nature. Beset with the strain of the sudden lift and tilt, the overly springy boarding bridge had come loose of the spikes and, snapping back from its forced arc, flung the wiry warrior bodily, as if hurled by a seige engine, up into the rigging of *Revenge*.

Sir Ali had learned to swim in the warm sea near his Arabian home and he did not fear this one, for all that it was colder by many degrees. He allowed the weight of his armor and weapons to bear him down, out of the dangerous area between the two hulls. Then, trusting in his sure directional sense, he struck out with strong strokes, leftward and upward, to finally surface almost at the very side of Bigod's sloop, *Lioness*, where willing hands first threw him a line, then drew him up from the sea.

By the time that *Lioness*'s grapnels had bitten deep and the sloop had been warped tight to the bow of the Frenchman, Sir Ali had drawn the wetted loads from his pistols, recharged and reprimed them, dried off his sword, borrowed a helmet and a spikebacked boarding ax, and wangled a place in the very first wave of boarders to clamber up onto the bow of the enemy vessel.

No sooner had any of them set foot on the galleon than did a suicidally courageous French gunner turn about and fire a long swivel piece. Had the two-inch bore been loaded with langrage or even with a handful of pistol balls, it might have done—like a huge shotgun—for the first wave, then and there. But it was loaded with but a single bore-sized stone ball . . . which chanced to take Sir John Hailey in the face left exposed by his visorless bascinet, wrenching off both helmet and head and flinging the blood-spouting body back down onto the heaving deck of the sloop *Lioness*.

The gunner turned to run, but had taken only a single step when Sir Ali's hard-flung ax took him between the shoulder-blades. As he wrenched the weapon free, the Arabian assumed the command that had been the responsibility of the so recently deceased Sir John Hailey.

Waving the red-edged ax, he shouted, "These damned gunners the most dangerous are. Let's get down below and from their warrens drive them up, away from their guns. You, there, and you, stay here and the next wave send after us to the main batteries."

Sir Ali and his force found no living men in the forecastle or on the deck immediately below their point of entry. Descent to the main gundeck revealed that they were blocked off from most of it by a smoldering, intensely smoky fire, so they all continued downward to the lower gundeck.

There they proceeded to wreak bloody slaughter among and upon the near-naked, ill-armed, or completely unarmed gun crews. The few French who survived the savage depredations only did so by dint of throwing themselves out open gunports. Then the red-handed butchering-party ascended to the main gundeck by way of one of the stern ladders.

*   *   *

Hurled high into the main shrouds, poor Nugai's helmeted head was slammed hard against an oak-and-iron pulley, stunning him, and he would surely have fallen the twenty-odd feet to the waistdeck had not a nearby archer grabbed, held, and steadied him long enough for him to regain full consciousness and equilibrium.

Before the Kalmyk could thank his savior, a large-caliber arquebus ball struck the Turk's forehead with a *splattering* sound and, with a gasp, the archer slumped limply against the waistband that held him secure in the shrouds, letting go his short, powerful bow.

A quick grab and Nugai had the bow, and taking the Turk's still-warm right hand he worried off the horn-and-copper thumb ring, which proved to be a fair fit on his own right thumb. Then he began to look about for the arquebusier.

A glance at the archer's death wound showed the Kalmyk that the shot must have been fired from almost on a level with its target, not much higher, surely no lower. The keen eyes of the nomad horseman searched the rigging of the enemy ship and presently spied six gunmen in a line on a long, narrow platform affixed in place of a true fighting-top to the mizzenmast of the French galleon.

Drawing out one of the short arrows from the brace of cylinders at the dead Turk's belt, Nugai nocked the shaft and fully drew the bow, aimed, then loosed. That first arrow was a clean miss. But the second one took a gunman low in his belly, between his belt and his crotch.

Nugai watched the distant gunman drop his long, heavy piece, then fall—arms and legs windmilling—from his perch. Blank-faced, he fitted another shaft to bowstring and with it felled another arquebusier. He had dropped all but two before they spied out his position and sent a ball humming in his direction, only to hit the dead Turk in the chest. Nugai skewered the one gunman while he was aiming and the second before he could finish reloading, spanning, and priming his weapon.

The Kalmyk checked the contents of the cylinders, combined them into one, and hung that one on his own belt along with the bow. Then he loosed the dead Turk's waist lashings, making sure that the body fell onto a deck and not into the sea. Taking the security strap in his teeth, he climbed higher in the shrouds, to where he had a better view of the battle raging on the decks of the enemy galleon.

It had been many years since he had had a bow of this sort in his hands, but such bows had been the principal missile weapon of the Kalmyks for untold centuries prior to their adoption of prods and crossbows from Teutons, Goths, and Magyars. He would enjoy himself with the bow as long as the arrow supply held out, then he would climb down to add his cunning and ferocity to the melee seething on those blood-slimy decks so far below.

CHAPTER ———————
THE FIFTH

When Walid Pasha saw desperate seamen, some of them with fresh, bleeding wounds, casting themselves out of the open gunports of the French ship, he breathed a long sigh of relief. Boarders apparently had reached and were clearing the enemy's gundecks, so there would be no more of those punishing salvos and he could safely put his carpenters to work on the damages already wrought.

Smiling, he turned to Fahrooq. "All right, you may commit the reserves. I'll have no more need of your men on the guns. Those are friendlies on those gundecks yonder, now."

The boarders from off the Bigod sloop grappled at the French galleon's stern were just killing the last gun crewmen on the main gundeck when Sir Ali and his boarders climbed up to it.

"Well, then, gentlemen." His smile flashed a brilliant white against a dark complexion darkened even further by an overlay of smoke grime. "Let us to see what to find above we may."

They found nothing but destruction and death on the lowest level of the sterncastle; whatever had exploded and however many explosions there had been, they had no way of ascertaining. Their horrified eyes could only witness and record the facts that every bulkhead had been blown down, every stern window and side window had been blown out. Some guns—there were sakers and minions on this part of this deck—had been completely or partially dismounted by the force of the explosion or explosions, others had been buried in debris, and bits and pieces of an indefinite number of men were splattered on every visible surface in the smoky slice of hell that that deck was become.

Halting the combined boarding force for the nonce in the deathly peace of the charnel-house scene, Sir Ali saw to it that every pistol was reloaded, then headed his command toward the blown-open double doors leading out to the open deck and the ongoing battle.

Bass had had the *cinquedea* dagger blade break about a span above the point and now was fighting with the Lochaber-style ax of one of the men he had earlier shot down. All of his pistols now were empty—as were all within easy sight aboard the ship—and matters were simply too intense to allow for reloading in safety. It seemed to him that the fight had raged on now for hours and he was weary unto death, but somehow he found the requisite strength and energy to fight on—chopping, slashing with the heavy, cleaverlike blade, stabbing with the spike, leaping aside and dodging thrusts of pike or blade, taking cuts on helmet or armor, sometimes able to deflect them down the iron-strapped haft of his captured weapon.

On his right fought a brace of his *galloglaiches* with their own long axes—of a somewhat different pattern from his but just as deadly and all showing close antecedents—while a knot of Turkish marines wreaked gory havoc with boarding pikes and cursive swords on his left and, beyond them, Sir Calum and the Barón Melchoro stood back to back, plying Irish shortswords and spiked bucklers to fearsome effect, while shouting gruesome jokes to one another and roaring out snatches of bawdy songs.

And Bass was worried. There were far too many familiar bodies out there, foot-trampled, on the deck. He and his score and a half or so of men here against the sterncastle and an approximate equal number backed against the forecastle were all that was now left of the boarders. Despite the singularly deadly slaughter, the French had fought hard and well, still outnumbered them, and were pressing them hard.

As he had done once before, at the cavalry encounter now famed as the Battle of Bloody Rye, Bass took out his worry and his frustration on the foemen facing him. Snarling, his lips peeled back from his teeth, he stamped forward, swinging his weighty ax as if it had been a feather, and Frenchmen recoiled from him, as much from a primal fear of the bestial growls and snarls as from the hacking steel blade.

The two *galloglaiches*, shouting with exhilaration, followed him closely, as too did Sir Calum, Barón Melchoro, the Turks, and all the rest, driving a steelshod wedge forcefully into the mob of Frenchmen.

Sir Ali's arrival with his relatively fresh force was timely in the extreme. The more numerous French had but just closed to completely encircle Bass and his following when the Arabian knight emerged from the sterncastle to smite the foemen with cold steel and hot lead. And although a degree of heavy fighting yet remained, the boarding of Fahrooq and his reserves was an almost unnecessary anticlimax.

In the aftermath of the fierce battle for *La Sentinelle du Nord*, as the commanders and ship captains toted up losses, it became painfully obvious that they must head directly for home port, praying constantly for fair weather, because the loss of experienced seamen—few of whom had gone into the fight as well armored or well armed as the soldiers—had been no less than staggering.

The prize galleon, moreover, could not be sailed in her present condition, with or without a crew, and the open ocean only a few leagues off the hostile French coast was certainly no place to undertake repairs of any save the most basic nature; all were in agreement on this. Therefore, Walid Pasha had two stout cables rove from *Revenge* to the prize, put Fahrooq and six Turkish marines, a carpenter's mate, three seamen, and a dozen *galloglaiches* aboard her, and took her under tow. By prearrangement, the caravel, *Krystal*, and the three Bigod sloops kept pace in clear sight of *Revenge* and the rich prize.

And if any doubt existed that she had been rich, one had

but to penetrate the ranks of full-armed guards ranged before the double-bolted door to Bass's quarters and gaze upon the gold, the silver, the uncut gemstones and pearls, plus the fine furs, the supple hides, shaggy robes, and light cotton cloth which were samples taken from bales and bolts still aboard the French galleon.

Within the confines of the now-crowded cabin, Baron Melchoro and Sir Calum—both of whom read French with some ease—pored over stacks of documents, notes, and ledgers, while Sir Ali and Nugai, with scales and quills and parchment, weighed and counted up the gold and silver ingots, coins, and jewelry. Close by the stern window, Bass was poring over one of the maps that had been taken from the prize, wondering at the so-familiar outlines all here labeled with alien names in unfamiliar languages.

"Let's see . . . hmmm, this *has* to be Greenland, therefore, this has to be Newfoundland, here's Nova Scotia and . . . aha, this hook shape couldn't indicate anything but the coast of Massachusetts.

"Huh, that's weird. According to this map, there's no East River; Long Island and Manhattan Island are joined. Hell, maybe they are, in this world. But where in the devil did the damned cartographers get some of these names? A few are French, yes, and some are obviously French adaptations of Spanish words, but some of these others look like no languages I've ever seen before. Indian? Maybe. These far northern ones are most probably Norse, at least the French transliterations of Norse."

With a shake of his head, he sighed in helpless frustration. "Well, maybe Melchoro can tell me more of this when he's done with the ship's papers; after all, he's soldiered in New Spain, years agone. Since they lay claim to all of it, surely the Spanish have at least some knowledge of the lands and people to their immediate north."

Laying aside the last of the pages of crabbed French script, the *barón* said, "Your grace, friend Bass, the ship we have but just taken at such dear cost was no more a ship of the French *roi* than are our ships of King Arthur. She was owned and financed by a group of French noblemen, true enough, but she was crewed by a multinational pack of pirates. They had spent the last score of months in robbing the coasts and commerce of New Spain, Great Ireland, New France, and the Norse settlements. Laden with plunder, they were making for Bordeaux when we chanced across them. No wonder there were so many of them aboard. Less wonder that they fought so long and hard and well—it was their profession.''

Leaving the Arab and the Kalmyk to their counting and weighing, Bass, Melchoro, and Sir Calum left the cabin and went up on deck to find Walid Pasha and relay to him the surprising truth about the supposed French warship, the battered hulk of which *Revenge* was now towing back to England.

They found the ship captain on the quarterdeck, but he spoke before any of them could do so. "Sebastián Bey, we must send at least a score more of your soldiers to the prize, immediately. They are needed to work the pumps and help otherwise. If any of your fighters number amongst their accomplishments aught of the carpenter or joiner trades, Basheer stands in sore need of more hands to repair damages to the hull of the prize, else we soon may be faced with the unpleasant choice of jettisoning valuable pieces of ordnance or seeing the ship sink in the sea.''

While Sir Calum stalked off to find some *galloglaiches*, the round-faced Barón Melchoro, happily practicing his Turkish, told Walid of his findings in the papers of *La Sentinelle du Nord*, ending by saying, "It would seem that they attacked and robbed and killed most indiscriminately—Spanish, Irish, Norse, red *indios*, even their own king's stations in New France.''

Walid pulled at his beard, nodding. "Yes, Melchoro *effendi*, what you here recount makes sense of matters I had pondered from early in our encounter with that ship. Culverins and demiculverins are long-range guns, painstakingly cast of fine bell bronze and hellishly expensive, designed to use a smaller caliber, lighter-weight ball, to provide finer accuracy at a distance than could any cannon.

"Cannon, on the other hand—your basilisks, cannon-royals,

true full cannon, and demicannon—are relatively cheap, being cast of iron, have no accuracy to speak of at any range beyond that of a common arquebus, but can throw stone balls weighing upward of seventy pounds. Consequently, most broadside guns—the lower-deck guns, certainly—are cannon, while the long-range, long-barreled, high-priced culverins are rarely seen mounted other than in bow and stern as chasers.

"I had thought it quite odd that yonder galleon mounted a broadside consisting almost entirely of bronze culverins, demiculverins, and saker-royals, with but a bare handful of true iron cannon, and these all amidships on the lower gundeck. Now I can see why she was so armed."

"And why was that?" asked the baron, his interest piqued.

"Weight, for one reason," Walid answered. "A full broadside of large-caliber iron guns, together with the stone balls and the huge amounts of powder necessary for them, would have been significantly heavier, *and* much bulkier, than that which they did mount and carry. The lesser weight and bulk meant that they could ship aboard more men and provender for them for a longer voyage, while still mounting sufficient ordnance to achieve the purposes of that voyage.

"Look you, *effendi*, their choice quarry was lightly built, lightly armed merchanters, for which their existing broadside was surely more than sufficient—observe how badly their broadsides damaged *Krystal*'s fabric, compared to the relatively minor damages they wrought on my ship. Most likely they ran from any true warships they chanced to encounter, just as they tried to run from us, to start.

"For land raids, their culverin broadsides were perfect, for they could lie out beyond the range of a fort's cannon and pound it with impunity, while their landing parties did their bloody work ashore. There exists ample proof that theirs was a most auspicious voyage . . . until they had the extreme misfortune to chance across this flotilla, that is.

"By the bye, the prisoners we freed from the hold of the prize are all anxious to express their thanks to his grace. One of them, a Spaniard, is most insistent. He has good English, far better than is mine own, but would Melchoro *effendi* care to meet with him before he is conducted to an audience with Sebastián Bey?''

Bass thought that the middle-aged Spaniard looked more Irish than Spanish, with his flaming-red hair and his sea-green eyes. The man was thick-limbed, obviously muscular, with a broad chest and a neck at least eighteen inches in circumference. He looks, thought Bass, like a slightly short-ened version of Buddy Webster, except for the face, of course.

Aside from a thick and flaring dark-red mustache, the Spaniard was beardless, his cheeks and chin deeply and profusely pockmarked. A new scar ran down one side of his face from a split ear to his jawline, and there was a profusion of other, older scars. His nose was crooked and canted and a mite flattened. He was missing all or part of three fingers, his right earlobe, and a goodly number of teeth.

He and the other prisoners had been found, heavily fettered, in the deepest, dankest hold of the French galleon. Two of them had been dead—long dead—and another had been so deranged that when he was brought up on deck for his fetters to be struck off, he had thrown himself overboard and sunk like a stone. Two of the survivors were Indians; this Spaniard was the other.

After his hour of conversation with the freed man, Barón Melchoro had sought Bass out and prepared him for the interview he must grant.

''Esteemed friend, your grace of Norfolk, this Don Diego is a belted knight, but more than that, he is a gentleman of the old school. To one such as is he, responsibility and honoring of just debts are of even more importance than are right and privilege.

''It is because he is what he is that he was residing in Nueva España, having willingly relinquished his patrimony in Old Castile to a younger brother. Don Diego feels that honor is now dead in Spain . . . and, considering certain of the shameful acts and base practices of the kakistocracy that presently controls the King of Spain, Don Diego may well be of a correctness, entirely.

"Don Diego has, alas, lost a large proportion of all he once owned in Nueva España, due to the depredations of the French marauders. He has replaced the verminous, filthy rags in which we found him with items of decent clothing taken from off the bodies of dead French officers, from whence source he also was able to reclaim his good sword, his daggers, and other equipment. But these are all that he now owns, he can pay no ransom, nor are there any who would ransom him. He will make you an offer of service. He means every word of that offer, I feel, and will fulfill his commitments to the very last jot and tittle, even unto his death."

The leased ship of the line, *Impressionant* arrived in Palermo harbor a full four days ahead of Cardinal D'Este's best estimate. That she did so was the sole responsibility of Le Chevalier Marc Marcel de Montjoie de Vires, who had seen to it that despite the long enforced stay in Livorno, the ship was kept ready for sea—fully watered, victualed, and supplied at all times—with no more than half of her officers and crew absent at any one time.

Moreover, *le chevalier* bore the power to enforce his will, both in his sharp sword and his strong arms and in the fact that whilst under lease-contract to the Holy See, *le roi*'s ship *Impressionant* and all within her were the royally assigned responsibility of said nobleman—in effect, he spoke for the king.

In actual practice, however, the young man needed neither his sword nor his royal authority to win over most of the officers and crew to his way to thinking, as might have many another French nobleman of equal rank. *Le chevalier* was no mere pompous, wellborn figurehead, no useless, royal supercargo such as the ship had borne far too often.

The twenty-five-year-old nobleman could read, write, and reckon; he could plot a true course and keep the galleon to it, by day or by night. Indeed, the grizzléd sailing master had been heard to opine that *le chevalier* was a born and most highly gifted navigator—generous praise indeed, from a man who in his forty-odd years at sea had seen most of the known waters of the world.

Le chevalier had won the worship of the crew in another way. He seemed intent upon learning every task and routine connected with the working of the ship and, not content to learn merely by instruction and observation, could right often be found hauling and drawing with the common seamen, or barefoot and shirtless high on a topsail yard when sailwork was ordered, he and his squire, side by side.

It was after the less surefooted squire had plunged to his death from high in the rigging that the sailing master was at last able to prevail upon the knight to eschew his own aerial activities.

"M'lord *chevalier*, you must know that the king's officers would have off my head were I to sail back with word that you had died while reefing sail. Not that they'd believe me, of course—they'd likely rack me until I told them I'd murdered you, then burn me, like as not. If you must have dangerous work to do, why I'll give you a cannon to captain. You've attended the gun drills, sir, so just pick the gun you want—bronze or iron, cannon or culverin."

"And if that gun blows up and kills me?" *Le chevalier* smiled lazily. "You'll still have to report a dead nobleman, Captain."

"There's always that, yes." The sailing master nodded. "But then I'd have pieces of a blown-out cannon to show, and such a death as that could be come by as easily ashore as at sea."

The young knight had been ineffably bored in Livorno, perpetual drunkenness, yarn-spinning, and the occasional dockside brawl not being to his interest. Invited to a tourney at the seat of a local count, he had been served well by his weapons skills, horsemanship, and strength, but his birthright of Norman ferocity in the fray had secretly horrified his hosts and opponents, to whom a tourney was become more an elaborate game than aught else. There were no more tourneys proclaimed while his ship remained in the harbor of Livorno.

Once the warship was securely moored beside a wharf in

the fine deepwater harbor of Palermo, a man in a strange but rich livery came aboard to announce the imminent arrival of one Sir Ugo D'Orsini, who would conduct *le chevalier* to his audience with Cardinal D'Este, Archbishop of Palermo.

D'Este, alone, received the French knight, in a small study in another part of his palace from the spacious solar in which he had received the Duce di Bolgia. Nor was any time wasted; once the wine was poured and the servant departed, the cleric got down to business.

"Sir Marc, your ship will be sailing in company with a brace of merchant galleons from this port to Anfa Antiqua, there to be joined by other ships, which then will sail by the most direct route north to Irland, the Kingdom of Munster, to be more exact.

"The two ships with which you will depart Palermo are being used to transport the noted condottiere Duce Timoteo di Bolgia, and his company. The landfall in Morocco will be for the purpose of picking up another condotta whose contract to the caliphate has expired."

"Your eminence," said *le chevalier* cautiously, "the Holy See might have leased four or even five transports of his majesty for the price of the *Impressionant*, and they would have carried more troops with less crowding and discomfort than a warship."

D'Este sipped his wine. "You misunderstand, Sir Marc. While your ship will doubtless carry di Bolgia and some of his officers and bodyguards, as well as my personal representative, Sir Ugo, the primary purpose of sending along *Impressionant* and the brace of Tunisian crompsters that will rendezvous with you off Malta is to protect the transports, which will be far too laden and overcrowded to fight easily or well . . . should fighting at sea become necessary, as I earnestly hope it will not."

"One would rather doubt that it will, save by purest chance, your eminence," *le chevalier* assured him. "No pirate in his right mind would be anxious to trade cannonades with a fine new ship of the line, nor would he be willing to close with a bevy of troopships brimful of professional soldiers, not to even mention the pair of Afriquan corsair crompsters he'd have nibbling at his flanks the while.''

Although, upon first introduction, each eyed the other boldly, almost to the point of impudence, like two strange dogs, *le chevalier* and *il duce* apparently liked what they saw in each other, much to the relief of Sir Ugo D'Orsini. The Roman knight had been fearful of an instant and mutual *dis*like, which would perforce have necessitated for him an exceedingly stressful voyage of striving to keep two dangerous but valuable men from each other's throats.

Bass and his battered but eminently victorious flotilla had been back in Norfolk for a bare two days when an old friend, Sir Richard Cromwell, and a small escort rode in from the king's camp under the walls of London. As they all dined in the lofty hall of the ducal residence, the officer of King Arthur's Horse Guards imparted them news of court and camp and the slowly ongoing siege.

His brown eyes twinkling, he announced, ''The Lady Mary O'Day did last month present his majesty with a fine, lusty boychild, having a full head of dark-red hair. His majesty is most pleased and proud. True, it is the fourth child born him since Candlemas, but the other three all were females, and one of those died at a week, its dam a fortnight later.

''Barely a one of the foreign ambassadors and their retinues remain within London, either from desire to eat regularly or due to knowledge that the city is doomed to fall soon. All of them have come bowing and scraping into the royal camp, of course, and the king has lodged them here and there at castles and manors around about the countryside, though all to date south of the river.

''His grace, Sir Francis, Duke of Northumberland, writes from the court of Emperor Egon that we need have no fear of the once-threatened Swedish-Norse-Danish Crusade. The prime mover of that business was, as all know, King Hans, and Emperor Egon simply assured his Danish majesty that was he so unwise as to embark upon that Crusade against England or Ireland, those Danish men so fortunate as to return at all would return to a much smaller and far less rich Kingdom of Denmark. Now, with King Hans busily occupied with strengthening his borders and adding to his fleet and his coastal defenses, the Swedish and Norse kings seem to have lost what little interest they once had in the undertaking.

"His grace went on to say that the emperor has sent word to both Rome and Genoa that any further attempted incursions of the Genoese against his ally, Savoy, will lead him to believe that it is the wish of his holiness, Pope Abdul, that a state of war should exist between Rome and the Empire."

"Damn, the boy is cracking the whip, isn't he?" exclaimed Bass. "Good for him! I'll bet old Abdul is chewing his motheaten beard in frustration."

"His grace further advises," Cromwell continued after a long draft of wine, "that his daughter, the Empress Arabella, was at the time of writing heavy with child. Emperor Egon and the imperial court were most pleased, he says, when he told them of the fact that no Whyffler woman has ever been delivered of a girlchild for nigh on two centuries.

"Your grace, his majesty has been kept minutely advised of your activities and exploits by Sir Paul Bigod and others. As ever, your grace pleases his majesty mightily in all regards, and he was reticent to ask that you halt your commendable sea activities for even a brief period, but you were asked for by name by a most distinguished personage, and he had no option.

"I bear with me, your grace, royal warrants granting to you the authority to break crown seals and to enter into rooms or buildings so sealed and secured. When once these have been placed in your hands, your grace must proceed posthaste to the episcopal palace of his grace, Harold, Archbishop of York, there to be assigned a mission and a task. This is as much as I know of the matter, your grace."

"Am I supposed to go alone, Sir Richard?" asked Bass.

The big guardsman smiled. "I doubt that his majesty would ask or expect his Lord Commander of the Royal Horse to go galloping off northward alone. But I was given a sense of some urgency."

As the tables were being cleared, about three hours before dusk, Bass was already giving orders, sending riders out to the cavalry camp and to the port. He had trained his staffs well, so that all was in readiness for his departure at dawn of the next day.

Two years ago, he could have ridden off alone or with a couple of companions and covered the intervening ground in jigtime. Last year, even, he could have ridden it with only Nugai and his gentlemen. But no more. Now no one, from the lowliest to the highest, would hear aught of his riding forth with less than at least two hundred *galloglaiches*, a pack train, a score of servants, and every officer who could manage to wangle a place in the resulting column.

Given his head and his choosing, Bass would have taken a cross-country route, camping under the stars, breaking those camps ere dawn. But burdened as the column was with baggage and civilians, they were forced to travel by road, and though he pressed them all as hard as was possible, the trip became a progression and did not come within sight of York for three weeks and two days.

Understanding the uncertain temperaments and tempers of his *galloglaiches*, Bass established his camp on part of the now weedgrown site of the royal encampment, with Sir Calum and the two hundred Irish mercenaries to guard it.

Having often expressed a desire to see firsthand Captain Buddy Webster's stock-breeding experiments, Barón Melchoro and his small entourage rode southwest toward the episcopal estate, taking Don Diego with them. Consequently, Bass arrived at the fine palace of the archbishop with a minimal escort—Nugai, Sir Ali, Sir Liam FitzAlfred, his bannerman, four squires, a dozen lancers, and Fahrooq, who had come along on the ride north that he might see more of this land called England.

Although he had been aware that conferences of a politico-religious nature had been going on for almost a year in York, Bass had not realized how deadly serious and how international the flavor of those discussions was until he entered within the walls of that city. It was well that he had brought his pavilion and adequate provisions for his entourage, for every inn was jammed full, and food, drink, and supplies seemed to be both scarce and dear.

Making toward the archepiscopal palace, the column could not manage any pace faster than a slow walk through streets thronged with foreigners—Scots, Irish, Burgundians, Germans from several parts of the Empire, Livonians, a scattering of Kalmyks or Tatars.

When finally reached, the palace complex was found to be much more heavily guarded than Bass recalled from any previous visit, nor would the grim, businesslike guards allow his lancers, mounted or dismounted, through the gate into the outer courtyard. At the gate between inner and outer courtyards, the party found itself stripped of squires, bannerman, and all of the horses, to then proceed under guard of a half-dozen pikemen to the gate of the actual palace.

Within the guardroom just inside that gate, a richly dressed, rapier-thin officer behind an ornate desk barely glanced at the warrants before casually shoving them back toward the bearer, shrugging languidly, and announcing in a tone little shy of rank insubordination, "Well, your grace, it were much better had you stayed in your camp until his grace, the archbishop, sent for you. There is but the barest chance that I could have an audience arranged for you any time this week . . . and if I can, it will be most expensive, most expensive indeed."

Dark face working, Sir Ali started to take a pace forward, but Bass laid a restraining hand on the Arab's sinewy arm. "Very well, what is the tariff for an audience today?" From within his buffcoat he withdrew a velvet purse that clinked musically as he bounced it in his palm.

The officer's thin lips parted to reveal bad teeth. "Your grace is most perceptive. Let us say that three onzas of gold would virtually guarantee an audience with his grace before sundown, tomorrow . . . ?"

Bass shook his head. "Not soon enough, man. I was sent here by order of both his grace and the king. I know—you will immediately escort us to his grace's presence, whereupon he and I will decide the actual worth of your services."

Shielded by the bodies of the men grouped around the desk, only the officer saw the second item that Bass withdrew from beneath the front of his buffcoat—a small-framed wheellock pistol boasting a half-inch bore in a two-inch barrel.

The officer's scornful "Impossible!" trailed off into a very weak squeak and the gaze of his two eyes locked upon that deadly cyclops now staring at him in all its inhuman coldness. All the blood drained from his face and his fine, soft-palmed hands began to tremble like leaves in a gale.

The guards lounging about at the other end of the big room saw nothing unusual in their noble-born officer's departure through the double doors leading out into the palace complex with this new-come lord and his gentlemen. One of the gentlemen, the dark-skinned, crooked-nosed one, had an arm thrown about the officer's narrow shoulders and was talking in a low tone but most animatedly to him. The lord himself walked close by the officer's other side, one arm looped in his, the other hand thrust within the front opening of his dusty buffcoat. The other gentleman—Scot or Irisher, by the look of him—and the Tatar trailed close behind the leading trio.

His skinny legs become weak as water, it was all that Guards Officer Edmund Bridges could do to place one foot before the other as the murderous duke and his Arab henchman supported the most of his weight and bore him along with them. He was keenly aware that, hidden by the buffcoat, the small pistol was pointed directly at his quaking body, and the Arab had assured him, besides, that he had ready an envenomed dagger. One tiny prick of the point would ensure him a protracted and agonizing death which no physician could ease or cure.

The small party trooped along corridors and through halls and smaller rooms without Bass's seeing anyone he recognized. He was getting desperate when they passed into yet another long, broad hall. A few yards down it to the right, a knot of men stood in converse. A brief glimpse of the face of one of them—a cleric, by his garb—tugged at Bass Foster's memory, and so he guided his party in that direction.

So immersed in their own affairs were the group that no notice was taken of the newcomers until Bass spoke. "Your pardon, it's Father Peter Aleward, isn't it?"

A beefy, broad-shouldered man in a floor-length cassock spun about to disclose raised, very bushy black eyebrows on a florid face from which a bulbous nose thrust out like the metal boss from a targe. Upon catching sight of Bass, his face lit up in a broad smile. "Your grace of Norfolk! Thank God you are arrived. His grace has been beside himself. He had expected you far sooner."

Turning briefly back to the group, he said, "We'll continue these matters at a later time. Just now, it is most urgent that I conduct the Duke of Norfolk, here, to his grace."

To the guards officer, he said, "Thank you for bringing these gentlemen to me, but now there is no further need for your guidance. You may return to your desk."

Sir Ali retained his grip on the unfortunate officer, however, looking questioningly at Bass, who said, "That might not be wise, Father Peter . . . unless it is your wish that this man go on with his odious little enterprise of selling audiences with Hal . . . that is, with his grace."

"Is this true, Bridges?" asked the priest sadly.

The officer shook his head violently, opened his mouth to protest his innocence of the charge. Then he took a single look at Sir Ali's cold black eyes, remained silent, and began to tremble again.

"He offered," attested Bass, "to arrange me an audience by sundown tomorrow for my payment of three ounces of gold to him. That's a bit steep, I feel, so I made him an offer he couldn't refuse." He drew out from his buffcoat his right hand and the small wheellock pistol it held.

The priest glanced hurriedly about, then waved a hand frantically. "As you love God, your grace, put that thing out of sight before one of our overzealous guards sees it and kills you! With the numerous recent attempts on the life of his grace, we have had to become a virtual armed camp here.

"Bring that piece of filth along. We'll hie us to the inner guardroom—we'd have to pass by it, anyway—and leave him there."

CHAPTER
THE SIXTH

Arsen Ademian took the quill in his left hand for a moment and flexed the cramped fingers of his right while, on the apron of the makeshift stage before him, the four drummers—his cousins Haigh and Al, his friend Sinclair, and his uncle Rupen—created rhythmic thunder from the *dumbegs*. As the drum section finished its allotted time, Buddy took up the quill and evoked the melody of the ancient Middle Eastern song from his treasured oud, joined now by clarinet, guitar, bass, tambour, zils, and the clapping and shouts of his audience.

The wind from off the river was fitful, and in the lulls, like this present one, the mosquitoes and other bugs zeroed in on the sixty or so people standing and sitting on the sloping riverside lawn. The audience did not seem to mind, but running on nearly pure alcohol as they were by this time, they may not even have felt the ticklings and bites.

As they neared the finale of this number, with the drums all booming and every instrument involved in the complex rhythm, while the three dancers swirled before the stage in their rich, if scanty, costumes, a bug bit Arsen just inside his right nostril, and his involuntary flinch caused him to hit a sour note.

"Aw, goddamnit!" he thought. "Hell, I didn' wanta make this damn gig in the first place! Sure, the fucking money's good for tonight, but it ain't like we do this for a fucking living, for Chrissakes. Besides, it seems kinda like un-American to play for these damn Iranian fuckers; why just last year, they and the fucking Arabs put that damn embargo on our oil because of a war with *Israel* that we weren't even fighting in. Now the fuckers're all bleeding us dry at the fucking gas pumps and if it keeps up, gas could go sixty, seventy cents a gallon, for God's sake, even a *dollar*, maybe.

"God knows, it ain't often I can agree with Uncle Rupen and John the Greek and their 'Kill a Turk for Christ' crap, but God love 'em, they're the onliest ones voted with me to not do this fucking mosquito gig tonight.

"Hell, anybody with half a brain would know why all the damn girls wanted to come out here tonight. They thought they could get this bunch of rich, foreign doctors so sexed up with the belly-dancing that they'd end up getting some really heavy bread laid on 'em for whoring before they left here. Heh, heh, none of the sluts knew these Iranian bastards was all going to bring their wives and, some of them, their kids, too, with 'em.

"It's harder to figger why Greg and Mike and Haigh and Al sided with the goddamn broads, unless maybe they thought they all might be able to score some good hash off of these fuckers here. Damn 'em, one day they're gonna get the whole fucking band busted for possession, and that is definitely not the kinda publicity we're in need of. Lord knows, I'm no goddamn puritan, I blew grass in the 'Nam, everybody did there, but that there was a completely different situa—*what the hell!*"

In the midst of his silent monologue, it had seemed for a brief flicker of a moment that the audience—men and women in folding chairs grouped around folding tables, under haphazardly strung Japanese lanterns—had disappeared along with the night itself, to be instantly replaced by another, strangely dressed group, none of them sitting, all standing with solemn expressions on their faces under bright sunlight in some open, grassy place. There had been the cloying reek of heavy incense all about and, at Arsen's very elbow, a man in jeweled brocade looking every bit as surprised and shocked as Arsen felt.

But even as he exclaimed, it all shifted back from glaring

light to near-darkness, from strange and silent people to the crowded tables of raucous, drunken Iranians on a sloping lawn above the Potomac River.

"God damn Mike, anyway!" thought Arsen. "Sitting right behind me, smoking weed and blowing it this way, and I'm getting high. Funny, though, I don't *feel* stoned, just hallucinating. . . . I wonder if that crazy Lebanese bastard has taken to smoking *opium*, now?"

As he shortly would learn to his sorrow, hallucinogens or narcotics had nothing whatsoever to do with the matter.

A light flashed on her private communications device, and Colonel Dr. Jane Stone depressed one of the switches and said, "Yes, Stone here."

"Doctor," a voice came from out the device, "Technic Peterson here. The stolen travel console suddenly reactivated a few moments ago, and we now have a firm lock on it in all dimensions."

"You follow orders well, Peterson," the tall, spare woman said, adding, "Hold that lock right where it is and prepare to beam me to the site and time the console presently occupies. Out."

Arising from behind her painfully neat desk, the woman crossed the spartanly furnished office to a range of lockers, where she removed her indoor uniform and shoes, replacing them with a field-dress coverall, boots, weapons harness, and a small pack. Going on to the end locker, she pressed her thumb into the niche for a print reading, then turned the handle and opened the locker.

After filling certain pockets and pouches with weapons and survival items, some reproduction coins of gold, silver, and copper, a water-purification set, and a supply of food-energy briquettes, she reconsidered for a moment, then added a medium-sized medical kit to her pack.

"Those traitorous bastards would not be trying to come back, knowing just what they're in for here, unless one or both of them are seriously injured or deathly ill, and I would not want either of them to die before I can get them back here to first answer for their crimes against the state, then undergo thorough reeducation. I might even take a leave of absence from here just for the purpose of overseeing the reeducation of Dr. Emmett O'Malley!''

The colonel doctor still seethed when she thought back on how the handsome, smooth-talking, lying bastard had wormed his way into her affections, won her very real love, then used her and her position to set his subversive schemes into motion. She and her intelligence network had gotten onto O'Malley and Dr. Kenmore Harold early on, of course, but they had all feigned complete ignorance just to see how far the two would go in their treasonous activities. And she and the network had waited, it developed, just a little too long to arrest the pair of traitors.

Less than two months ago, during the President's Birthday Holidays, O'Malley and Harold, feigning a state of inebriation, had crossed over from the residence complex to this one by way of the subriverine railway, assaulted a guard, entered the room housing the time-travel projection equipment, and activated it.

"The activation, of course, set off a silent alarm I had had installed as soon as I was made aware of O'Malley's treachery," the colonel doctor mused. "But before I could get down here to the operations level from my quarters, they had gotten everything set, had the projector on automatic, and before I could stun them down, they were gone to who knows where.

"The cagey scum must have switched off the console immediately they arrived at wherever/ whenever, for our attempts to track it with the computer have been fruitless and burned up so much of our allotment of energy that we had to stop the search. It wasn't until last week when they apparently tried to use that console to project one of the labs to wherever/whenever that I was able to convince the board of the real danger of allowing them to remain at large with our equipment.

"But now they've done it right. The equipment has been turned on and left on; otherwise our rotating scanner couldn't have picked it up just now. And I'll get them and bring them back. And I'll see the bastards broken in every conceivable way. I just hope that I, personally, can wangle control of the breaking of Dr. Emmett O'Malley.''

The last item she took from its rack in the locker was a heavy-duty shoulder-model heat-stun weapon and a pouch of spare power units for the device. With the familiarity of long usage, she retracted the folding shoulder stock, then clipped the weapon to her harness so that it hung muzzle down with the handgrip close to the normal hang of her hand, easy to swing up and use, should the occasion demand.

Loaded for bear, ready to fetch back the traitors to their just and richly deserved punishments, Colonel Dr. Jane Stone closed her office door behind her and stalked down the corridor toward the descending lift.

''As you may or may not know, Bass,'' said Harold, Archbishop of York, ''His majesty has decreed that a church be raised on each of the five battlefields whereon the various armies of Crusaders were smashed, in the last two years, and I had journeyed up to the environs of Hexham to dedicate the chosen plot of ground and also to symbolically break the earth for the construction.

''Then, in the very midst of the high mass, which was being sung out of doors, of course, before the gathered throng, eight men and five women appeared—one of the men at my very side—then disappeared so quickly that one might have thought to have imagined the entire sequence of events, save that it repeated twice over. Then, while still the folk all were exclaiming and calling on God and the saints, those eight men—musicians—were *there*, before the very altar! Two wantons stood amongst them and three more, almost nude, were whirling in some lascivious Byzantinic dance.

''Bass, I am become an old, old man, and my mind has lost some of its flexibility, alas. I was shocked, deeply shocked, thinking for a brief moment that this was but another plot hatched by Abdul and the thrice-damned Romans; then it dawned on me what must have happened. I knew myself the terror of the unknown that these poor men and women must feel and cursed myself roundly for not making useless that hellish device up there under Whyffler Hall, long since.

"As my own terror melted away, however, the understandable terror and horror of the assembled throng had mounted, and as one they moved forward, blood in all eyes and weapons in right many hands, while their voices roared out their common intent to do fatal violence to those whom they saw as evil warlocks and witches.

"It was a near thing, Bass, a terrifying near thing. Had my guardsmen—of whom I had brought along a goodly number, both horse and foot—not been easily to hand, belike the bemused throng had taken and messily done to death those poor involuntarily projected men and women. But a few prearranged signals brought the guards to me, and twoscore of my pikemen and halberdiers proved quite sufficient to halt the ill-armed folk there congregated. Once my horsemen had cloaked the intruders and ridden them out of sight, it was still an hour or more before we could quieten the folk, but it was done, and the mass was concluded."

"Where are the poor bastards now, Hal?" asked the Duke of Norfolk. "Christ, what a shock to them that must've been!"

"Well cared for, Bass, although their movements have been restricted, for their own good, of course, you understand. I felt it wisest not to bring them into York, especially not into my palace, not with all that is here going on these days. They are all being held at the Abbey of St. Olaf. You recall its location, do you not? It is the place where his majesty kept his—aahhh—'ladies' when the royal camp was hereabouts three years agone.

"From my brief conversations with various of them, from their dress—the men, that is—and from the dialect that they all seem to speak, I would guess that they are plucked from a time far closer to yours than to mine own; therefore, I would like for you to take them over, try to ease their transition into this world of the here and now which will be so new and strange and terribly frightening to them."

"And what am I to tell them of exactly how they got here, Hal?" inquired Bass. "Do I troop them all down into the ground level of Whyffler Hall and show them the console to which you've so often alluded? Is that what these damned royal warrants are for?"

The archbishop shrugged. "It's in your hands entirely, Bass. Your judgment has proved itself good; tell them as much or as little of the actual truth as you think they can understand or believe.

"As to the warrants, that is another matter entirely. Bass, at the far end of the main cable of that console lies a world of technological savagery beyond the imaginings of you or any other man or woman here. That world has almost exhausted its ores and fossil fuels, has poisoned its best croplands and its waters, and its people will do the same or worse here, if once they discover this rich, unspoiled place and know the proper console settings to get here.

"That console and the building full of equipment that backs it and powers it was developed by a project the avowed purpose of which was to find and plunder earlier eras of Earth history, but they would jump at this world just as fast and like it even better.

"I showed you one of the heat-stun weapons from that world, Bass, demonstrated it on that pig, remember? How long do you think even your fine cavalry could stand up against men armed with such weapons? No, every second that that device is turned on—and it must be turned on, else those poor men and women would not have been projected here—is a second that this world lies in the direst form of danger.

"So I want you to take a small force, and those warrants, and ride as fast as horseflesh will bear for Whyffler Hall. There you are to break the seals, have the masonry blocking that archway broken down, descend to the old cellar, and ax the power cable in twain, thus permanently severing all connection with my own world as Emmett and I should have done when first we came here one hundred and fifty-eight years ago."

*   *   *

Bass decided that the newcomers could wait a bit longer. Gathering his lancers, he rode back to his camp at a stiff clip. There he gave a staccato stream of orders and began to change from his more formal clothing into attire more suitable to a hell-for-leather cross-country ride up to the border and his estate of Whyffler Hall.

The Norfolk Lancers had made a fine, brave, colorful military show for the procession into York, but for the kind of ride he now planned, parts of it through the traditional haunts of outlaws, brigands, and the like, an entirely different variety of mounted man-at-arms was needed, so he had ordered Sir Calum and Sir Liam to select fifty *galloglaiches* to accompany him, and the rest of his gentlemen on the long, hard ride up to the Marches.

He only spared the necessary time to send a galloper over to the archbishop's estates to fetch back Barón Melchoro and Don Diego because he knew that did he not, his lady-wife, Krystal, would most likely not see the jolly nobleman again before he had to return to Portugal and his family, estates, and affairs.

They set out for Whyffler Hall in the manner in which he would have preferred to set out for York from Norfolk—sixty-six armed men, no pack train, no servants, no tents; horse grain, powder, and absolutely necessary equipment were packed on the spare horses' backs. Quickly inspecting the men chosen from the *galloglaiches*, Bass silently doubted that any brigands of sound mind would risk a tangle with such specimens, and for the umpteenth time he thanked his stars that they and their comrades of the Royal Tara Squadron of *Gallowglasses* felt and evidenced such fanatic personal loyalty to him.

What with wind and rain and mist, plus unseasonal chill in the mountains, Bass Foster had occasional cause to regret forcing his unit to travel so light, but they did make good speed and on the only night of really hard, driving rain were able to camp in the partial shelter of the crumbling, weed-grown ruin that had once been a place of cheer called Heron Hall.

Despite the sadness that Bass felt in the ruin, having many far more pleasant memories of the place and its late owner, Sir John Heron, that sadness was allayed with a sense of satisfaction, for a dawn departure from the place would see them at Whyffler Hall by midafternoon of the following day.

"You do not love us, do you, Brother Prospero?" asked Pope Abdul in a mild tone tinged with sadness.

Cardinal Sicola, who had been summoned by the pontiff within hours of his return to Rome from Palermo, reflected that the faded blue eyes were radically incongruous in that lined, dark-olive-hued face above that raptorial beak of a nose; they should rightly be black or at least brown to properly match so predatory a face.

In reply, he shrugged, saying candidly, "No, I do not, your holiness, I never have. Nor did I love your holiness's predecessor . . . but he, at least, was *properly* elected."

"And you feel that we are not, Brother Prospero?" probed Abdul, in the same mild, sad tone.

"Let us not fence, your holiness," said Sicola bluntly. "I know and your holiness knows that that election which saw your holiness elevated was fraudulent; it flew in the very face of every written and oral agreement that has held the various feuding, infighting factions of the College of Cardinals together for above two hundred years.

"It was the sainted Khalil I, your holiness will recall, who personally hammered out that very wise and far-seeing policy: that the Papacy would alternate between the Moorish-Spanish faction and the Italian–Northern European faction, each faction also to have equal numbers of cardinals and bishops. Khalil di Granada knew human nature, your holiness, he knew the power of not only the Church, but of Rome, the State. Rome's power is great, but power is based upon wealth and influence on other states, as well as upon internal cohesion and the willingness of all within to work for and toward the state's good without.

"Because of what was illegally done in electing your holiness, a millennium and a half of painfully garnered wealth and power is being at best risked and at worst frittered away on causes of a most questionable nature. Because of your managed election, your holiness, the College of Cardinals has today lost every scintilla of proper cohesion; it is rather splintered into a dozen or more fractious factions all spending their every waking hour in plots, counterplots, amassing private armies and planning assassinations of personal and political enemies, rather than working—as they should—together for Rome.

"Rome, the city, may well be eternal, as is claimed, your holiness; but the power of the Church and the State of Rome is definitely not, nor should we delude ourselves with claims to the contrary. Recall what happened three centuries ago to the Papacy of Alexandria; *that* could easily happen to Rome, like it or not. I'll not besmirch the dead, but the treatment of the Kingdom of England and Wales and of King Arthur III Tudor and his family by your holiness's predecessor *and* your holiness himself was most imprudent and unwise, to put the matter in the most charitable of terms. At best, Crusades are very risky business, as should have been learned from the sad example of Galerian IV, the last Pontiff of Alexandria.''

The Pope snorted derisively, "Oh, surely this silly business abrew in York doesn't frighten a man like you, Brother? Rome has weathered more and worse, over the centuries—Arianism, Manichaeism, Maximianism, Rogatism, Circoncillianism, Donatism, Catharism, Monophysitism, Baldarism, and at least a score more—this Yorkism, too, will burn itself out, die, eventually be stamped out.''

Sicola shook his balding head. "I think not, your holiness, not in this particular case. Roman agents report that far more than just England and Wales are herein involved. All save a few of the Scottish bishops favor York over Rome, and over half of the Irish bishops do. Moreover, there is firm support from many of the Burgundian bishops, both lay and ecclesiastical authorities of the Empire and its allies, as well as interested observers from a number of other as yet uncommitted states. Even Prince Sidônio of Portugal has commented before his court that a Papacy located somewhere to the west and north of Rome would surely breathe new life into a patently moribund church-state.''

Abdul shook his head slowly. ''So much does he then hate the other Spanish kingdoms and principalities. He could have no other reason for making so false a statement in public, you know, my brother.''

''Of course his inherited hatreds have something to do with it, your holiness,'' Sicola agreed. ''And there also is the fact that the Princes of Portugal have always been on better terms with the English than have most of the other kings and princes and caliphs on that peninsula. But your holiness must also recognize that regionalism, nationalism, these are but parts of a whole, small parts, really. The bigger, more important parts of that dangerous whole are widespread distaste for the way in which Rome attempted to make a virtual satrapy of England and Wales, coupled with a recognition of the fact that Rome is become, in the wake of the utter rout of the Crusaders in England and our proven inability to even resupply our folk besieged in London, far weaker, poorer, and less influential than at any time in the last five centuries.

''We can expect more defections, your holiness, unless we can quickly regroup and present to the world a strong, united front, something that we cannot do, cannot show, cannot achieve or give any aspect of achieving so long as we leaders remain riven and thus keep our Roman State riven.''

''We suppose that our brother has a plan of some sort to achieve these ends?'' was Abdul's response, delivered with raised eyebrows.

Sicola nodded. ''One formulated not solely by me, your holiness, but by a sizable body of the College now in Rome and participated in by letter by certain cardinals who are elsewhere.''

''And just what are the salient points of this plan, Brother Prospero? For instance, what are its provisions for us?''

''It is felt in consensus, your holiness, that the first order of affairs must be a lifting of the excommunication of Arthur and of the interdiction of England and Wales, these to be coupled with immediate reestablishment of normal relations betwixt Rome and the Kingdom of England.''

"Impossible of accomplishment, Brother," snapped Abdul. "In order to do that it were necessary to wash our hands, withdraw all our support and protection of the rightful king and his mother, the regent, leave them and their few remaining faithful supporters to the mercy of a ruthless usurper. No, we'll not see such done!''

Sicola sighed. "Yes, your holiness's unflagging hatred for King Arthur of England and Wales is known far and wide, and that is one of the reasons that it is felt that overtures of friendship, of a reconciliatory nature, would be more believable were they to emanate from a Papacy other than that of Abdul. But more on that subject anon.

"As regards the abandonment of the so-called regent and the boy who may or may not be the actual son of Richard IV Tudor, they should never have been supported in the first place, not to the ridiculous extremes that they were. It is a precedent that has earned Rome no friends and a plentitude of enemies.''

"But," protested Abdul vociferously, "she is the niece of—''

"Your holiness's pardon if I interrupt. That your holiness's predecessor chose to have the daughter he always called a niece wed to him who then was Crown Prince of England and Wales was not a new or a novel idea. Many of *his* predecessors had arranged good, sometimes royal, marriages for their offspring and relatives. But when King Richard IV died, Rome should have accepted the choice of his brother to succeed him, not tried to force a foreign-born widow and an heir that many believe to be a non-Tudor bastard on the kingdom. Some pity can be felt for the transgressions of the predecessor of your holiness, of course, because he was after all the father of the widow and grandfather of the possible bastard in question.

"But your holiness himself has no such extenuating circumstances to excuse *his* intemperate actions. Your holiness had been most well reded—as many attempted at that time, myself included—to rescind the excommunication of King Arthur, send congratulations and Papal blessings, invite him to Rome and arrange to have him meet with a fatal accident somewhere along the way. But no, your holiness felt compelled to compound matters by first placing England and Wales under interdict, then by preaching a Crusade against them.

"And that Crusade of your holiness's concoction . . . I think that never before in all history has a military operation been so ill coordinated and generally mismanaged. Granted, the English and Welsh were fighting on their own land and for it and the king they had chosen, but the combined strengths of the crusading forces should have been overpowering, had there been any sort of timing and coordination of the attack, the invasions of England. But no, the forces were allowed to invade when and where and as they saw fit in no less than five integuments, which Arthur and his army easily defeated. Now, so many gallons of Crusaders' blood have been absorbed by English fields that few bishops from Riga to Garama but are loath to continue to preach this Crusade, and it is become exceeding difficult for Rome to hire mercenaries without signing agreements beforehand that service contracted will not include any possibility of fighting on English soil.

"Nor can your holiness apparently learn from his mistakes. I herein refer to the Irish business. Could your holiness not realize that such harsh measures over so petty a matter could do nothing, would do nothing save drive the high king and most of the petty kings into, directly into, the English camp?"

"What was done to Cardinal Mustapha, a prelate whose very person is holy, a prince of the Church, a . . ." Abdul was become so angry that he fairly spluttered.

"An old and personal friend of your holiness," added Sicola. "Yes, I know. But think, your holiness, is the sacrifice of all of Irland not too high a price to pay for a bit of salve for the bruised pride of his eminence?"

"There will be no sacrifice of Irland, doubting brother," Abdul declared hotly. "The Crusaders of God will—"

"—most likely never make an appearance, this time around, your holiness. The ill-fated English Crusade has virtually exterminated all the glory-seekers, the religious fanatics, the suicidal types from those lands over which Rome holds sway; the barrel scrapings who'll crawl from behind the wainscoting now will not be worth having—lunatics, thieves, brigands, and their unsavory ilk.''

"If so," snapped Abdul, "we shall have His Holiness of the East have the Irland Crusade preached to his people."

"It would not be wise, your holiness, to attempt any such thing. For one reason, his holiness in Constantinople pronounced a pest on both houses, as it were, early on in the English debacle, feeling he said then that both your holiness and his predecessor had been and were using the Church in what was a purely personal affair. More recently, his holiness of the East has had all that he can do, this according to his letters and messengers, to prevent a declaration of war against Rome by Sultan Omar."

Abdul's puzzlement appeared sincere. "But, Brother, why would Sultan Omar wish to declare war against us?"

"A little matter," replied Sicola dryly, "of a Turkish galleon sent on a diplomatic mission to Naples, crippled and driven into a Roman port by a tempest, then impressed entire into the last fleet sent to try to supply the besieged City of London. It was one of those fine four-masted galleons of Omar's, mounting a king's ransom in bronze guns and captained by one of his pashas. That all would be enough, but it seems that a brace of the sultan's favorite nephews were aboard, too."

Abdul shrugged. "This all is made right easily enough, Brother. When the fleet returns from England, we—"

"No, your holiness, nothing about this is going to be easy. That fleet is not coming back . . . ever, none save the one fast sloop that did make it back to bear the sad tale. The fleet was brought to battle by the English fleet, and those that were not sunk in the Thames River were all captured. One of the leading galleons blew up, and the captain of the surviving sloop thinks that that galleon was the Turkish ship."

"But why, Brother?" queried Abdul fretfully. "Why would

any Roman officer take it upon himself to cause us such trouble through impressing a Turkish ship?''

Reputedly, your holiness, it was a brainstorm of Ammiraglio Pietro himself. It seems that the fleet was awaiting the arrival of a leased French galleon, which ship was very late. The now deceased *ammiraglio* was loath to sail with less than four of the heavy-armed four-master galleons—for all the good they eventually did him. Then came word of this Turkish ship in harbor with relatively minor damage. It was a piratical scheme, but I suppose that he assumed that any infamy was acceptable was it but done in the name or the cause of the Holy See. We'll never know, really, just what he thought or planned, for he died at sea of a seizure of some sort, a day's sailing out of Oporto.''

"May the bastard rot in the deepest pit of hell!" snarled Abdul feelingly. "How we wish . . ."

"Were wishes horses, your holiness, all the world would be neck-deep in horse dung," Sicola attested. "What is done is done. What now must be done is to attempt to extricate Church and Roman State, alike, from the sorry pass into which they have been cast by all the mistakes and excesses of your holiness, his predecessor, and their various agents.

"Your holiness has two choices only. He may very quietly retire to a comfortable, very secluded hermitage, whereupon Rome will announce his death and the College will be gathered to elect a new pontiff.''

"And if we choose to not do any such foolish thing, Sicola?" snapped Abdul. "What then? What can you and the other malcontents do?''

"Regretfully see to it that your holiness expires in all truth . . . and with some rapidity. Your quiet retirement was my own choice, your holiness; the second, more violent option was supported by a larger number in the beginning and still is favored by most. This is why I feel it is so important that your holiness allow me to change his mind, to persuade him to steal away and spend his waning years in the comfort of, perhaps, a small monastery near to Tunis.''

*   *   *

The westering sun lay no more than two fingers above the hilly horizon when Sir Sebastian Foster, Duke of Norfolk and Lord Commander of the Royal Horse, rode at the head of his column of dusty, dog-dirty, dead-tired horsemen along the winding way through the cannon emplacements still remaining from the invasion of King Alexander's Scots Army. Next, they passed through the gate in the stone walls that enclosed what had long ago been the outer bailey of an earlier fortified dwelling place, walked their stumbling mounts up the graveled carriage drive to come at last to and draw rein before the gracious mansion called Whyffler Hall.

"Sir Geoff," her grace, Krystal Foster, Duchess of Norfolk, replied in answer to her newcome husband's question as to the whereabouts of his steward and castellan for this his barony, "is away these last five days with his lances and those of Laird Michael Scott on a hunt for a band of brigands who robbed, blinded, and viciously mutilated a wandering chapman lately, and have otherwise been afflicting both sides of the border. I thought you'd approve, so I gave him permission to go so long as he left half the lances here."

"Damn right I approve, honey," Bass said. "It's a sign of these new times, you know, English borderers and Scots borderers working together for the common good. Less than five years back, each would have blamed the other for the atrocities of those brigands, and eventually, reivings or raidings would have been the result, followed by vengeful burnings and ambushes and battles and then the whole damned bloody border might well have gotten involved. And of course, Sir Geoff had no way of knowing I'd be riding up here . . . hell, I didn't know it myself, hardly, before I was on my way."

She squeezed her husband's hand. "I must say, I'm flattered, Bass. I know that's not an easy ride, even in slow stages, and from the looks of you, your men and your mounts, you came damned fast. Or was it little Joe you rode up to see? I doubt he'll know who you are—he hasn't seen you in a year, and that's a long time to a child as young as he is."

Bass squirmed in his chair. "Krystal, honey, you know

how much I miss you and the baby, the only son I've ever had, but my duty keeps me down south, mostly, and you're up here. Much as I wish I could say differently, it was duty brought me up here, this time—a royal warrant at Hal's request. Somebody or something has been screwing around with that devilish machine down under the old tower keep, and Hal has ordered me to break down the wall sealing the doorway, ax through the cable connecting it to his former world, and end the menace forever.''

"You seem to be able to find time, Bass," said Krystal coolly, "to sail off playing pirate whenever the mood strikes you. I'm told that it's a far shorter and easier journey by sea up to one of the Northumberland ports, then only a week or less by horse to arrive here . . . if you really wanted to come.''

Bass sighed. "Honey, there's still a war going on, you know, and I'm still a soldier of the king. Every ship I prize goes either directly or indirectly into King Arthur's service, every cargo benefits not only me but the kingdom, which has been starved of foreign imports for years now. I don't enjoy the bloodshed and the killing at sea any better than I did ashore. I just do what I have to do to keep faith with King Arthur and with England. I'd thought . . . that is, I'd hoped you understood, but . . .''

She took his hand back in hers, looked at him levelly, and said, "I *do* understand, Bass. I hate myself when I start to slide into bitchiness, but . . . but I just get so goddamned lonely up here . . . or down at Rutland, for that matter. There's nothing but the boy and your letters for company. And the gallowglasses you use for post riders all speak such a garbled, guttural dialect that I can't talk to them without Sir Geoff or someone to translate for me.''

"Can't you talk to your household staff, honey? Your ladies? What about those two maids you used to get on so well with, aren't they still here? Trina and Meg, wasn't it?''

Krystal grimaced. "There were three of them—Trina, Bella, and Meg—but only one still is here and she's become as big a yes-man as any of my ladies, since you became a goddamned duke. I think I'd have become insane if dear Wolf hadn't come up here to hunt a couple of times. It was he who told me of how well you're doing as a pirate, you know. Your letters never say one damned thing about all your ships and ill-gotten gains. Just how rich are you now, Bass?''

He shrugged. "I'm sure I don't know, Krys. Sir Ali and Nugai might be able to tell you, though. They both seem to delight in keeping track of things like that.''

"I'm sure I don't know, Krys.'' She postured, mocking his tone and mannerisms. "Bass Foster, you're becoming as arrogant as any of the born nobility, dammit! Do you ever try to recall just who and what you really are anymore?''

"Krys, my lady-wife,'' he said soberly, "what I and you really are, who we are, is the Duke and Duchess of Norfolk, Markgraf und Markgrafin von Velegrad, Earl and Countess of Rutland, and Baron and Baroness of Strathtyne; there is and will never be any going back, honey. We'll live out the rest of our lives in this world, and we'd best learn to live and behave as we are expected to, as our peers do, as our subordinates expect us to; I've accepted these truths and I'm striving to adapt. You must too.''

"Oh, I know, I know, Bass,'' she answered dispiritedly. "All you've said is true, I know that, but that doesn't make me like it, any of it, any better. Being what I know I'm going to have to be for the rest of my life around most people doesn't come easily to me, and I get frustrated and angry when I see you adapting faster than me.

"I guess it all boils down to the differences in our backgrounds. From what you've told me about your life and your family, you came of what some people in that other world refer to as 'the Tidewater Aristocracy,' families who'd been in America for two or three hundred years, owned a lot of land and farms, rode horses, lived on inherited money, and supported the Republican Party, mostly. You were an officer in the army, too. So all this would naturally be easier for you to stomach and become a part of.

"Bass, all of my grandparents were immigrants, from Russia and from Latvia; my father was even born there. He grew up in this country—I mean, in the America of that other world—though, and he lived his democratic and fanatically egalitarian ideals. And he instilled them in me, Bass, to a degree that I hadn't really known or realized until I started trying to act the part of a great lady, here. I truly hate what I am becoming, what I am expected to become, what I must become; I miss people disagreeing with me, telling me I'm full of shit, sometimes. I just want to be a normal, average human being again, Bass."

Seeing her dark eyes swimming with tears, Bass Foster slipped from his chair—albeit a bit stiffly, his muscles sore from all the long, hard days in the saddle—to kneel beside her and take both her hands in his own.

"Look here, Krys, why don't you plan to leave here when I do? With my force and some of Sir Geoff's lances to escort us, we should be in no danger taking the old wagon track to York. Hal's palace is overrun with delegates to this religious thing he's presiding over just now, but Buddy Webster is just rattling around on Hal's country estate. You could live there for a while, until the weather warms up, then come down to Norwich."

"Another cold, drafty, smelly medieval castle, like Rutland?" she demanded.

"It was when first I moved in, still is, in some ways, honey," he replied, adding, "but it's being made more modern, more livable, every day, Krys. At least, it would mean we'd be together more."

She sighed, then nodded. "I'll think about it, Bass. But, God, how I miss the other world, miss all the simple, beautiful things I and everyone else there took for granted—central heat, flush toilets, hot showers, cars and decent roads to run them on, good lighting, running water, people to talk to, argue with, new books to read whenever you wanted.

"I love you, Bass, and I know that if I hadn't come . . . been brought here, I'd never ever have had you and our little son, but if only there were a way for us all three to go back together . . ."

*　　*　　*

Colonel Dr. Jane Stone strode out of the lift on the level housing the projection laboratory, then went the few paces down the wide corridor to the pair of steel-sheathed doors flanked by well-armed guards. She reflected that basic human nature had not changed much over the years. It had taken the defections of Drs. Kenmore and O'Malley to get her superiors to heed her often-reiterated demands to beef up internal security measures at the facilities here and across the river. Locking the barn door after the horse was stolen. She tried to recall if she ever had seen a horse in the flesh, wondered if they, like so many species of once-plentiful animals, were now extinct.

The guard officer saluted smartly, then opened the door for her. Inside the anteroom, she paced directly over to the desk of the director on duty. The balding, cadaverous-looking man came to his feet at her approach.

"Well, Ackerman," she snapped, "have your people gotten the location of that stolen console locked in yet?"

His head bobbed up and down on his skinny neck, and she noted that his sunken, dark-rimmed eyes contained the proper amounts of respect and outright fear of her; she noted these things with a sense of satisfaction.

"Has anyone bothered to check out the location of the console? I don't enjoy the prospect of possibly projecting into three or four meters' depth of water."

His almost fleshless lips slightly aquiver, the man nodded again. "Yes, Colonel Doctor, I have just come back from checking out the site. The console is sitting near one wall of a large, high-ceilinged space with a floor of packed earth, stone-walled, windowless, unlit save by the glow of the console. It appears to be possibly the cellar or ground floor of some sizable building."

"How about doors, Ackerman? How am I to get out of this place? Any signs of life there?" She deliberately injected a note of exasperation she did not really feel just for the pleasure of watching the already abject man cringe still more.

The effect was gratifying. He almost stuttered the reply. "It . . . a stairway . . . there is a stairway angling steeply up two walls and ending at a recessed archway on the next level. The only life I could see was traces of rodents.''

She nodded curtly, without thanks for the report, and strode on into the main room of the laboratory and directly over to the circular silvery plate set in the floor. Deferentially, the senior technician situated her at measured distances from the edge and center of that plate, then stepped back to place his hands on a bank of controls.

"Colonel Doctor, as the receiver plate seems to be some seven and one-quarter centimeters lower than is this projector plate, it might be wise to flex your knees so as to absorb the shock of impact. Please indicate the moment you are ready to be projected.''

"I was ready for projection when I came in," she half snarled. "Get on with it!''

The man's hands moved over the bank of knobs and buttons and levers, as she watched. Then he and everything else within her sight became wavery, cloudy, misted, hard to focus upon. For a brief time that seemed to last for an eternity, there was utter, unrelieved darkness—a darkness even darker than darkness, empty formless nothingness, eons old, immortal—then, from out a wavery, mint-green mist, appeared one of the small consoles and, behind it, big blocks of black and gray rectangular stones. A wall reached up beyond the limits of light, all streaky with slime and niter. Slowly, she turned about, then her right hand went to the grip of her heat-stun weapon, her forefinger seeking the activator, while she stepped off the plate, recalling that the field of the projector had been found to deflect some other types of beamings.

"Damn that Ackerman!" she snarled under her breath. "I'll have that bumbler strapped onto a shock table until his brains, if any, congeal! Nothing but rodents, hey? I wonder what he'd call *those*?''

Those were six or eight men clad in archaic clothing, bearing swords, what were probably some sort of primitive firearm, and at least one big, broad-bladed ax. Two or three of them were carrying blazing torches, and more torchbearers were coming down the steps behind them. Even as she brought up her weapon and stepped forward, the foremost of the men drew his sword with a sibilant *zweeep* and a silvery-blue flash of fine steel blade.

The royal seals were first chiseled off, entire, and set aside, then the *galloglaiches* went at the walled-up doorway with picks and sledges and coarse, hoarse Gaelic curses and obscenities. These became louder and more vehement when a second wall, every bit as carefully laid and well mortared as the first, was found some foot behind the outer one. It proved to be slow, hot, very exhausting work in the confinement of the archway, which was too narrow to allow for a full-arm swing of the tools, so Bass had the initial crew of wall-breakers replaced with a second when the first wall had been cleared away. Even so, it was nearing midnight before the last stones of the second wall had been dragged from their places and the open passage, pulsing with a faint, greenish, eldritch glow, yawned before them.

Bass had patiently explained to all of them well beforehand that the device that lay down the stairway beyond the walled-up doorway was lifeless, soulless, only a machine no whit different from such familiar machinery as wheellock actions, clocks, and mills, that the glowing was simply akin to the glowing of heated iron. Still, when the first dim radiance welled up out of the long-deserted space, there was a ripple of movement as the hard-bitten warriors crowded back toward the honest Christian light of the torches, crossing themselves or clasping tightly the silver crucifixes strung about their sinewy necks.

But regardless of their evident fright—these men who feared nothing living—when Bass, Sir Ali, Nugai, Don Diego, Sir Calum, Sir Liam, and Fahrooq entered the archway and started slowly, carefully, down the steep, unrailed stone stairs, every one of the *galloglaiches* took up weapon, heavy tool, or torch and followed their chosen war leader.

Just as Bass reached the foot of the dangerous stairs and took a step toward the brightly glowing, green-gray, boxlike device and the silvery plate on which it crouched, uttering

barely hearable sounds that seemed to raise the hairs on his
nape and set his teeth on edge like a thumbnail dragged
across a slate, everything changed. The noise became truly
audible—a whining-humming—and the glow heightened to
fully illuminate every cubic inch of the earth-floored room—
side to side and top to bottom—then, for the barest eyelid-
flicker of a moment, complete and utterly black darkness
enveloped the room and the men within it, bringing a gasp of
surprise from Bass and a chorus of terrified moans from men
who saw that not even the brightest torch would penetrate the
suddenly stygian place into which they had trespassed.

But then, just as suddenly, the too-bright green light returned and, along with it, something new had been added. A
tall, slender personage stood upon the silvery disk close
beside the boxlike device, but facing away from them all,
facing toward the bare stone wall. The figure was clothed in
some gray-green garment that covered it from neck to wrists
and to just above its ankles, where the legs of it met its
low-topped boots. It wore no sword, but was hung all about
with pouches of various shapes and sizes, from among which
jutted the pommel and ridged hilt of a knife or dagger.
Another, smaller hilt stuck out from the top of the figure's
right boot.

Slowly, the figure turned, stood for a moment staring at
them all while its lips moved soundlessly. Then, bringing up
a something hung from its right side to point a slightly belled
length of metal ahead, it stepped off the disk and strode
toward Bass and the rest.

He cursed himself for not bringing down at least one pistol.
The others might not recognize the thing being pointed as a
deadly weapon, but he certainly did. It was probably one of
those things that Hal had called a heat-stunner, and here he
was with only a sword and a couple of daggers and none of
them properly balanced for accurate throwing. Nonetheless,
he impulsively drew his Tara-steel sword from out its sheath,
stepping out to meet the figure with his weapon at low guard.
It was not until the flat-chested creature spoke that he realized
he was facing a woman.

The dialect was not too different from his own 1970s American English, far less different and more understandable than had been the English of this world when he first came here. "Drop that sword, man, or I'll kill you! Drop it, I say! All right, you ————!"

The final word was unfamiliar to him, but it its meaning was as crystal-clear as the tightening of her finger on what he decided must be the trigger of that strange weapon. Bass leaped sideways, then lunged forward, his body in a sidling crouch, his sword pointed very high, his intent to stun the menacing woman with a sword flat to the temple while he used his free hand to jerk the weapon from her grasp.

But a split second before he had come within range to try to accomplish his risky purpose, the familiar-looking hilt of a kindjal was standing out from her chest, a look of shocked pain was on her face, and she was falling backward onto the floor.

Bass, however, had not lived through many a hard-fought battle through allowing mere surprise to slow him down. He continued his forward movement until he had his left hand clasped on the short barrel of the woman's weapon, but when he essayed to jerk it from out her grasp, he discovered it to be fastened to the webbing belt cinching her waist. Dropping his sword, he used his freed right hand to unsnap the clip, then tore the buttstock from her weakened grip and hurled it beyond her reach. When her emptied hand immediately started to move jerkily toward the square butt of what might have been some variety of automatic pistol, holstered at her right hip, he beat her to it, drew it, and threw it in the wake of the larger weapon.

The gaze she fixed on him for a moment was distilled of pure, unadulterated hatred, but then she sagged back in defeat, moaning, "Please . . . ? Take . . . it . . . out . . . never . . . felt such . . . pain."

"You won't feel it long, either," said Bass bluntly, "That's a deathwound. You'll be dead in five minutes . . . maybe less, if I try to pull that blade out of you now."

A voice spoke from just above him then. "Iss vay, mein

Herr Herzog . . . might be. Blade did not directly into zee heart to go. Iss strange, for to at distance so short, miss." The squat little man knelt beside his victim, placed one yellow-brown hand palm down on her chest, and grasped the hilt of the kindjal with the other, gingerly, at first, exerting just enough pressure to see how deeply the blade was imbedded and to ascertain if point or edge was stuck in bone. He nodded to himself, then took a better grip on the hilt and drew out the full length of the blood-slimed blade in one smooth, swift motion, seeming to not hear the gurgling scream of the woman as the steel came free of her chest.

Carefully cleaning the kindjal blade on the leg of her breeches, he then returned it to its scabbard at his waist. That done, he retrieved the sword Bass had dropped, checked it from end to end for possible damages, then held it until his master might again require it.

"How long do you think she'll live now, Nugai?" asked Bass.

The little nomad shrugged. "Might be two minutes, mein Herr Herzog, no more than four."

With Nugai's assistance, Bass unsnapped the dying woman's belt and harness and, as gently as was possible, removed them and the various packs and pouches they held from her body. He beckoned over Sir Calum and said, "See that black thing at the base of that box, the thing that looks like a thick, shiny rope? Take your ax and sever it as close to the box as you can. Do it now, at once! Do it before another of these murderous people is projected into here."

Turning back to the woman, he noted for the first time the silver oak leaves on her shoulderboards, which previously had been obscured by the straps of her harness. These insignia, coupled with the name strip affixed above the right breast pocket of her coverall—STONE, DR JANE—jogged his memory.

"You're Colonel Doctor Jane Stone from the Gamebird Project, aren't you? You came after Hal . . . that is, Dr. Harold Kenmore, didn't you?"

Her reply, though weak of voice, was perfectly clear.

"Yes, but who are you? I don't think you're of this time, but then I know you're not of mine, either."

"You're right, Dr. Stone," he replied, "but it's a longer tale than you have time left to hear. Suffice it to say that I was sent here by the man you knew as Kenmore to break the connection of that box to your world, lest someone like you came into this world. Needless to say, I was almost too late."

She tried to snort a scornful laugh, but ended moaning with agony, then after a moment said, in a weaker voice yet, "Cut that cable through if you wish, whoever you are, but it will do you no good now. The lab has a firm lock on the coordinates of this console and can project through another if this one fades out, disappears from the scanning instruments.

"You say Kenmore sent you? Well, why didn't the traitor come himself?"

"For one thing, Dr. Stone, it's a long, hard journey and he is a very old man," said Bass. "Perhaps you are unaware of just how much he has aged since you saw him last."

"How much can anyone age in two months, man? Talk sense. Where is Kenmore? Where is that other traitor, Emmett O'Malley?"

"Hal thought something like this, and he once told me about it, Dr. Stone. Time must be different in your world from time in this one. Your two months there has been more than a hundred and fifty years here. As for O'Malley, the evidence is that he's dead, killed in a battle several years ago. Even had they both been alive and you had gotten out of here and sought them out, you'd hardly have recognized them, either of them. They lost most of their longevity boosters, you see, and . . ."

He fell silent when he realized that he was speaking to a corpse. Colonel Doctor Jane Stone was dead.

Sitting on the ground between the old tower keep and the hall stables in the bright sunlight, with a sack containing the effects and clothing of the late Colonel Doctor Jane Stone atop it and the silvery disk leaning against it, the console did not look one whit so imposing as it had in the benighted subterranean room. Moreover, the greenish glow had faded so much with exposure to the sun as to be almost invisible.

A party of the *galloglaiches* had hoisted the heavy, bulky device up to the first floor of the tower, while another group painfully pried up the disk on which it had rested. Bass meant to deliver both to the archbishop in York; if he didn't want them, maybe Pete Fairley could make use of the metal alloys and wire. Recalling another thing that Hal had told him of that sinister world from which Hal, O'Malley, and the dead woman had come, Bass and Nugai had stripped her to the very skin, then poked and probed at her cooling flesh until they had found what they sought—a tiny metallic disk implanted just under the skin of one inner thigh.

After giving the corpse to the galloglaiches to bury, he ordered the walls rebuilt in the archway. With the walls once more firmly in place, he reset the royal seals in the fresh mortar, then went out to order the organization of transport for his wife and son, her household, and the other-world items down to York. He had now successfully carried out yet another mission for King Arthur. He wondered where the next one would take him, and he was beginning to wish that Hal and the monarch would find another errand boy before loneliness bred of protracted separation completely soured his relationship with Krystal.

Harold, Archbishop of York, sat in the study cum alchemical laboratory of his palace facing the newly returned Duke of Norfolk across the width of a heavy, much-scarred table. The top of that table was cluttered, end to end, with the effects of the late Colonel Doctor Jane Stone. Directly before the cleric lay an opened case containing row upon row of small green-and-yellow capsules. Beside it, a similar case held two transparent ampoules and four hypodermic syringes.

The old, old man shook his white-haired head yet again. "I do not understand, Bass. I can understand why she might have brought the four dozen booster capsules, since they can be very useful as general antibiotics and she had no idea just what kind of a world she was projecting into. But why in

God's holy name she brought along enough longevity serum for four initial dosages, I cannot imagine."

"Will they help you, Hal?" asked Bass.

The archbishop nodded slowly, his lips turning upward in a faint smile. "Oh, yes, my good friend, the capsules would prolong my life . . . if I choose to take them, that is. An intravenous injection of an eighth to a fourth of an initial dosage of the serum will do even more, serving to partially reverse the effects of aging already present in the body. It was to obtain the lab equipment and supplies to make this that poor Emmett O'Malley attempted to project the drug and chemical laboratory building from the Gamebird Project into this world and ended in what appeared total failure but actually succeeded in bringing you and the others here, years ago. Youth, the appearance at least of youth, meant so much to Emmett. It doesn't to me.

"So, no, Bass, I'll most likely just keep these longevity treatments and booster capsules as I did my own supply, years agone, for medical emergencies. Most of these other items she brought along are weapons of one sort or another, some of which I may be able to teach you the use of. You might want her canteen, too—it's unbreakable to the extent that I doubt even an arquebus ball would hole it.

"The thick brownish disks in the tubes are food concentrates spiked heavily with vitamins, minerals, and a powerful stimulant. A soldier such as you are may find them helpful, on occasion."

Bass fingered one of the disks—about the circumference of a dime and some four millimeters thick—dubiously; it did not look or feel or smell very appetizing to a well-fed man, but if he were hungry, now . . . "What do you do with these, Hal—chew them first or swallow them whole?"

"Either, Bass, though chewing them probably puts the stimulant into the bloodstream more quickly. They taste far better than you would suspect from sniffing them, incidentally. You should drink at least a pint of fluid after taking one.

"I think it best that I keep her writers, Bass. An archbishop stands less likely to be accused of witchcraft than do you. That is the same reason I'm keeping a number of other items for which I really have little or no use. But I am turning a couple of the heat-stunners over to you, along with an admonition to use them with due circumspection. I'll give you a supply of the power units—one size fits all the weapons, from the largest to the smallest—and I'll show you how to change them; never throw an expended one away, Bass, for a few days of exposure to strong sunlight will recharge them."

"I have a favor to ask of you, Hal," said Bass, "a very personal one. I'd like to park my wife and her household and my little son out on your estates, where Buddy Webster is, until the weather has warmed up enough to make Norwich Castle a little more habitable."

The archbishop displayed still-strong, though yellowed, teeth in a broad smile. "It will be my very own pleasure to have the delightful Dr. Krystal Kent Foster guesting at the estates for as long as she and you wish, Bass. I have always enjoyed her conversation, and it will be far easier for me to journey out to the estates for a few days than to find enough time for the long trip up to the Border Country. Why don't you plan to have her live there until you get back from Ireland?"

"Until I get back from Ireland?" shouted Bass. "Since when am I going to Ireland, dammit? Please, Hal, please tell me this is just a sick-humorous joke, *please!* Because if it's not, it's going to be your job to tell Krystal the when and where and, most importantly, the *why* of it all. What good am I to anyone in Ireland, Hal? Why, I can't even speak the language."

"You are a proven superlative military strategist and tactician, friend Bass," replied the archbishop soberly. "In addition, you are a fine warrior, personally brave, considerate of those under your command, and you therefore inspire loyalty. War leaders of your caliber are a rare and a precious treasure to monarchs, you must understand, living gems, as it were. And as you or I might loan a relative a bauble he admired, so is King Arthur loaning you—your unmatched abilities, that is—to his cousin King Brian VIII for a particular mission."

"What kind of mission, Hal?" demanded Bass, grim-faced.

"I really don't know," the archbishop answered. "Perhaps his majesty does, but if so his letter did not contain information of that nature—which is understandable, considering that he and I are not the only persons who can read Latin and this is, after all, a matter of state."

Bass stared hard at the aged man for a moment, then asked, "Hal, what would likely happen to me and my family if I refused to go? After all, I've been constantly at war or at least in the field every spring, summer, autumn, and sometimes winter since I got to this world. I think I deserve some years of peace and relaxation with my wife and my son. Poor Krys is becoming a bitch because of my long absences and her resultant loneliness, plus her difficulties in adapting to this world and her new station in life. Joe, my son, didn't even know who the hell I was after not seeing me for a year or more. Hal, I think I owe Krys and Joe as much as I owe Arthur . . . and a whole hell of a lot more than I'll ever owe the *ard-righ*, Brian. Brian the Burly, my *galloglaiches* call him."

"Bass, before I answer your last questions, let me say this: You say that you do not even speak the Irish language, yet you have just used two Irish terms, *ard-righ* and *galloglaiches*, and furthermore spoken them with exactly the proper accent; nor have you ever seemed to experience difficulty in mastering the various regional dialects of this English language, dissimilar as many of them are, one to the other. Sir Ali feels that you are well on the way to becoming fluent in basic Arabic. You seem to have acquired a decent command of German and not a little Khazan and Kalmyk from your man, Nugai, and from the Barón Melchoro a smattering of Portuguese and Spanish. You, my friend, are blessed with an ear for languages; you may not truly speak Irish, now, this minute, but if you put yourself to it, you will in short order.

"You have earned his majesty's gratitude many times over in your service to him, his just cause, and the kingdom, Bass, so I doubt that he would be overharsh were you to refuse his request in this instance . . . had you a reasonable reason to so refuse. But you do not, Bass. . . . Now, hold your tongue, let me finish, please.

"You, at least, have a living family to which to return at the eventual conclusion of hostilities. Arthur, alas, has only his memories of his young wife and infant children, all of them done to hideous deaths by his sister-in-law, Angela, his dead brother's demonic widow and her minions. Think you, also, on how many others of his majesty's loyal supporters have been as much or even more absent from their own families and lands as have you from yours.

"No, friend Bass, I strongly urge you to accept and carry out his majesty's request, in this instance. It is a reasonable assumption that you won't be in Brian's service long, in any case, for London soon must fall; that will be the bitter end of war in England, and Arthur most assuredly will want all his great captains and high nobility hard by him to aid him in setting the kingdom aright once more.

"So far as concerns her grace, your lady-wife, I have learned a great deal concerning human nature in more than two centuries of living and dealing with human beings, so trust me to win her over in your absence."

CHAPTER
THE EIGHTH

When his grace, the Duke of Norfolk, and his road-weary column arrived back at Norwich Castle, Sir Richard Cromwell was awaiting them with an order to escort his grace to the presence of King Arthur III, at Greenwich Castle, his majesty's current residence.

But while sitting at meat with his own officers and Sir Richard, Bass declared, "I have just saddle-pounded my poor arse from here to the Scottish border and back by way of York, and I'm damned if I mean to further tenderize said arse so soon after such a ride, not when I've some fine, large, comfortable, and speedy ships moored half a day away from Norwich. The king did not say specifically that you bear me to him on the back of a horse, now did he, Sir Richard?"

The king's emissary laid aside his knife, dabbed at his lips with a fine, linen *panolino*, and replied, "Why, no, your grace, no method of transport was specified in the royal orders. And speaking personally"—he grinned—"I would dearly love to go to Greenwich aboard one of the rightly renowned warships of your grace's flotilla. My troopers can take the horses back by land."

The matter was thus decided, and within the hour, Bass had dispatched a galloper to Walid Pasha, that *Revenge* might be ready to lift anchor and sail when he and his party arrived at the port.

Forewarned by Hal as to the reason for this royal summons, he left many of his usual entourage behind to attend to the preparation of the Squadron of Royal Tara *Gallowglasses* for what would most likely be another campaign—this one, however, on land and on horseback rather than at sea and aboard ships, though they all might do some of the latter too, for all he knew.

Abbot Fergus felt it to be his holy duty to personally escort the patently murderous, thankfully recaptured Sassenach madman to his nursing order's parent house, for all that the journey would take him across the widest width of the Kingdom of Scotland to the Western Isles. Having lost four brothers, some of his structures, and a number of his animals, the abbot simply felt that so proven-dangerous an afflicted one as Uilleam Kawlyer would be far better off in the larger, older, better-staffed parent house on the Holy Isle of Iona. Immuring him on Iona would serve a further purpose: Should he manage to again escape, there would be nowhere for him to go, precious few hiding places from which he might again stalk and murder the unwary, which was precisely how he had subsisted during his weeks at large.

The trip was made some easier for Fergus and the brothers who rode with him in that Sir Tormod, the Laird of MacGaraidh, had generously offered the loan of not only the five fine riding mules they all now forked, but an ancient wheeled bear cage in which to safely transport the madman to the far west, a span of sturdy draft oxen to draw it, and a sturdy lad to goad and tend the oxen and mules. The influential laird also had arranged for the defenseless monks to accompany a party of MacGhille Eoin clansmen back to Mull, the clansmen having served out the time that their chief had pledged them to the military service of King James. The noncombatants were to return in company with a similar party of MacDhughaill clansmen bound to Edinburgh to commence their year and a day of pledged service—which would protect them (and, incidentally, Sir Tormod's mules, oxen, bear cage, and serving lad) in traversing the still-wild stretches of the lowlands. Abbot Fergus was most thankful for the laird's generosity, and he had silently vowed to pray thrice every day for him and his.

The filthy, stinking, rag-clad madman spent most of the journey crouched in one corner of the tall iron-bound cage, muttering to himself in what either was gibberish or some heathen tongue which Fergus could not understand. Occasionally the lunatic would stand erect and scream out at the world in that same or some other variety of incomprehensible speech. But he did not often try to stand, for staying on his feet in the springless conveyance as it bounced and jounced from rut to rock to pothole along the ill-tended track was an effort foredoomed to failure, even given a plenitude of thick, stout oaken bars to which to cling.

To the knowledge of Abbot Fergus, this particular madman had never spoken an intelligible word to anyone from the very first day he had been brought to and placed in the care of the nursing order. Therefore, it was a distinct shock to the good abbot to hear himself addressed as he walked past the cage at dusk one day, addressed in excellent, if strangely accented, Latin.

Looking quickly about, he immediately realized that there was no one of the monks nearby and that the words could have come from none but the chained and caged Sassenach madman.

"You called me, my son?" he replied in the same tongue, still more than half convinced that the syllables uttered by the poor, murderous lunatic had only accidentally resembled Latin words.

"Is it your intention, Holy Father, that I die of the effects of exposure?" the madman inquired, sounding as sane and rational as any man Abbot Fergus had ever heard speak. "If you have no blankets to spare, can you not at least have this cage lined in straw or dried grass, wherein I can burrow when the cold winds of night beset me?"

The abbot caught himself beginning to move closer to the cage and hastily fell back a few paces, recalling that this pleasant-spoken man had, with only his bare hands, murdered a priest of God and at least seven other persons. "You are mad," he replied. "Lunatics, like beasts of the fields, feel not the ravages of weather, everyone knows that. Heat afflicts them not, nor cold."

With a rattling of chains, the madman shook his shaggy head and said, "Not so, good Father, there is no truth in that old, outmoded adage. And, in any case, I am not mad."

"Ah, but you are, my son, my poor son." Fergus assured the madman. "If anyone should know it is I, who heard you raving from the cell you inhabited in my order's house night after night for years. Yes, my son, you are indeed mad, alas."

"Have you any idea, Father, just who and what I am?" queried the madman.

Fergus nodded gravely. "I know that you are a Sassenach, most likely of noble birth, else the powerful men who send silver each year to defray the expenses of your care would not so do."

"Then know you this truth, as well, Father," said the madman, just as gravely, "I am William Collier, Earl of Sussex and loyal subject of the one and the only rightful King of England and Wales, Richard V. At great personal danger, I pretended loyalty to and liking for that disgusting thing, the Usurper who styles himself Arthur III, but through mischance, I was found out. While spurring hard for the border, I made the error of seeking a night's shelter, a sup of food, and a fresh mount at the hall of an old and trusted friend. My friend betrayed my trust and I was taken. But then, with me in custody, my captors thought more deeply on the matter and decided that a mere killing were too mild a punishment for me.

"Father, though you may know it not, for it is somewhat of a secret, the usurper is a foul, godless, Satan-serving warlock, and right many of his demon spawn serve him. The leader of my captors was one such he-witch, and there, that cursed night, did he wreak his evil will upon me, ensorcelling me, laying upon me a foul curse of madness to encompass most of my waking life, with brief snatches of sanity interspersing to torture me further with the realization of what I had become."

At the first mention of witchcraft, the old monk had crossed himself, an act he rapidly repeated each time any allusion to sorcery was made. Through lips become pale and tremulous, he half-whispered, "Och, my lord, I didnae ken!" His educated Latin was clear forgotten in his shock and horror at the revelations.

The man long supposed mad continued in a sad, wistful tone, "As for the howling of nights, Father, imagine how a man must feel when he awakens from dreams of the bygone days when he was a rich, respected peer, owning lands both broad and fair, living in comfort, faith, loyalty, and God-given peace with those he loved all about him; when such a man awakens shivering in cold, dark squalor, immured in a tiny, stone-walled cell, near naked and filthy, with no furnishings save a malodorous tick of straw and no companions save the vermin infesting his body, what then can such a man do but howl the long nights of torment away?"

Fergus had moved closer and closer as the sorry tale was spun. Now he was hard by the cage; extending a hand, he laid it upon the bony shoulder of the man he had thought mad and asked, "My poor, persecuted lord, what can I do to ease your unwarranted torment?"

"First of all, Father," replied the caged man, "withdraw to a safer distance, for such is my curse that reason can depart in a bare twinkling and madness return, and I would not have your blood on my hands.

"I would like to be let out and unchained long enough to wash. Surely, with four monks and twoscore men about you can mount sufficient guard to restrain me should the unholy madness suddenly reafflict me the while.

"I will be in far more comfort can this cage be scoured and a foot or so of straw or dried grass placed within it. And cannot one of the brothers trim my beard and hair and pick out some of the lice? Even the lowly ass sometimes is curried. Pleasant, also, would it be to have a clean cassock and a blanket or woolen war tartan in which to wrap my body of cold nights."

*   *   *

Three days after Bass Foster's departure for Norwich on the heels of a stormy final meeting and "discussion" with his wife, the Archbishop of York made one of his excessively rare visits to that portion of his estates being currently used by former Captain Buddy Webster and, most recently, by the Duchess of Norfolk, her son, and her household. His grace made the journey in a horse litter slung between two huge shire horses, while his capacious coach trundled along behind, crowded with ten men and women he had had brought in from the Abbey of St. Olaf; the other four, who seemed to know one end of a horse from the other, rode along behind the coach on rounseys.

Arrived at long last at their destination, the archbishop had his "guests" ushered into two connecting suites of rooms on the second floor of the wing he had sent retainers ahead to clean and open for his use. After personally ordering cold food, ale, and water for washing for them, he sent for the eldest and apparently most sensible of the lot.

Rupen Ademian, for all his fifty-odd years, was still a thick-limbed, powerful, intensely vital man; his hands were big and square, his palms and blunt fingers hard with callus. He was rapidly balding in the scalp area, but his beard and flaring mustache were thick and blue-black and a little curly, and he grew more and denser body hair than any human being that the archbishop had seen in more than two hundred years.

Judging solely from brief earlier conversations with him, Harold of York had hopes for this elder of the two Ademians. Unlike his nephew, Rupen was open-minded, adaptable, and, though clearly no stranger to violence, not easily prone to wreaking it.

Harold had thought on the matter and had decided that quite probably the answer to this man's easygoing nature and willingness to try new and different things, to do things in novel ways, or to rearrange his thinking modes to consider the possibility of the once-impossible derived of his background rather than of formal education, of which he had partaken but little.

Rupen had been born in Damascus, Syria, in 1920, of parents who had been prosperous farmers before Turks and Kurds butchered most of their kin, took their land and all that was on it, and transported them and millions more to Syria, then—in 1916—a Turkish province. That fraction of those who had been torn from out Armenia strong enough or lucky enough to make it to Syria alive had been simply abandoned there with only the pitiful bits and pieces of their previous lives to sustain them.

In 1923, Rupen's family enjoyed the extreme good fortune of being one of the families chosen to go to America, sponsored and provided tickets by Armenians already resident in that Land of Promise. Arrived in New York, however, with almost no English or money, only train tickets, they had somehow wound up in Orange, Virginia, rather than the Midwest location to which they had been bound.

But it worked out well for the immigrants who had suffered so much for so long. Orange County, Virginia, breeds some of the finest horseflesh in the nation if not the world, and in addition to being an expert farrier, Rupen's father knew horses and had a God-given "way" with them. So, once more, the little family began to prosper and grow in size, now safe from Turks and Kurds. They never grew wealthy, even after the family farrier supply and hardware business in Fredericksburg, Virginia, began to do as well as the horse-trading sideline, for Rupen's parents squirreled away every spare dollar to bring over those relatives and friends who had survived the atrocious treatment to which the Armenians had been subjected.

In the depths of the Great Depression, Rupen's father had mortgaged his business and even the small truck farm on which they then resided in order to invest in and keep operating a small local factory that just then gave employment to many of the selfsame immigrants his hard-earned dollars had brought to Virginia.

As the nation girded itself for the certain onslaught of a second worldwide war, that little factory, which had been making brass curtain rods, lamps, and the like, was visited by government men; shortly, adjoining land had been purchased with low-interest government loans which also were funding a rapid expansion and modernization of existing facilities, the road was widened and resurfaced to take frequent and very weighty traffic, and the railroad built a spur from the main line to the factory. Half a year before the Japanese, in support of their so-called Greater East Asia Co-Prosperity Sphere, tried to destroy the United States' Pacific Fleet at Pearl Harbor, the Fredericksburg Factory #1 of Ademian Enterprises, Incorporated, was already turning out brass shell casings under contract to the Department of Defense.

Rupen had not had much childhood; he had grown up working. All of the Ademian family worked and, regardless of their actual ages, were expected to be as responsible as adults. Rupen had operated the roadside stand at which vegetables and eggs from the Ademian family farm were sold until the twins—Haigh and Mariya—were old enough to take his place. Then he had gone to work in the factory. Rupen's father did not believe in coddling anything except eggs and sick horses. Therefore, neither his eldest nor Haigh, who later joined him, received any preference in their employment; they started at rock bottom, drawing no more wage than did any other beginner—two dollars a day for eleven and a half hours of work, when Rupen started, though it had increased to almost three dollars by the time Haigh came.

The Armenian employees afforded the brothers a measure of respect initially simply because they were the sons of Der Vasil Ademian, but the two soon enough earned respect and friendship on their own. As the plant grew in size, however, the workers of Armenian antecedents became a smaller and even smaller percentage of the total work force and Rupen began to make friends not related to him by ethnic background or race, just as he had in the public schools; he made friends easily, always had, fighting only when he had to do so as a last resort, but then hard, to win.

At the time of the sneak attack on Pearl Harbor, Rupen was twenty-one years of age and Haigh had just turned nineteen. Due to the nature of their employment—in a vital defense industry—neither expected to be drafted, and they possibly would not have been, at least not until much later in the war, but war fever was gripping the nation, government and citizenry as well. And on a snowy day in January 1942, Rupen's father summoned him and his brother to the executive offices, newly refurbished, refurnished, and extensively modernized, in the older part of the plant.

"Sit down, my sons," he said in his heavily accented English. When they were seated, he set a small glass before each of them and himself and filled all three from a bottle of fiery arrack. He offered the dark, strong Egyptian cigarettes he preferred, lit Rupen's and his own, then spoke again.

"It is time that we speak now of debts and of the repayment of debts."

Rupen had squirmed and forced a straight face, wondering just how in hell the old man had found out about his highly profitable small-scale gambling enterprises.

After a long drag on his cigarette, Vasil Ademian said, "My sons, the accursed Turks and the Kurds, they took all that we had, your mother and me, they tore the girlchild, the infant, who was our firstborn, from your mother's arms and threw her tiny body high into the air, catching it on their sharp bayonets. They drove us all like cattle from off our land to the deserts of Syria, where you two and your sister, Mariya, were born, given to your mother and me in the mercy of God that our family and race live on and become again strong. It was also through divine mercy that we were able to leave Syria and come to America.

"As you both know of old tellings, when we came first to Orange County, I had in my pockets less than six dollars and your mother had ten dollars in gold hidden on her person. But the country was good to us all, the people and the land, they gave us all we now have, and now the time comes to repay that debt, that just debt.

"These Nazis and Japs, my sons, they are evil, evil people. They are just like the Turks and the Kurds, and they must be both stopped before we find them trying to drive us from America, too. These Nazis may even have learned their evil from the Turks, for I am told that these Nazis are mostly Germans and I remember that the Kaiser of Germany was a friend and ally of the sultan in the last war. From all that I am told of the brutalnesses of these Nazis, they sound very Turkish to me.

"I have but just this morning earlier returned from the place where they take men for soldiers to fight these Nazis and Japs and keep their evil from out of this fine country that has been so very good to us all. But they will not have me, my sons, they say that I am too old for their use, even though I am more man at my age than many they said they would have for soldiers.

"And so, my dear sons, since I cannot go to repay the debt that the Ademians owe to this great and generous United States of America, you must go in my place."

There was never any questioning the dictates of Vasil Ademian, not by his progeny; they went—Rupen into the Army, Haigh into the Marine Corps—and by the time that Corporal Ademian, Rupen S., landed in North Africa, Marine Private Ademian, Haigh R., was already dead at Bloody Ridge on Guadalcanal.

By the time of the Sicilian invasion, Rupen was a platoon sergeant. His sister, Mariya, having completed her nurse training at the Medical College of Virginia, had been ordered by their father into the U.S. Navy Nurse Corps, and seventeen-year-old Kogh Ademian had forged his father's signature and followed his dead brother into the Marine Corps before Vasil knew anything about it all. In the fierce fighting on the drive from Palermo to Messina, Rupen became by attrition first platoon leader, then company commander, was awarded a battle-field commission of second lieutenant by his own army and a 7.9mm rifle bullet by some rifleman of the Hermann Göring Division, but had recovered in time to lead his platoon ashore into the hell that they called Anzio. More than half his platoon were killed or wounded, but Rupen lived to see Rome.

Commanding a company of infantry in the bitter, muddy, rainy mountain campaign that followed the fall of Rome,

First Lieutenant Ademian, Rupen S., received another German gift, this one so meaningful that he was shipped back to a hospital in the United States. By the time they were ready to release him from that facility, the war for Europe was ended and that against Japan on its last legs, and the United States Army seemed not at all anxious to retain the services of one slightly battered citizen-soldier who still was more or less convalescent and consequently in no shape to be considered for the upcoming invasion of the Japanese homeland.

A week after he arrived back home, his sister's ship docked at Norfolk, Virginia, and Lieutenant j.g. Ademian, Mariya Z., came up to Fredericksburg with her friend, Lieutenant j.g. Bedrosian, Margaret L., the first blond Armenian woman Rupen had ever seen. She was not pure Armenian, of course, only a quarter Armenian, in fact; her father's father's family had come to America in the nineteenth century and she did not even speak Armenian, but she was beautiful, charming, and vivacious, and Rupen had made up his mind less than a full day after he first met her.

Marge seemed to like Rupen, too, and she wrote often to him during the five months that she and Mariya nursed aboard ship ferrying ill and wounded servicemen home from the European Theater of Operations.

Meanwhile, Japan had surrendered and Vasil informed Rupen that for all that he fully approved of the proposed union, no marriage could or would take place until the younger Ademians, Kogh and Bagrat, had returned to witness the ceremony, and that was that.

It was during the preparations for his wedding, which finally was celebrated in the summer of 1946, that Rupen first got the idea of organizing and forming talented and musically minded local Armenians into an ethnic-type band; his father had had to pay to bring one down from Massachusetts. But it was years before Rupen did any more than think or occasionally talk about that idea.

It was at the wedding itself that Vasil, chock full of arrak, vodka, and old-country spirit, made an announcement to his three sons who had managed to survive the war that was to have considerable influence on the future of Rupen's marriage and life.

"My sons, my brave sons, you don't know it, of course, and that's why I tell you now, but Ademian Enterprises is worth ten million dollars, the lawyers tell me. And I told the lawyers and now it's down in writing with them and I've signed it that the whole damn business will go to the first one of you who gives me a grandson and names him Haigh, in memory of not only your brother what the Japs killed but my brother, your uncle, what was murdered by the damned Turks."

"Goddamn it all, Papa," Kogh had burst out, momentarily forgetting just to whom he spoke, "that ain't fair! Rupen, here, you're giving him the fucking edge on us both, me and Bagrat . . . and Mariya, too, we ain't even married yet!"

Vasil allowed the red-faced young man to get all of two sentences out before his still-hard fists clubbed him down. "This is a day for joy, Kogh," he addressed the stunned, dazed man where he half sat, half lay getting grass stains on his flashy dress uniform, "so you should not have made me to do such a thing on this day. Perhaps it is because you have been long away in the company of men who had no respect for their elders, but *your* people, the Armenians, and especially the Ademians, do and have always done and you will do as long as there is strength in my right arm. Do you understand me?"

Rupen had pulled his brother to his feet while Vasil was speaking, and while Bagrat's khaki muslin handkerchief absorbed the blood that trickled from the corner of Kogh's mouth, the old man went on in jovial tones such as he had used before their sibling's exercise in insubordination.

"What I've said, my sons, is the way it's going to be. As for Rupen having a what you say edge, maybe so, maybe not. If the girl he was married to was pure Armenian, yes he would, but this new daughter of mine, she's only one part Armenian to three parts English, and you know these English, they don't get kids very fast, mostly. So you two look around here today, find yourself a good, strong, healthy Armenian girl, and bring her to me. Don't worry none about a dowry, us Ademians don't need one anymore.

"Your sister, Mariya, she's already brought a medical doctor over to meet me, earlier today. She met him when the both of them were learning at the Medical College of the Commonwealth of Virginia, in Richmond, and he will live and work there now that the war is over. He is of the Panoshians, his father and mother came to America from Van in 1917, and he is their oldest son. He will make a good brother to you all, I think, and it will be good to have a medical doctor in the family."

Vasil Ademian's pronouncement at Rupen's wedding festival made the year that followed a very bad one for sheep, lamb being the meat of choice for Armenian festivities; there were three Ademian weddings within eleven months. But the Massachusetts-based Armenian musicians and the railroad that shuttled them back and forth had reason to rejoice. So did the employees of the Ademian Enterprises, Incorporated, Plant #1 and Plant #1 Annex, as they all were given a paid day off in order that they might attend the huge, raucous outdoor wedding receptions and gorge on Armenian foods, American barbecue, and Brunswick stew, with unnumbered gallons of draft beer to wash it all down.

Rupen and Marge tried their damnedest to produce a grandchild for Vasil, but fourteen months of more than merely frequent sexual athletics left them exactly where they had started. So Rupen made an appointment, then he and his wife drove down to Richmond and availed themselves of the services of their new brother-in-law, Boghos Panoshian. He examined them both thoroughly, took some assorted specimens, and said he would be in touch. A week later, he telephoned Rupen and suggested that he come back down to Richmond.

In his deserted office, after his normal hours, Boghos had Rupen strip for a second examination. "These scars in the neck of your scrotum, Rupen—do you know what might have caused them and when?"

"Shrapnel," said Rupen casually. "In Italy, back in '44. Most of it got me in the ass and the backs of my legs, but a couple of little bitty pieces did have to be taken out of my scrotum, too, as I recall. Why? I can tell you plain, it never affected my performance in bed or anywhere else, that's for damn sure."

"Get dressed." Boghos sidestepped the question. "I'd rather look at your ugly face than your hairy ass. Did you ever consider applying to replace Gargantua? You've got as much body hair as any ape I've ever seen. Come to my office when you're dressed and we can have a drink or three."

A quarter hour later, Rupen swirled the ice cubes in his vodka and asked, "And just what the hell do you do if you have this a-zoo-spermia, Boghos?"

The doctor shook his head slowly. "To be truthful, Rupen, I may not be able to do anything. You may just have to live with the knowledge that you're sterile, to all intents and purposes, that you and Marge are out of the running in your father's silly little race. Of course, the only way I can tell for sure is to get a good look at the inside of your scrotum, and that means some exploratory surgery. It's entirely up to you."

"So far as Papa's baby derby is concerned, Boghos, you may consider ten million plus dollars silly, but damned few other folks do. Not that any of us, baby or no baby, is going to get it anytime soon; the old man comes of folks who always lived a good, long time if somebody didn't kill them first, and just look at the little guy: he's nearly twice my age and still strong as a fucking ox. Why, at my wedding feast, Kogh gave him some lip and the old man just reached up and knocked that kid silly and flat on his back. No, anybody who is crazy enough to sit around waiting for the old man's pile to drop into his lap will die of starvation long before Vasil Ademian kicks off."

"Mariya and I do worry about him, though, Rupen. He drinks far too much alcohol and he smokes those foul, stinking Egyptian cigarettes at such a rate you'd think he owned stock in the Egyptian monarchy." The doctor's real concern was evident.

"Knowing the old man, he just may own that stock, Boghos." Rupen grinned. "But back to me, when do you want to cut?"

Boghos shrugged. "Whenever you're ready, let me know

and you can drive down here and check into a hospital; almost any of them, take your pick—MCV, Grace, Johnston-Willis.''

Rupen did and Boghos did but none of it did any good; Rupen simply would never be able to sire children. The first person Rupen told was, of course, Marge. The second person he told was Vasil. It was the first time that he could remember having seen his father cry, and Rupen could have wished to be almost anywhere other than in that room on that day, watching the tears streaming between the fingers of the thick, scarred, hairy hands that covered Vasil's face, seeing the massive, corded shoulders heave and shake spasmodically, hearing the whipped-child sobs tearing up from out that horselike chest. In that terrible time, he came to the full realization of just how intensely he loved his father.

A few days later, Vasil sought out his eldest son and led him to the little tramway which bore them to the new executive office building in the annex section of the plant. Seated once more in his father's new office, which reeked of strong, acrid tobacco smoke and anise, just as had all his earlier offices, Rupen was apprised of Vasil's decision.

''My son, it was not really the Turks . . . ahem, the Nazis who did this maiming to you, no, it was me, Vasil Ademian. No, no.'' He held up a broad hand, palm outward. ''You will please to let me to finish before you speak, Rupen.

''It is true, what I just said. The life of your brother, Haigh, and this thing that has been done to you, they are the price that was given to repay all the good things that America gave to me and your mother and your brothers and sisters. Because you have given so much to America and to me, my debt, it is not right that I should not give to you something in return, something more than I would give Kogh and Bagrat and Mariya, who came from out of the war whole.

''My offer still stands . . . so far as the others are concerned, but them only, Rupen. I have this morning had transferred to your name a substantial amount of Ademien Enterprises stock, enough of it to pay you a minimum of six thousand dollars a year, so that no matter what you do, Margaret will not have to work and can stay at home and rear your children properly."

Rupen could not maintain silence at this. "*What* children, Papa? Oh, I get it now, you've changed your mind about the artificial insemination."

"I have *not*!" declared Vasil bluntly. "Still do I say that this artificial in . . . this nastiness that Dr. Panoshian told you about is, *must be*, just another new name for a kind of adultery; and adultery is a *sin*, Rupen! Go ask Der Mesrop, if you don't believe me.

"No, I have arranged for two Armenian orphans to be brought to you from Syria. The boy is two years of age, the girl is still an infant. A man needs a family, it is good for him, better for his wife. You will see, my son, you will see."

It was probably fitting that it was the dead Haigh's twin sister, Mariya, who first gave birth to a son and, of course, named the boy Haigh Vasil Panoshian. But Boghos politely declined the controlling share of Ademian Enterprises, which finally went to Kogh on the birth of his firstborn, Arsen David Ademian.

THE NINTH

The aged archbishop combed at his long white beard with his fingers. "Our last conversation was, I believe, abruptly ended by some crisis that called me away, Mr. Ademian, but I recall all that you had told me of yourself up to that point. Your father had arranged for your adoption of two orphans and had settled a sum of some six thousand dollars per annum on you. Was that a goodly income, then?"

Rupen sipped at the goblet of sweet honey mead, savoring the barely perceptible tang of herbs. He nodded. "Der Hal, in 1948, fifteen hundred dollars every quarter was a princely sum indeed. Not that I intended to take it any longer than was absolutely necessary. I was at last able to talk my father into holding off on his ready-made family for me and Marge until I got an education of some kind better than just a high-school diploma.

"We moved down to Richmond, Marge and me, and I enrolled at a college there, under the GI Bill. She got a job as a nurse at one of the hospitals, and she and I both joined reserve units—active units, so as to draw a day's pay for each weekly drill. It worked out fine for about a year, but I'm no scholar, not in any formal sense; when I found that I needed every available night to study, I started missing drills, and after a while they gave up on me and transferred me to the inactive reserves. I wasn't even aware of it at the time, I was working my tail off trying to keep up academically, with classes full of bright kids just out of high school. I was succeeding, too, Der Hal. In June of 1950, I finished my sophomore year with really good grades. But then, all hell broke loose on me and a whole hell of a lot of other poor folks around the world, and by the time it was done, none of us and none of our lives was ever the same again."

The Archbishop of York had been right about the desire of the king that Bass and his condotta go to Ireland, but the old man either had not known or had not bothered to tell Bass that the monarch had another task for him first, this one involving his flotilla.

Now, in company with Admiral Sir Paul Bigod and a sizable portion of his Royal Navy, the Norfolk Squadron was beating down toward Cape Peñas and the Port of Gijón, which lay a little alee of that promontory.

"This Grand Duke of León calls it a continuation of the Spanish portion of the Crusade of Abdul," King Arthur had said, "but, gentles, it truly is more in the matter of a family and personal vendetta—vengeance against us for the death in battle of the elder brother of the grand duke, the late and unlamented Principe Alberto, who so disastrously led and wasted the cavalry of Count Wenceslaus's army of Crusaders last year.

"Now the Crusade has cost Spain heavily, gentles, not only in treasure, but in noblemen, soldiers, horses, supplies, and equipment, not even to mention the three ships prized and generously presented to us by our valiant Lord Commander of the Royal Horse last year, or the several others taken by our Lord Admiral's ships whilst the Spanishers tried to run up the Thames to resupply London.

"Now true, gentles, the Spanishers are possessed of a large fleet of ships, well found and modern, but the most of these are located in and about the waters of New Spain, whence comes the bulk of Spanish wealth. And if there had been any thought of bringing any of those warships eastward, despite the constant pressure put upon portions of New Spain by the Irish, French, Norse, and Portugees, who encroach further and ever further on the lands which the Spanishers falsely claim to own entire, that thought was forgotten completely after recent events.

"It would seem that several privately financed groups—predominantly French, though not representing the French Crown, at least not openly—dispatched to the west a number of heavily armed, heavily manned large galleons to cruise for prizes of opportunity, mount raids on coastal and riverine settlements, and suchlike. We know this for fact, because our own Duke of Norfolk and his flotilla overhauled, fought, and prized one such of these French pirates, and what little her log and papers failed to tell, the freed prisoners from her hold did.

"In consequence, gentles, this grand duke has been hard-pressed to find not only men, horses, and the sinews of war, but bottoms to bear what he could scrape up to our shores. The only thing for which he does not seem to lack in this venture is money, it being a secret but ill kept that the Spanish Crown, the Caliph of Granada, the King of Morocco, and eke certain well-heeled, red-behatted clerics have been surreptitiously, albeit generously, befunding him."

Burly Reichsherzog Wolfgang—brother-in-law to King Arthur by way of the monarch's murdered wife, uncle of the present Holy Roman Emperor, Egon—snorted, "But tcheap at zee price, nonezeeless, *mein Brüder* King. Gained hass Engelandt in zee last few years, zee appellation *der Hackmesser* . . . no, meatgrinder of armies. No matter how supposedly holy zee cause, no monarch his own subjects to cast unto such a certain death desires, now, I think."

"Just so," agreed King Arthur, "and in such a pass, a lunatic of the grand duke's water is doubly valuable to those desirous of feeling to do something while actually doing nothing injurious to kingdom or subjects. Even so, gentles, the case of the grand duke's project is a mite precarious, for one may not sail the seas aboard golden onzas, nor yet place armored ducatos astride dirhams, nor expect pesos to learn pikedrill.

"He has, we have heard, emptied jails, freed slaves, impressed freemen of nearly every nonnoble rank and age, vainly offered unheard-of sums for mercenaries, and even offered amnesties to brigands and condemned felons in return for service. Now he does have a force of a sorry sort, most of which is presently encamped around and about the Basque coast port of Gijón.

"In order to transport his choice collection of gaol scrapings and gutter scum, the grand duke has bought and brought to Gijón the most complete assortment of antique ships recently assembled. It is said that some few of them sailed or were rowed into Gijón unaided, but many had to be towed. He has truly scoured the sides and the bottom of the barrel to get these ships, and should he lose even a few of them, he can never hope to replace them and so must cancel, perforce, his entire ill-starred scheme.

"We have a plan, gentles, to bring to pass such a cancellation."

When Bass got back to Norwich and placed their assignment to his own staff, he once more thanked the lucky star under which he had captured the then-Crusader Barón Melchoro years ago, for the Portuguese nobleman averred to know the Port of Gijón quite well and was able to elucidate certain things left unclear by the charts furnished Bass by agents of the king.

"It once was the Freeport of Gijón, friend Bass, a place in which any honest seaman—and many a one not so honest, as well—could sail in to take on water and victuals, sell loot or other cargoes, trade goods, and even careen ships or repair battle-wrought damages. Moreover, all these things might be accomplished in Gijón-port without worry of the unwelcome attentions of the Spanish Guarda Costa or payments of the heavy import-export levies exacted by Spanish customs officialdom. During a few years at sea in my wild and tempestuous youth, my shipmates and I made right frequent use of Gijón-port. Of course, that was a score of years agone, back when el Conde Don Hernán Padilla and his issue still held their patrimonial lands thereabouts."

"They lost their lands in war, then?" asked Bass.

"No, my friend." Melchoro shook his head. "Their relatives would never have permitted that; the family was quite old and was related to the royal houses of Castilla, León, Granada, and Navarre. Agents of the monarchs then reigning thoroughly investigated the sudden extinction of La Casa de Padilla and concluded that they all died along with not a few of their servants and retainers in the space of a bare fortnight of the effects of some rare and most deadly pest. For some year or more, the *condado* was administered for the King of León and Catalonia by a royal commissioner, then was added to the holdings of the *ducado grande*, which lands it abutted.

"Purely in the cause of sentiment, I had the ship that bore me and my party to Scotland enter the Port of Gijón, and I spied much activity, even then, last year, though of course I did not know or guess its purpose."

Walid Pasha, who still had somewhat less understandable English than did his captain of marines, spoke rapidly in Arabic, and Sir Ali translated. "The Pasha would know just what sort of harbor defenses this Gijón-port mounts, my lord Barón."

"At one time, years ago, under the rule of the *condes*," replied Melchoro, "they were *muito formidable*; they then had to be, when one is to consider the varieties of clientele entertained by the port, then. But I noted last year that the smaller *forteleza* is become little more than a crumbling and uncared-for ruin, bare of any ordnance, while the larger, the main *castillo*, though in fair repair, has been stripped of all save only the very largest pieces, mostly aged bombards not suitable for shipboard use, though very dangerous enough if one chances to sail within range of the stones they cast.

"I could not understand the decrepitude of the port defenses then, but I do now. If Gijón is become no longer a trade port but rather a naval basin, marshaling port, and embarkation facility, then there is scant need to defend it with land fortifications, not with the intelligence abroad in Europe that all of the larger ships of the navy of England either were destroyed fighting each other in the early days of the civil war that preceded the crusade or were scuttled to prevent capture by one or the other side years agone.

"Naturally, his grace, the *duque grande*, lacks the current information of the numbers of galleons, carracks, flutes, and other larger ships now owned by or at the use of his majesty, King Arthur. And he, I take it, means to have Gijón attacked and razed before any Crusade can from there be launched? Therefore, when, my good friend, your grace, do we to set sail?"

Of a dark and rainy night, some of Paul Bigod's smaller vessels sailed into a tiny rockbound bay, holding their positions in the chop with sea anchors while the longboats they had towed ferried a well-armed party of three hundred *galloglaiches* onto the beach at the foot of the eroded cliffs.

The retainer who had drawn the chancy mission of awakening his grace, the most illustrious Don Esteban de Alcabória, Duque Grande de León, did so by voice alone and from a fair distance, for the grand duke had been known to strike out at those who awakened him on many past occasions with pillow sword or hanger, often following up the slashes with a thrown dagger . . . and ofttimes he did not miss.

When the nobleman had shoved and kicked away his bed mate—a plump young girl—and struggled more or less erect in the deep feather bed, to sit glaring out of bleary eyes at the man in the doorway, the retainer said, "Your grace, a coaster reports that a Papal fleet—five or six big galleons, at the least, with numerous smaller sail in company—are bearing in from the west, clearly bound for Gijón-port."

"Capital!" Don Esteban crowed, showing very bad teeth in a very broad smile that split his scarred, pox-ravaged face above his red-blond chin beard. "At last, the Holy See has recognized my efforts to enforce the will of his holiness upon the heretical *ingléses*. With even four galleons, I can forget repairing and refitting that woebegone collection of hulks down in the harbor and get to the holy business of crusading on enemy soil.

"Fernando, notify my captains to get their troops ready to

go aboard ships upon my imminent command. My gentlemen and my guards are to assemble in the courtyard in parade dress, immediately; we will be on the quay to meet and to greet and to render all due honors to these, our brothers in the Faith.''

''Uhhh . . . your grace, the *castillo* should long since have seen the fleet and at least signaled as much, but they háve not.'' Fernando sounded worried, fearing the certain violent outburst should the Papal ships bypass Gijón-port as he secretly suspected that they would.

But Don Esteban shrugged even as he threw off the down coverlet and swung his hairy legs over the edge of the high bedstead. ''Fret not, my old, you know as well as do I how often Don Pedro strives to climb into a bottle of brandy of nights and how long it takes him to resume normal life on the mornings after. Have a galloper sent to the *castillo* with my orders to draw the stones from out the guns and replace them with thick wads. I want salutes fired as the Papal fleet enters my harbor. Every ship with mounted guns is to do the same, you hear? That is my order, Fernando.''

The entry channel to Gijón-port was well marked with buoys and wide enough for two galleons to sail abreast safely, so that was how they headed in—*Revenge* to starboard and Bigod's four-masted *Royal Arthur* to port, sails filled and drawing, embroidered, silken Papal ensigns and banners snapping in the stiff breeze, freshly painted and regilded upper works and hulls sparkling and gleaming brightly in the morning sun.

The leading pair were followed closely by another brace— the recently prized French four-master, now *Thunderer*, and another of Bigod's royal galleons, *Honor of Wales*.

They had lain off the harbor mouth as long as they thought they could without arousing wonder or suspicion while vainly awaiting the prearranged signals that would reassure them that the squat *castillo* had fallen to the *galloglaiches*, but now they simply sailed into Gijón-port, leaving the other galleon and the carracks to guard their rear and perhaps keep the *castillo* gunners so busy dodging balls and stone shards that the four galleons might emerge intact after doing their work in the harbor basin.

Inside the harbor, it was immediately clear that there would be but precious little space for maneuver of the huge galleons. The right side of the almost circular basin was all old stone quays, new wooden wharfs, and ships of every conceivable size, age, type, and degree of decrepitude tied up to those quays and wharves. The left side was a newly expanded careening yard and drydocking facility, and between right and left sides lay a section of some score or more of temporary floating wharves, these as crowded with ancient, battered, rotting ships as any of the other, more permanent structures. Moreover, those ships for which there was as yet no room at quay or wharf or drydock, as well as the few either not needing extensive work or with repairs and refitting completed, lay anchored wherever space existed for them, most of them lashed gunwale to gunwale in order to conserve to the utmost that precious space.

Anxiously scanning, searching the shores to either side with the one pair of binoculars and several long-glasses, Bass and the sailing masters could spot no earthworks or any emplaced guns of any description. Apparently, the only, the sole fortification that Gijón-port any longer owned was that afforded by the *castillo*. Not that that measure of menace to the invading ships should be underestimated or discounted, for it was real, within narrow limits, true, but real nonetheless, that menace.

Stripped as the *castillo* now lay of the smaller-caliber, more accurate long guns—probably by the present lord of Gijón, the grand duke, so that he could mount them on his heterogenous fleet—the fortification could return nothing more than arquebus fire so long as the galleons stayed within the harbor basin. It was when they essayed the exit-entrance channel again that the danger of those yawning metal maws grinning down from out their emplacements in those ancient stone walls would become most real and pressing.

Large as those black muzzles seemed at the distance, they

were assuredly mostly the bombards—archaic, large-bored, primitive guns antedating true cannon and heavy, clumsy to handle, with barrel walls and breeches too weak to throw iron balls. Even so, if they happened to be manned and commanded by gunners of sufficient competence to hold fire until the targets came to bear, they were quite capable of achieving horrific damage to a galleon with but a single hit of a stone ball that might weigh as much as a quarter ton and be a foot or more in diameter. And there were at least a score of these monstrosities emplaced on the three lowest levels so as to cover the channel to and from Gijón-port, which fact stood to compensate partially for their slow rate of reloaded fire.

"And you can bet your arse," thought Bass, instinctively giving his armor-clad arms a rub to lay the gooseflesh he felt arising on them, "that those *castillo* gunners know the ranges from shore to shore to the inch. All it will take them is one shot, no overs or unders, just one and we'll be either minus a galleon or, at best, nursing a crippled ship back toward England . . . and it could just be one of mine as easily as not."

The *castillo* had been described in some detail to Bass, Sir Paul Bigod, their sailing masters, captains, gentlemen, and staffs by Barón Melchoro, and in light of his descriptions—he had many times over the years been entertained by various of the *castillo*'s commanders—it had been decided that should the landing party of *galloglaiches* somehow fail to take the place by night, no open attack by day would be essayed, lest they get themselves bogged down before those strong walls in a lengthy siege. For they must always recall that the King of León and Catalonia had troops not too far distant from Gijón and that San Sebastián, a short sail to eastward, was that monarch's principal naval base on the Bay of Biscay, with not a few fine, modern, well-found warships at instant readiness should word come of English pirates raiding this coast. And one of King Arthur's closing injunctions had been to the effect that until matters within his kingdom were more stable, he wanted no formal troubles with other secular monarchs; a general crusade was one thing, a declaration of war for cause was another thing entirely. Should any of the ships involved in the attack on Gijón be sunk or run aground or prized, should any of the soldiers or crewmen or nobles be captured, they were completely on their own and King Arthur would disavow any slightest knowledge of them and their nefarious ventures into kingdoms with which the Crown was at peace. He was in no position to do or to say other.

As the grand duke, Don Esteban de Alcabória, meticulously inspected his personal guards, at the same time rapping out a stream of orders to three clerks concerning matters military, matters nautical, and matters domestic (that is, just what he wished served at the great feast for the newly arrived Papal allies), the town that rose up the terraces below the palace was aboil with its own preparations for the coming custom.

Innkeepers rolled out barrels and pipes of wines of varying qualities, slaughtered beasts and fowl, and heated up ovens for the baking of breadstuffs. Whores donned their finest and most revealing garments, and some of them even washed before dousing themselves with strong scents. As ordered by the agents of their grand duke, all households hung out brightly colored cloths from upper windows and balconies, while musicians and dancers gathered in the squares to await the official commencement of this unexpected fiesta.

In the basin, all of the ships were aswarm with life as flags and ensigns and banners and buntings of every description and a veritable rainbow of color were run up halyards and draped here and there, guns were polished, loaded with powder and waddings, run out ready for salutes of honor.

The faithful retainer, Fernando, pulled deferentially at his lord's sleeve. "Your grace, the galloper has not yet returned from the *castillo* and I feel . . . I fear that something is amiss with Don Pedro . . . ?"

The grand duke shrugged impatiently, foot already in stirrup, groom waiting to give him a leg up into the gilded saddle of his prancing, showy golden-chestnut barb. "Fernando, you maunder like some old crone! You know that the *castillo*

garrison is understrength; no doubt Don Pedro kept the galloper to fill out a guncrew. Or the man might have stopped at
any of a score of places for any of a hundred reasons. Get
you gone about your duties. If you have none, I'll give you
some, and that right speedily!''

But immediately the grand duke and his party had departed
the palace environs, the still-worried Fernando dispatched a
second, completely unauthorized galloper—this one a griz-
zled veteran—with orders to cautiously spy out the place at
close range before making to enter it.

Down on Calle Embarcadero, Don Esteban drew up his
guards and gentlemen in ranks and waited patiently, trying to
ignore heat and sweat and insects while the four huge, elegant,
high-masted galleons slowly maneuvered themselves about
the cramped harbor in search of anchorages that suited their
masters. At some length, they arranged themselves in an
extended crescent, with one four-masted galleon standing out
from the old wharf section and one out from the careening
yard and drydock, the bow of each of these pointing roughly
toward the harbor exit. The two three-masters lay off the long
section of new wharves.

''Hummph!'' remarked one of the grand duke's gentlemen,
Don José de Zuera. ''If I didn't know better, I'd say that
those ships were all afire, your grace. Look at all the smoke!
We couldn't see it when they sailed in, of course—the wind
would've dispersed it—but with them anchoring, it's there for
any to see. What does your grace suppose it portends?''

''Incense, most likely,'' opined Don Esteban languidly.
''They are no doubt saying a mass to celebrate the safe
conclusion of the voyage from Italy.''

''But aboard all four ships at the once, your grace?''
probed Don José. ''It seems not a little odd, to me.''

''As you live longer around clerics, Don José,'' the grand
duke stated, ''you will find them to be a queer, singular breed
given to habits and ways most odd to secular gentlemen.''

''Strange that they've not loosed off a single gun in salute
as yet, your grace.'' This statement came from another of the

gentlemen, Don Nasir de Guadix. "They should have been firing from the moment they entered the channel, one would think."

"It is as I but just told Don José," said the grand duke. "The clerical mind is right often difficult of the understanding of the laity, even of noble-born laity. Look you, though, Don Nasir, they are making ready to salute; see, the gunports are all being opened and the guns run out."

"I hope they loose all at once," said Don Nasir. "What a fine, brave show *that* would be, eh, your grace?"

A thought then struck Don Esteban, and he beckoned to a young knight, saying, "Don Sergio, my compliments to Don Pedro at the *castillo*, please. Tell him that I feel it is long past time for him to fire salutes in the honor of our visitors."

Reining about, the knight cantered off in the direction of the *castillo*, his silk-lined velvet cape floating out behind him.

Major Rupen Ademian, USA, returned to Virginia a few weeks before Christmas 1953. A bit surprised that Marge had not driven to meet him at Broad Street Station, he allowed a smiling redcap to wheel his footlocker and B-bag out to where a long line of taxis awaited, settled back, and gave the driver the address of the apartment to which Marge had moved some months after he had been recalled to active duty and sent to Korea to command a company of infantry in the war that was called a "police action."

The thirty-two-year-old officer now wore ribbons denoting some impressive decorations, far more impressive to the knowing eye than the mere Bronze Star and Purple Heart from World War II. The taxi driver, a WWII vet himself, whistled softly between his teeth, then asked diffidently, "Welcome home, Major. How was it, sir? As bad as the big one?"

Rupen sighed. "Yes, it was bad. There's no such thing as a good war, but this one was especially stupid, pointless. Nothing at all was accomplished to justify the expenditure of lives."

"But we won, didn't we, sir?" stated the driver.

"In a pig's asshole we did!" was Rupen's quick response. "It's not over, man, not by a long shot. Those talks in

Panmunjom are just a truce, a temporary cease-fire, not peace, so don't let anybody kid you.

"By the way, driver, don't take the gear out until I say so. My wife's a nurse. She may be on duty at the hospital, and I don't have a key to this new place yet, so unless she is home or I can find another way to get in, I may have to have you drive me out to my sister's place on River Road."

The driver crinkled up his forehead and, as they were just then stopped at a light, turned half around to look Rupen in the eyes. "Major, as one old soldier to another, you won't spend as much to go out on River Road if you switch over to a county cab. I'm on a meter, see, and a run out there would end up as high as ten, fifteen, even twenty dollars."

Wordlessly, Rupen reached into a side pants pocket and drew forth a silver money clip, then riffled through the thick fold of greenbacks. The driver smiled, his eyes lighting up. Nodding, he turned back to his driving.

"You're the boss, Major. You tell me where you wanta go and that's where we'll go, by damn."

Lucky at cards and dice, as ever, Rupen had left a high-stakes poker game at the main O-club at Fort Benning with something over twenty-three thousand dollars; the pudgy-looking bulge around his middle was, in reality, a moneybelt stuffed with hundred-dollar bills—around eight hundred and eighty dollars per month for a bit over two years of fear and pain and privation. And he still would have felt cheated at double the figure. World War II had been different to his way of thinking; he had gone willingly and had been basically responsible for all that had happened to him. But there was no truly adequate recompense for two years plus of involuntary servitude.

The inequity of it galled him, too. During World War II, damned nearly every swinging cock in the whole country had been in one of the armed services—those not too old, too young, or crippled in some way—and quite a number of women, too; it had been a truly democratic, citizen army. But those doing the bleeding and the dying in that slice of very hell called the Korean Police Action were mostly the unmarried and the unlucky minority, while the majority of American men stayed Stateside—fat and happy and healthy and unbidden, making money hand over fist and precious few of them giving a rat's ass whether Korea was won or lost.

The address was a three-story house of the late-Victorian era on Floyd Avenue not far from the college. In comparison to the similar houses on either side, it looked a little run-down, shabby even, and Rupen wondered why; for what with her income from nursing and the monthly monies from him and the army, Marge should be able to live quite comfortably, and in any emergency, she knew she could always draw from his accounts or ask Papa for help.

The bell inset in the peeling door had been painted over so many times that it was a sure bet it did not work. Rupen tried the knob, turned it easily, and stepped into the foyer to peer at the names scrawled in dim pencil on the battered metal covers of some half-dozen small mailboxes. There it was, "Ademian 2fl rear."

Major Rupen Ademian, mindful of the taxi waiting outside, started briskly up the shadowy stairs with their covering of cheap, threadbare carpet toward a horror that might have broken a lesser man.

The climb up the cliffs of rain-slick, crumbly rock from the shallow beach was costly to Sir Ali and his party of *galloglaiches*. Sir Sean Jernigan and a sergeant were resting briefly on a narrow ledge a bit over halfway up when that ledge abruptly tore loose from the cliff and plunged them both to their deaths on the rock-studded sand below. Moreover, debris knocked loose no less than three other climbers, and one of these unfortunates chanced to fall directly atop a man standing still on the sand at the base of the cliffs, breaking his neck. All that could be done was to strip the bodies of still-usable weapons, equipment, and supplies and leave their dead where they lay.

Once the survivors were atop the cliffs, they found themselves on a rocky plateau grown with tall, wiry grasses, gorse, and heather, almost flat and featureless as far as any could see through the cold, driving rain.

The sudden demise of Sir Sean left Sir Ali and his two English squires, along with a young Irishman who had been one of the Irish knight's squires, as the only noblemen in the party with but some fourteen vintenary sergeants and three centenary sergeants to assist them in handling almost three hundred men who, though near-matchless fighters in actual breast-to-breast combat, were almost undisciplined, undisciplinable, and savagely insubordinate on occasion, and too many of whom spoke a variety of English that even native-born Northumbrians and Lowlander Scots had difficulty in understanding.

There were, however, a few points in Sir Ali's favor with these rude *galloglaiches*. One was that they knew him to be not only the man of their chosen chief, his grace of Norfolk, but a close personal friend of that worthy, as well, so they were unlikely to murder the Arabian knight or to see him harmed by enemies. One other favorable factor was that most of the sergeants and quite a few of the other ranks spoke a type of French—an archaic Anglo-Norman-Erse dialect still spoken in certain parts of Ireland and some of the Western Isles of Scotland—much better and more understandably than they did English, and Sir Ali spoke French, too. The third favorable factor was that all of these Royal Tara *Gallowglasses* had seen Sir Ali ibn Hussein fight, and they respected him, to a man.

Sir Ali also owned a matchless sense of direction, so that by dawn he and the raiders, now all draped over in white surplices adorned with reddish crosses, were almost under the northwest wall of the Castillo de Gijón. Although this pile had been described to him by the Barón de São Gilberto, still the Arabian knight hissed softly through his teeth when he finally saw it close up.

The place was built on, built into, the very stony core of an extrusion of the cliff line. For long previous centuries, it and the fortifications that had preceded it had been the stronghold of those men and families that had held Gijón. In earlier parlance, the site of the present *castillo* had been the motte and the older section of the upper town to the southeast of it had been the bailey. Probably, mused Sir Ali, much of the stone for the walls had been quarried on the spot, which fact would account for the broad, deep dry moat that encompassed it on all sides visible from his vantage point. The sides and verges of that moat seemed too regular to be natural.

Before Sts. Rogiero di Pancetta and Bertramo al-Iswid had given Believers the secrets of gunpowder, this *castillo* would have been impregnable, could only have fallen to treachery from within or lengthy, hideously expensive siege. Even today, in modern times, with siege guns, a determined garrison could hold that *castillo* almost indefinitely if attacked from this side, the northwest, as the land hereabouts offered little or nothing with which to try to fill that moat and allow attackers to get at any breach their guns might batter through the walls.

The only alternative in this instance was guile, which method Sir Ali had planned to use all along. He would get himself and a few of his steadier men inside, then drop the bridge and open the gate to admit the bulk of his force.

Leaving all but a score of his force concealed in a fold of ground some quarter-mile distant from those ancient walls, Sir Ali proceeded slowly, striving to appear utterly exhausted. He and the rest of the smaller party had deliberately torn some of their clothing and left most of their armor and weapons behind, though their long, full surplices adequately concealed others. A few men had inflicted dagger cuts in their own flesh just deep enough to bring sufficient blood to make their "bandages" look convincing.

When ready, he and his score or so came up out of the declivity and slowly straggled on across the rough, brushy ground toward the *castillo*, taking pains to stay in plain view of sentries and to make noise. They apparently succeeded well in being noticed, for by the time they came to the verge of the moat opposite the raised bridge, a corporal's guard were gathered on section of wall above the entryway, covering the strangers with arquebuses and cocked crossbows.

"*Alto!*" rang the shout, "*¿Quien es?*"

Having fought both with and against knights from most portions of the Iberian Peninsula over the years, Sir Ali was become apt at aping not only their speech but their air of superiority, their overweening arrogance, and their utter contempt for any of nonnoble birth.

In the Castilian dialect, he shouted a snarled "What the hell *can* I do save halt, you ill-begotten rogue of a ninny? Men walk upon clear air only in fairy stories. Inform your commander that Don Ali ibn Hussain de Al-Muñecar y de Castro de Castilla and what is left of his retainers and crew have arrived at his gate, having survived shipwreck in that Satan-sent tempest last night, and drop the bridge, you peasant pigs, or it will go hard for you all. Hear me and heed my words, you nameless spawn of syphilitic goats!"

The gentleman had clearly identified himself, and his manner and speech left no doubt as to what he was, so the most of the guards set themselves to lowering the bridge that spanned the moat and raising the portcullis, while one of their number ran to Don Pedro's quarters to breathlessly gasp out the news to the old *borracho*. They all knew that it was invariably a most unhealthy practice to anger Castilian knights and noblemen, whose hot tempers and matchless cruelty were become a byword. God and all the saints be praised that Don Pedro was not a Spaniard of any description, but a Leonese Basque like most of the rest of them.

Don Pedro had slowly come back to consciousness out of a drunken stupor in the midst of a great stench to discover to his chagrin that once again he had fouled his breeches and his bed. He had but just laved off his legs and lower body from a pail of tepid water, donned clean small clothes and breeches, and was breaking his fast with brandy and barley bread when his long-suffering squire knocked and entered, trailed by one of the men of the *castillo* garrison, this latter sweating, panting, and wide-eyed.

Breathing as shallowly as possible in the reek of the small, close, windowless room, Escudero Juan Galliñanes said, "Don Pedro, Alberto here has just come from the north gate. A party of about twenty Crusaders led on foot by a knight are just on the other side of the moat and are demanding entry and aid. The knight says that their ship went down in the storm of last night, which most likely accounts for a few screams that the winds brought down to us from the north while you were . . . ahhh, sleeping.

"They are mostly wearing Crusader surplices, Alberto says. All are torn, battered, and dusty, and some have bloody bandages, as well. Everything about them would seem consistent with the knight's tale of shipwreck. Now true, Don Pedro, the storm was not all that severe, but then we know not in just what condition was the ship, either."

Galliñanes knew that this last would bring a smile to the face of his knight, even in his hungover condition, for Don Pedro's opinions concerning the numerous maritime disasters that the grand duke had had towed into Gijón-port over the last year or so were well known about the *castillo*.

"Alberto says that even as he left, the corporal and the rest were making to lower the bridge lest they further anger the knight, who seems to be either of Granada or Castilla . . . and you know how badly those types terrify humbler folk, even when they happen to be in a good mood. So the knight will no doubt present himself to you in all his superciliousness and in no long time, Don Pedro."

Losing his brief smile, the Basque knight nodded and arose, then swayed for a moment, supporting himself against the table edge, while muttering curses damning all Spanish knights to the deepest, foulest pits of perdition. "All right, Juan, hold the bastard off as long as you can. I must change clothes. Have you seen my sword lately?"

Even as the squire and knight spoke, however, the corporal and his gate guard all lay dead in their blood and the column of Sir Ali's main body of *galloglaiches* were trotting across the lowered drawbridge and streaming under the menacing points of the raised portcullis and through the angled tunnel beyond it to emerge within the *castillo* and fan out in small units seeking out the rest of the resident garrison.

They found them quickly enough, and most died without waking on the sacks of straw which were barrack beds.

Squire Juan's final scream was drowned in a gurgle of his own blood, Sir Ali's backhand stroke nearly decapitating him. *Don* Pedro had his head and both arms buried in the doeskin pourpoint into which he was wriggling when the slim dagger blade went in under his left scapula and pierced his heart. Of all the garrison of the *castillo*, only the two busy cooks were spared and encouraged to continue their accustomed tasks, though tightly guarded by the hungry raiders the while.

When a single rider appeared at the southern gate, Sir Ali had the man speedily admitted. Within the courtyard, however, the horseman took but a single look at the strange men, the scattered corpses, and frantically reined about, to earn a brace of crossbow quarrels in the back, whereupon Sir Ali cursed; he had wanted the obvious messenger alive, and now he could only hope that they would send another to seek after the first.

From the walls of the *castillo*, it could be seen that all the town was aboil as the four galleons sailed in from the sea. Up around a gleaming-white building that was probably the palace of this grand duke, men and horses were assembling, weapons and armor flashed in the morning sun, while bugles blared and drums rolled and horses neighed over a continuous, though distance-dim and incomprehensible babble of human voices.

Down on the ships at the quays and wharves and anchorages, men scurried hither and yon, running up ensigns, it seemed, while others worked on deck guns—which could mean expectation of imminent combat or not. Sir Ali had no way of ascertaining this and could do nothing about it in any case, since no one of the archaic battery left mounted in the *castillo* pointed toward the harbor or the town, and the monster bombards were just too heavy to move to locations from which they would. Nor was Sir Ali at all sure that he would like to be the one to order men to try to serve and fire the ill-kept relics. All he was willing to do was to spike them all, then roll the balls and casks of powder out the embrasures to tumble down the cliff and so into the sea.

The second rider was more astute. He realized that something was wrong while still on the bridge, reined about, and was quarreled out of the saddle. The panicked horse galloped off toward the town, while the brace of *galloglaiches* dragged the still-twitching body into the *castillo*.

The third horseman did not arrive until the four galleons were already dropping anchor within the Gijón harbor basin. Arriving astride a frisky red-bay palfrey, wearing silver-washed parade armor and a sword with a gilded, bejeweled hilt and a matching dagger, he was exactly the stripe of Spanish nobleman that Sir Ali had earlier aped so successfully.

Drawing rein in the *castillo* courtyard—which had by then been circumspectly cleared of cadavers—and barely deigning to glance at a rank of *galloglaiches* now garbed in garrison clothing and equipment and bearing a miscellany of polearms and crossbows and arquebuses, the Spaniard glared at Sir Ali and demanded to see Don Pedro de Haro at once, adding that he came directly from the grand duke himself.

"Don Pedro is not to be seen by anyone," replied Sir Ali, adding, "He lies gravely ill in his quarters."

"Donkey turds!" snapped Don Sergio coldly. "Either dead drunk or hungover, you mean. And just who in seven hells are you?"

Sir Ali extended his leg in a courtly bow, a mocking smile on his dark face. "Don Ali ibn Hussain de Al-Muñecar y de Castro de Castilla, at your service, Don . . . ?"

"Don Sergio Mario Felipe Umberto de la Torre de Fuentesauco y de Gata, Señor," the rider replied a little less stiffly, now that he knew himself to be addressing a fellow Castilian knight. "The fame of your *casa* is well-known, Señor, but why have I not seen you before? There are few enough of us genuine *hidalgos de Castilla* hereabouts, amongst this rabble of Catalonians and Basque sheep-fuckers."

Sir Ali thought it well to change the subject and did so: "What does his grace desire of me, Don Sergio?"

"Ah, yes, that matter. Don Ali, his grace dispatched me to tell you that it is past time for the salutes to be fired from the *castillo* in honor of our Roman visitors."

"Salutes from this *castillo* are now impossible, Don Sergio." Sir Ali grinned and added, "For the very good and sufficient reason that all those antique bombards have been thoroughly spiked and the powder and balls dumped down the cliff. Don Pedro is not really ill, nor yet drunk; he is dead, along with the rest of the garrison. The name I gave you was mostly an arrant lie told you with an abundance of joy in the telling. I actually hight Essayed Ali ibn Hussain, a knight of Arabia, in service as herald to his grace, Sir Sebastian Foster, Duke of Norfolk, Markgraf von Velegrad, Earl of Rutland, Baron of Strathtyne, and Lord Commander of the Royal Horse of his majesty, Arthur III Tudor, King of England and Wales. You, Don Sergio, unless you are of the opinion that you can digest a half-dozen crossbow quarrels so early in the day, are my prisoner; give me your parole and you can keep your sword."

"But . . . but . . . but . . . ." The red-faced, utterly flabbergasted Don Sergio could not seem to find words or get them out.

"We are come here," Sir Ali further enlightened him, "to burn your master's pitiful little armada where it floats and thus end his Crusade before it starts."

"But the Kingdom of England and Wales is at peace with the Kingdom of Catalonia and León!" Don Sergio finally found words.

"Just so," agreed Sir Ali mildly. "And this is a purely private action, mounted by my master against yours, nothing more."

Just then, from the harbor below, came the answer to Don Nasir's stated wish. All four galleons thundered forth four broadsides, sending red-hot shot from every gun that would bear into ships, docks, wharves, quays, warehouses, stacks of supplies, and drydock facilities. The crews reloaded fast and did it all again, continuing the horrific bombardment at point-blank range until all the waterfront was become one blazing and lifeless inferno along all three sides of the harbor basin of Gijón-port.

CHAPTER
THE TENTH

Not bothering to summon a servant, the archbishop refilled Rupen's drinking vessel with his own hand, then said gently, "Mr. Ademian, if this recountal is become unpleasant to you, there is no reason to continue it, not today. I simply was trying to learn of your life and experiences so that I might judge how best we can fit you into this world and society. I began with you because you seem to be far more responsible and adaptable than those other men and women who were projected here with you."

"I'm sorry, Der Hal," answered Rupen, wiping at damp eyes with the hairy back of a hand that was become a little tremulous. "It was more than twenty years ago, but still it hurts. Maybe if I'd talked of it more over the years. . . ? But I didn't, couldn't, it was just too painful to me."

"My God, but I wish you'd let *us* know when you were coming into Richmond," said Boghos Panoshian, with evident feeling. "Mariya and I would sure have met your train, brought you out here, and told you what you had to know, what you would have learned sooner or later, but given you the facts a lot easier than you got them today. What an utterly rotten, traumatic thing to come home from a war to!"

"It's hard to believe, even with all I saw, all I've been told. *Why,* Boghos, why? Marge is . . . was . . . a bright, smart young woman, a former naval officer with a decent profession which, while it was not as lucrative as some others,

174

certainly offered a steady income and was highly respected by everyone. For her to have become in only two years a dope fiend, a whore, and a les . . . lesbian just seems completely unreal, some dark fantasy from the sick mind of a lunatic. How could it have happened? How could she have fallen so low so fast, Boghos?"

But Mariya answered him first. "Rupen, we—Boghos and I—hired an investigator about a year ago, shortly after Marge's first arrest for prostitution. . . ."

Listening to his sister, Rupen shuddered, the words— "arrest," "prostitution"—smashing into him like the bone-jarring blows of heavy cudgels. Marge, his Marge, sweet, pretty, blond Marge. His wife, the woman around whom he had woven all his lonely dreams for the nearly two years in Korea. How? Why? Had it been in some way *his* fault? What could he have done so far away?

". . . lesbian thing apparently came first, when this Evelyn Mangold moved in to share your apartment with Marge. The Mangold creature had a record of abusing narcotics when she could get at them, and after she and Marge had become lovers—"

"But, dammit, Mariya," burst out Rupen in some heat, "Marge was never . . . *that* way! I was married to her, you know, lived with her for four damned years—you think I wouldn't have known a thing like that?"

"Probably not, Rupen," said Boghos dryly. "I discussed the whole matter, all that our investigator turned up, with one of my associates, Dr. Saul Fishbein, a neuropsychiatrist down at MCV Hospital. He says that not only can bisexuals be very cagey, cover their dual natures very cleverly and well, but that quite a few of them never realize that they are what they are until a situation arises which brings their aberrations to the surface. That might well have been the case with Marge, this Mangold woman being merely the catalyst."

"And all because they took me away into the goddamned army to fight a war that we weren't allowed to win, in the end," said Rupen bitterly. "Chalk up another one for the fucking politicians and the Commie-loving fellow travelers in the State Department!''

Mariya shifted in her chair and clasped her hands tightly, then said, "It may not have been just that way, Rupen. There . . . there were some . . . ahhh, rumors, years ago, during the war, on shipboard. The way I first wound up with Marge as a roommate was because her roommate moved out the day before I was logged in. Marge always said that it was a case of the other girl's disliking Armenians, and that particular nurse was very intolerant of any person who was not of pure-English descent, preferably born and bred in Boston, Massachusetts, which made her stories about Marge sound like just some more of her racism.

"Rupen, as you know, women hug and kiss each other normally, but Marge seemed always to be touching me, brushing against me, and once, when we had both come in very drunk from a dance in Norfolk, it . . . it went a bit farther than that. She was still in my bed when I woke up the next morning, too, though she always swore she had no memory of anything from shortly before we left that dance. But now, for over a year, now, I've wondered. . . .''

"The investigator's report states, Rupen, that after Marge and this Evelyn Mangold became lovers, Marge began to acquire drugs for her, then started using them herself, it appears. I even wrote her prescriptions before I started to become suspicious. It seems that when she finally had exhausted all legal means of laying her hands on drugs, she commenced to steal them from the hospital at which she then worked, and eventually she got caught at it. They declined to report it to the authorities or to prosecute, but they did fire her and quietly blackball her at every other facility in the area.

"She tried working private duty, nursing in patients' homes, for a while. It was during that period that she went through all of your savings buying drugs illegally. When that money was gone, she borrowed from your father, from me, from Mariya, from damned near everybody she knew and quite a few she didn't. She sold both your cars and everything else of any value, then she and this woman moved out of the apartment and into that place on Floyd Avenue. With her mind occupied entirely on ways to get more drugs, she was not able to do a very good job of nursing, of course; a number of patients let her go after thefts of small valuables and sums of money. Then she was apprehended trying to get a forged prescription filled and the State Board of Nursing lifted her license. It was shortly after that that she began to sell herself.''

"And this, this Mangold woman," demanded Rupen, "she was whoring, too?"

"No." Boghos shook his head. "She apparently does no work of any kind. There's not even a record of her having a Social Security card. She's had two husbands that we know of. One was killed in the Pacific during the war. The other is in prison up north, serving a ninety-nine-year sentence for a murder he swore his wife actually committed, very grisly one, too, or so the investigator said.

"No, Rupen, her *modus operandi* seems to be to move in with a woman—there were at least three others before Marge— seduce her sexually, get her addicted to drug use, then live off her as long as she can keep her."

"Well, for the love of God, Boghos," burst out Rupen, "if you and Mariya knew all this a year ago, why didn't you *do* something about it? Why didn't you write and tell *me* about it, man? With a letter like that to show, I could probably have gotten the Red Cross on it, maybe gotten compassionate leave to come back here, even."

Mariya sighed, reached over, and laid her hand on Rupen's. "Don't you think we tried, my brother, my poor brother? But Marge had convinced herself that she was deeply, passionately in love with Evelyn Mangold, that she couldn't live without her. Boghos pulled every medical and political string he could get hold of to try to get her nursing license restored so that she might give up her new profession, but it developed that the board had discovered more and more heinous offenses than the forged prescription that she had perpetrated, and they wouldn't budge.

"Finally, all else failing, Boghos's attorney was instructed to offer the Mangold woman money on the condition that she leave the state permanently. She took the money, some thousands of dollars in cash, and even let herself be seen boarding a Greyhound bus . . . but she only stayed on it until she got out into Henrico County, then she took a local bus back into town.

"Boghos and I pondered writing to you, among other measures, but we at last agreed that Marge was just too far gone in drugs, perversion, and serious mental disorder for your presence here to do her or you any good. Anyway, there was continual talk of an impending cease-fire in the news and we both figured that you'd be back soon enough; nobody here had any idea that they'd drag that cease-fire business out for as long as they did.

"Boghos thought of getting Marge committed—to a private place, not Eastern State, Rupen—and he and his attorney did get her into Tucker's . . . for a little less than three weeks, then the Mangold woman went in there, told everyone that she was Marge's sister, and signed her out to go downtown shopping, and that was the last that anyone at Tucker's saw of either of them, of course."

Rupen cradled his face in his big, powerful hands, elbows on knees, his voice muffled, cracking slightly. "I'm sorry, Mariya, Brother Boghos, I should've known you both would do the best you could. Well, poor little Marge is at peace now, thank God. Now I have to see to it that that conniving harpy pays full measure for the life she corrupted, ruined, degraded, and finally took away."

The sack of Gijón-port, such of it as was not either blazing or heaps of smoldering ashes, was necessarily brief, for both Bass and Sir Paul Bigod were frantically anxious to be out of the deathtrap harbor, away from the rockbound coast and well out to sea before a *guarda costa* came sniffing along or some troops of better quality than the grand duke's "crusaders" marched over the surrounding hills, it being a certainty that numerous riders had gone out in every landward direction during the initial bombardment.

Had it been entirely up to him, Bass would have allowed no sack of any duration or description, but Sir Ali, Sir Liam, Sir Calum, and even Nugai pointed out that all of the soldiers, sailors, and noblemen expected one, eagerly anticipated an opportunity to get themselves a little loot and engage in a little casual rapine, and that to deny them, especially the half-savage *galloglaiches*, could easily breed trouble. Bass had had no option; he had acceded.

Sir Paul Bigod, like most people at most times in this world, had completely misunderstood the motives of the Duke of Norfolk, attributing it not to other world squeamishness and hatred of bloodshed, but to a high degree of caution regarding the welfare of his ships. "Look you, your grace, four galleons, your carracks, and one flute are all that are in the harbor anyway, and these be ready to cut cables and beat out to sea with a minimum of work, should that prove needful. Any foeman that would make to block that channel would firstly have to deal with the galleon and the other, larger ships standing out just off it. Furthermore, all my sloops and smaller vessels—flying various ensigns, of course—are patrolling west and east from this place all a-watch for incipient trouble from the Spanishers, never you fear."

Bass did not fear; he would, indeed, have welcomed any diversion that would have brought the raiders back aboard the ships and then caused the ships to put out to sea. After a few quick, long-distance glimpses of what was going on in the steep streets, terraces, and plazas of the port town by broad daylight, he put away the binoculars and tried to find other things to occupy his hands and mind, but nothing seemed to work.

Locked in his flagship cabin, lest his squires or servants see what he was about and horrifiedly relieve this high nobleman of the inappropriate manual labor of burnishing a breastplate, he tried to think out the matter of the sack and his feelings on the subject.

"In my world, most of the killing and maiming in formal warfare had been placed on a long-distance, completely impersonal level. Since it was so damned seldom that flyers or artillerymen ever got a close look at the people they were killing and wounding, the making of war had become a job very much like any peacetime, civilian activity for them—hard work, sometimes, and not always done under ideal conditions, in ideal surroundings, but virtually bloodless.

"Even the men in infantry or armored units often did their work at long range, directing their fire—rifle, machine gun, rocket, mortar, recoilless rifle, and so on—toward places where they had been told there were groupings of enemies, not toward men they could actually see.

"But warfare here, in this world, is bloody and savage and very, very personal and done at such close range that a slain man's lifeblood often splashes onto the man who kills him. Now in the heat of battle, when it's your life or his and your life is clearly on the line, natural instincts take over, invariably, and you do what you have to do, *anything* that you have to do to make damned sure that he dies for his beliefs instead of you for yours. And you do what you do then instinctively, without regrets.

"You impale living, struggling men on lances and spears, hack and slash and cut and stab with the sword, gape open skulls with the ax, crush them with mace or morning-star, blow them apart with horsepistol or arquebus, and then on to your next opponent, heedless of the wounded and dying man your horse kills or further injures under his steel-shod hooves.

"And there's that particular barbarity, too, here. In my world, most military units of most of the more civilized countries looked with at the very least official disfavor upon the mistreatment of wounded foemen, and their medical services quite often gave those wounded care in no way inferior to that that they gave their own wounded. But not here, not in this world.

"Of course, as Krystal long ago pointed out, what passes for medical care here is so basically useless if not actually harmful that it's often a real mercy to put down wounded men just as you put down badly injured horses—far better a bullet or a quick dagger thrust than a lingering, hideous death of sepsis or gangrene. Even so, that was one current custom that came damned devilish hard to me when first I came here . . . still does, for that matter. But I do it when I have to.''

The Duke of Norfolk would have certainly been even more perturbed, just then, had he been aware that his obvious reluctance to grant the mercy stroke or shot to wounded foemen on many occasions had been drastically misread. He was widely considered to be a hard, cold man, utterly callous and unfeeling when it came to enemies, even suffering, wounded enemies. His *galloglaiches* loved him for these supposed qualities. Other men deeply respected him and strove to remain on friendly terms with him, for all that they found so patently cruel a man difficult to truly like.

Bass hung the breastplate back on the rack and took down a spauldron that seemed a little dull to his eye.

"It's not really the killing that tears me up, though. I'm at least that much of a realist. I know that if I should pull my stroke or consciously miss my shot, the man I spare will possibly kill me or one of my friends or retainers. No, it's the thinking about it all later, when those dead men whose names you never knew, those men with the twisted, bloodless faces come into your mind and dreams in the dark of night, sometimes with weeping women and starving children, and you wake up sweating and gasping or screaming.

"But even that worst part has gotten better—I hope, I *pray*—with time; I don't get that kind of nightmare nearly so often now as I did two, three years ago. I think those long talks with Hal helped immensely. "Our Archbishop of York is a damned good shrink in addition to his many other talents.

"No, the facing of armed men in battle is one thing. I've had to learn to live with it and more or less accept it. It's the same with killing wounded, too; when a man arms and goes into a battle, here and now, he has to expect to lose his life in one way or another. I've even—God forgive me—learned to live after a fashion with using the misericorde, though my personal preference for the act is a pistol.

"But what's going on ashore, there, is another thing entirely. The turning loose of armed men, especially of those heartless *galloglaiches*, on a trapped, terrified, and mostly unarmed

civilian populace constitutes to me an unforgivable crime that
I know will haunt me—waking and sleeping . . . if I ever can
sleep again, after this, that is—for the rest of my life. I can
think of nothing that would in any way justify what I just
have countenanced doing to those poor Spanish civilians of
Gijón-port, and I'm more a criminal than those sailors, soldiers,
and *galloglaiches*, for I *know* that it's wrong . . . yet I am
condoning it all. I doubt that even Hal has the ability to ease
my mind of this enormity.''

Duce Timoteo di Bolgia thanked his private gods that this
contract did *not* call for him and his command to make a
fighting landing in Ireland, for if it had, they all would have
been slaughtered on the beach like so many helpless sheep.
Mercenary companies almost invariably marched from one
contract to the next, and consequently precious few of his
officers, sergeants, or other ranks had ever been aboard anything more prepossessing than a mule-drawn canal barge or
the Neapolitan craft in which they had been towed over to
Sicily from the Italian mainland.

As a mercantile-minded Cardinal D'Este might have put it,
the goods failed to travel well. Most of Timoteo's company
became ill shortly after leaving Palermo harbor, though a
largish proportion had recovered, gained their "sea legs" as
it were, by the time the coast of the Caliphate of Granada hove
into view on the western horizon. But as the small fleet
passed through the Gates of Hercules and breasted the heavier,
less predictable seas beyond, *il mal di mare* took its toll once
more, even harder this time, striking down not only the
recently recovered victims, but claiming others who had seemed
immune on the relatively placid waters of the inland sea they
had just traversed.

There was a spate of recoveries whilst the fleet sat in the
calm harbor of Anfa Antiqua, taking on fresh food and water
and waiting for the small contingent of Afriquan mercenaries
to get themselves, their gear, and their animals aboard the
ships that would be joining the fleet. As Timoteo wisely let
his officers and men go ashore for a while, recovery was

complete by the time the fleet was ready to set sail northwest-
ward for Ireland.

However, as luck would have it, the first of what was to
prove a seemingly endless succession of fierce Atlantic Ocean
storms struck them only two days out of Anfa Antiqua, and
before even this first tempest had run its course, Timoteo had
five shiploads of men whose highest present aspiration was to
immediately die. And before it was done, before the battered
fleet finally reached its Irish destination, some of those men
were dead. Most of them had perished of the effects of utter
dehydration—being unable to hold even water on their
stomachs—some sufferers crept up from the foul 'tween-
decks to be swept overboard by the towering, crashing seas
that swept the vessels end to end and necessitated constant,
twenty-four-hour use of the pumps by the overworked seamen
and the few mercenaries capable of it. Some of them found a
dagger thrust perferable to ceaseless, unbearable suffering.

So the proud, justly famous company that had departed
Palermo landed on the river quay in Ireland as a sorry-
looking, draggle-tailed lot indeed. Many of the wan, cadaverous-
looking men were too weak even to crawl up the ladders from
the holds and had to be hoisted up and over onto the quay,
some dozen or so at the time, in cargo nets. Those who
essayed to walk stumbled and swayed on weak and wobbly
legs, looking like nothing so much as helpless, hapless inebri-
ates as they sprawled on the slimy stones of the quay. Timoteo,
who had for long prided himself on having the best, the
hardest-fighting, the most victorious, and the finest-appearing
company in the length and breadth of Italy, was appalled at
the sight of the filthy, unkempt, emaciated men in their
unwholesome rags and tatters, his sole consolation being that
the Afriquan mercenaries looked, if anything, far worse.

The horses, on the other hand, had survived the long
voyage in fine flesh. Only a single charger had been lost of
all the horses belonging to the officers of Timoteo's company—
that of his brother, Roberto—along with a couple of coursers
and one saddle mule. No one of the Afriquan contingent's

mounts had died, but some few were in poor flesh and would require nursing ashore before they could be ridden.

Timoteo had not allowed himself to become ill during the whole of the voyage. Lacking his steely self-control, Roberto di Bolgia and Sir Ugo both had succumbed during the spate of fearsome storms, but both were again in fine fettle by the time that the fleet had docked in Ireland. Therefore, it was these three, plus *le chevalier,* who donned their finest attire, mounted led horses, and accompanied the guard of honor sent down to fetch them by King Tàmhas only some hour after the first ship had sailed up the river to the quay and begun to discharge passengers and their gear.

King Tàmhas proved to be a tall, slender man with a full head of hair—once raven's-wing black, but now thickly interspersed by strands of white—a double-spade chin beard, and a thin, drooping mustache, their blackness in distinct contrast to his wan, sallow face and his pale, watery-blue eyes. He had no Italian, of course, and Timoteo owned only a smattering of the guttural, difficult Irish tongue, but it soon developed that this kinglet did speak an archaic dialect of Norman French quite fluently, which fact made for ease of conversation between the monarch and his new-come captain-general.

Of conservative tastes, as are many professional soldiers, il Duce di Bolgia silently deplored this pocket king's taste in clothing. That it was long out of date was something to be more or less expected in this cultural backwater so far from the true center of the civilized world, but that was not the worst of it. The outfit was so garish as to set edge to edge the teeth of any modern man with a sense of the proprieties and an innate eye for the balancing of colors.

The old-fashioned slashed doublet was of umber lined with a glaring, flame-red silk, while the separate slashed sleeves were lined with green silk, but two different shades of the color, one shade to each arm. The slashed breeches were of gold brocade all interwoven with silver threads and trimmed with seed pearls, the lining being of a saffron hue . . . but not the same saffron hue as either of his stockings. The ankle-high shoes were of an elaborately tooled purplish-crimson leather, with gilded heel and sole edges, which also were set all around with semiprecious gemstones. Among the ten fingers of his monarch's hands could be counted sixteen jewel-set rings. A ruby-set earring and a tourmaline stud decorated his right ear; he was missing his left ear. More jewels and large pearls depended from links of the solid-gold chain that rested on his shoulders, held in that unnatural drape by bronze brooches of ancient designs, all inlaid with turquoise and mother-of-pearl.

"The warrior lucky enough to capture this bugger," thought Timoteo, "would not need to wait for a ransom, by God. That chain alone would buy a rich county, and the worth of those rings would keep a man in luxury for life and his heirs thereafter. Only a fabulous fighter or a cocksure fool would display so much wealth about his person."

After a few minutes of conversation, Timoteo decided he distrusted this Irish kinglet and could easily dislike him as well. For one thing, Tàmhas seemed ever unwilling to give a man a look into his eyes, keeping them carefully averted at all times whilst he spoke on any subject at all, a habit which in di Bolgia's wide experience indicated a man with something he hid, did not tell, or at least failed to tell in full.

The advisers present were an unprepossessing lot, to be very charitable in the phrasing—one tall and lanky, one shifty-eyed like the king with a head too small for his corpulent body and pudgy limbs, one short and ferret-faced and endlessly rubbing his hands together. All three, when introduced, bore the same patronymic as the royal personage and so were surely related to him, dependent on him, and therefore likely to tell him always what they knew he wanted to hear rather than the truth, which made for damned poor advisers.

Moreover, despite their protestations, Timoteo was dead certain that at least one of his advisers had a command of Italian, for when he was translating a remark to his brother—who was experiencing some difficulty with the archaic *francese criollo*, peppered as it seemed to be with Germanic and Gaelic loan words—and chanced to refer to the fat adviser as *il maialesco,* that worthy reddened and glared balefully at them both. Immediately, Timoteo switched his translations and asides to the Umbrian peasant dialect. Even born Romans and Neapolitans had trouble understanding that one.

"That king is no *irlandais,*" remarked *le chevalier* to Timoteo, Roberto, and Ugo, as they all rode back to the ships. "He's a Norman. I've an uncle who is his spit and image. So far as is known, my *grandpère* never visited *Irlande* . . . so, mayhap his majesty's *grandmère* . . ."

Le chevalier perforce broke off as his mount, stung by a forceful dig in the flank by the dull point of the metal chape of Timoteo's swordsheath, reared and essayed to bolt. When he had once more brought the beast under control, the captain drew up close beside the French knight and spoke rapidly, in a low voice and in modern French. "*Pour l'amour de Dieu,* Marc, watch your tongue, if you'd keep it and your head! This is not France, nor yet one of the Italian states, wherein sophisticated humor is enjoyed. Had I allowed you to finish that which you had started and had one of those with us taken it back to this kinglet or, worse, one of those so-called advisers, you could have put us all into a pretty pickle. A few outsized boulders from the bombards up there"—he gestured with a gloved hand at the crenellated walls of the glowering stone riverside fortress—"would put even your galleon on the bottom of this muddy river. Then I'd likely be stuck in this cold, damp, foggy backwater for the rest of my natural life . . . and I'm homesick for Italy already, Marc; hell, even those bare, brown Sicilian hills would look good to me, just now! And our just-concluded audience with this monarch has bred in me a vague but gnawing presentiment that this will be an ill-starred contract."

At the indictment hearing, no single tenant of the Floyd Avenue house would admit to having heard enough of the proceedings on the day that Evelyn Mangold had beaten Marge Ademian to death to be able to identify the voices of the persons then within the apartment, even as to whether they both were female. In the end, all that the well-meaning and thoroughly frustrated young Commonwealth Attorney was able to do was to get the woman indicted and convicted of resisting her arrest and assaulting two police officers while in performance of their duties. She was sentenced to eight months in the city jail, but given credit against this sentence for the nearly four months she had spent in jail awaiting trial.

His innate sense of fairness, of rightness, deeply offended by this turn of events, this particular Commonwealth Attorney quickly became a willing—eagerly willing—accomplice of Rupen, Boghos, Mariya, Kogh, Bagrat, old Vasil, Boghos's attorney, a city police sergeant of Armenian antecedents, a local private investigator and his staff, and a sometime public defender from New York State (half Armenian, by chance happening) who still was galled by his belief in the innocence of a convicted client.

Large inputs of cash by Kogh, Vasil, and Boghos lubricated the gears of the device that mutual effort and a desire for justice had assembled. And Evelyn Mangold herself made it even easier, her first vicious actions upon her release from durance vile playing directly into the hands of the family she had wronged.

It was Rupen who received the first batch of obscene photographic prints, and it was all that his family could do to prevent him from throwing over the meticulously laid plans and going after the evil woman with tooth, nail, and hard, scarred knuckles.

Richmond attorney Greg Zaroukian—he who had once before tried to bribe Evelyn Mangold into leaving the state—telephoned the number included with the photos and set an appointment to meet with the murderous woman in his downtown office.

"Them pitchers got to the damn furrin bastid, din't they, huh?" crowed the tall, big-boned, flat-chested woman, a dirty grin on her broad face. "I got lots an' lots more of 'em, too, lawyer. An' I got some spools of tape, too, with her tellin' me how I'm a better lover than any goddamned *man* she ever had afore. I wants ten grand fer the lot, lawyer. But none thishere shit 'about me leavin' town, this time; I likes it here, I a'ready got me a nice lil gal lined up fer to move in with at a apartment up on Monument Avenue. Met 'er the same damn day I got outen thet fuckin' jail, I did, too!''

Greg Zaroukian knew all about that part of it, although he was careful to keep a blank face. The investigator had found the "lil gal" for them—an attractive actress, somewhat older than she appeared, with four years as a WAAF and a thorough grounding in combat judo behind her, plus a few more years in undercover aspects of law enforcement. Her services had not come cheaply, but the Ademians had been more than happy to foot the bill.

The purpose for the hired woman had been dual. For one thing, they had not wanted Evelyn Mangold to even consider leaving the Richmond area; for the other, the furtherance of their plans for her called for her to have immediate access to enough money to allow her continuance of her interrupted addiction to injected narcotics. Considering her history, Boghos had estimated that a mere two weeks would guarantee her being again firmly hooked.

"You know, you slimy bitch," remarked Greg Zaroukian, "I should immediately turn you over to the police. Extortion is frowned upon in this area, and you just might wind up on the Women's State Farm, a couple of hours' drive west of here. You wouldn't like it there, I think; no sitting around, like in the city jail. There they'd put you to work—hard, manual work, in the fields—and beat the crap out of you three times a day."

He placed a hand on the receiver of his telephone and regarded the ugly woman seated across from him as he might have some vile creature born of filth under an overturned rock. She sat stiffly, tensely, obviously ready to bolt from the chair in an instant, and he noted with some satisfaction the glitter of true fear in her muddy-brown eyes.

He slowly, grudgingly, removed his hand from the receiver. "But, alas, I have specific orders from my clients in your regard, you perverted sow. I can't get that large a sum for you at once, you understand. However, I should have it all in about a week. But I must insist, for that much money, that I receive all of the prints and the negatives as well, and also all of the copies of these tapes you just mentioned. Should you hold out on us and try this again, we will have no choice but to have you killed . . . slowly, painfully. Do you understand me, bitch?''

Evelyn Mangold was quite pleased in regard to her progress, so far. True, she had not yet managed to get into the new girl's pants, but that would come, and the girl was already regularly, obtaining prescription drugs for Evelyn's "affliction." The Monument Avenue apartment was large-roomed, airy, and exceedingly comfortable after that bare cell in the city jail and the Floyd Avenue dump that had preceded it.

She was convinced that Millicent Mavore had at some time been in bad trouble with the law, no matter how often and vociferously the girl denied it. She knew too much, understood too much for it to be otherwise, but Evelyn was assured that she'd get everything out of her latest victim, eventually. Silly women—and men, too, for that matter—would stupidly tell anything and everything to a lover, holding nothing back, even when it was clearly to their best interests to do so.

The accused murderess was overjoyed when Millicent expressed a desire to drive her out to the midnight meeting scheduled by the Ademians' attorney near the Duck Lake in Byrd Park. This involvement of the girl in extortion would be another unexpected club to hold over her head when the time came for threats.

Millicent's Ford Victoria had been parked in the agreed-upon spot for barely five minutes, lights out but engine purring softly, when another vehicle pulled in behind and cut its own lights. Evelyn's hand was already on the door handle when a second vehicle came up from behind and pulled in to park in front of the Ford.

"Sumpthin's fishy 'about thishere!" she snapped. "Git us out'n here, Milly!"

It looked to Evelyn as if Millicent tried, but ineptly. She first ground the gears, then let up on the clutch at an inopportune moment and the engine stalled. When she tried to restart it, she flooded it. Seeing men emerging from the two cars, knowing that she lacked the wind to outrun them, Evelyn used her right elbow to depress the door lock. Then she began searching through her commodious handbag for the big switch-blade and her brass knuckles, the blackjack, too, though she wasn't sure she'd remembered to bring it along on this occasion.

But before she could lay hands to any of her arsenal, there was a clicking and a big, burly man had opened the locked door with a key, grasped her upper arm in a bone-crushing grip, and jerked her out of the car as if her big body had been that of a rag doll. In the dim glow of the Ford's courtesy lights, Evelyn could see the squat, powerful man's face . . . and she felt real fear. She could sense without conscious thought that this man despised her and that, furthermore, he was every bit as calculatedly cruel as was she herself.

"Give me some trouble," he softly rumbled from his barrel chest. "Please, give me some trouble. They done told me I can't hurt you none, 'less you give me some trouble."

Evelyn found herself unable to take her gaze off his face—a face scarred by the effects of knuckles and sharp knives—his thin lips that barely moved as he spoke, his black eyes that were as flat and expressionless as those of some deadly serpent. She only half felt her bladder empty, soaking the crotch of her slacks and then beginning to spread the hot moisture down her thighs. From close behind, she heard a voice that sounded a lot like Millie's, but harder, far more mature.

"Better get that bag away from her, one of you. I took the knucks and a six-inch switchblade out of it before we left, but could be she has other little playthings hidden in it that I didn't find. She's as bad as they come, worse than most I've ever seen. Don't trust her an inch, I'm warning you."

Evelyn could see lights moving along the drive far, far over on the other side of the lake. Opening her mouth, she screeched, "*Help! Help! Po-leece! Helaarrgghh! Stop It!* Aanngghh, you *killin'* me!"

But the pain not only continued, it intensified, and at some point in her unbearable agony, consciousness left her and she slid gratefully into the painless nothingness of darkness.

——————— CHAPTER
THE ELEVENTH

Thanks principally to Barón Melchoro, bales of documents and correspondence had been captured at the palace of the grand duke, along with selected works of art and a goodly quantity of gold. All of the voyage back to England, the *barón*, Don Diego, and Sir Ali had spent the best part of their time in sorting the paperwork, reading and rendering or at least dictating renderings of translations or synopses.

Information gleaned from this work was most significant, of as much value as the minted gold, or more. They learned for one thing that London had now been as good as written off by the Holy See. For another, they learned that High King Brian VIII's archenemy, King Tàmhas of Munster, had been or soon would be reinforced by Rome to the tune of a company or two of mercenaries and a famous mercenary captain, one Timoteo, the Duke of Bolgia, secured by the Holy See to endeavor to hammer the Munster troops into a true army along modern lines.

Upon hearing this last, Sir Calum and Sir Liam had both snorted derisively. "The only certain sure outcome of that," declared Sir Calum, "is that the whole host of career *galloglaiches* and *bonaghts* are going to be a-march to north and east and west out of the Kingdom of Munster and straight into the employ of King Brian or any other who conducts war and leads armies in the old style of Ireland rather than in the new and alien manner of an Italian captain. Mark my words,

Tàmhas na Muma will soon have no retainers save those
bound to him by blood, by honor, or by Papal gold.''

The papers in another batch made it abundantly clear that
there would be, could be no Crusader activity expected from
Spain in the foreseeable future. The holy Christian Caliph of
Granada was already at war with his most Catholic majesty of
Spain in all save name. And in the New World, on the
northern continent of that world, Spanish forces and a coalition of *indios* were making war against the French and another coalition of *indios*.

The Kingdom of Hungary seemed to be about to plunge
into a civil war again, with various of its neighbors waiting
hungrily along its borders like jackals, hoping to snatch bits
and pieces of territory when the time seemed ripe.

The French and the Burgunds were snarling a little more
loudly and viciously than normal and had even engaged in
several skirmishes at odd points along their borders. The
French were also picking at the borders of Savoy, and the
Holy Roman Emperor, Savoy's ally and patron, was known
to have issued to the King of France the same threat he had
issued to the Holy See last year.

The King of Naples was consolidating his hold on Sicily in
the face of a sometimes stiff resistance, and he seemed to
have as his next objective the Grand Duchy of Sardinia,
which would surely plunge him into a war with Genoa. Since
both Naples and Genoa enjoyed special relationships of alliance with Rome, which might be expected to attempt to
mediate a row between two of the Roman allies, the letter
noted that that particular time might be an ideal one for
Catalonia to pick for the seizing of Sardinia *and* Sicily for her
own, as had been long planned.

Another letter discussed the feasibility of having the Duke
of Valencia assassinated, then speedily marching in sufficient
force to seize the duchy and city for the Catalán Crown,
while a fleet set sail from Barcelona to occupy the Valencia-
owned Balearic Islands, as well.

Bass shook his head. ''This King José of Catalonia is a
damned acquisitive bastard, isn't he?''

Melchoro nodded grimly. "There were but a bare handful of Catalán knights on the Crusade last year and the year before. Now one knows why, eh? And this Duque de Valencia, gentlemen, is King José's own half brother."

A letter from yet another batch urged strong and concerted action against Malta. It seemed that the Maltese, taking advantage of the unsettled conditions, had commenced raiding the southern and the western coasts of Sicily and were offering slaves captured in those areas at far below the prices agreed upon by the slave traders' guilds. Bass silently wondered how and why such a missive had been where it had been found—in a small port on the Bay of Biscay.

The voyage back to England was quick, quiet, and uneventful. The few sails that hove into view on the distant horizon made haste to disappear from the view of so many warships as speedily as they could.

On arrival at Thames-mouth, Bass had the sealed casks containing the reams of documents and letters and the king's share of the loot of Gijón-port rowed over to Sir Paul Bigod's flagship and keeping, then set sail for his own port with his personal fleet, now grown to seven ships. The first phase of his commission was now completed. Next would be the Irish expedition.

But arrived at Norwich, he found another messenger awaiting him.

The two men met in the dead of night in a place that few if any of the superstition-ridden folk of this world and time would have willingly frequented at such an hour. Their two horses placidly munched at the grasses growing around the canted or tumbled ancient gravestones while the riders squatted on their heels and conversed in a language that no other man or woman within two thousand miles could have comprehended.

The two men were much alike; not only did they wear similar styles of clothing and weapons, but their almost identical physiologies and physiognomies indicated an affinity at least of race if not of family. Indeed, the only obvious difference was that one seemed somewhat older than the other.

"It is something that might well go into records and be noted by those who would use that information ill. Far too many persons witnessed that particular projection. Many are persons of note in their world and time, and their elimination would cause even further disruption, cause more records to be put down, and some future examiner might correlate the oddities, to our detriment. This is why I arranged for Foster Bass to be summoned here once more so soon. I knew that you surely would accompany him, and I need your help in setting this matter aright."

The elder squatted in silence for a moment, then said, "Yes, I agree, younger one. They must be returned to the exact place and time of projection. Do we use our projector or that one brought down here from Whyffler Hall?"

The younger shook his head. "Most of that more primitive device has been disassembled and bits of it scattered from the archepiscopal palace to the Royal Manufactory of Arms and Gunpowder. No, we must use our own."

The elder shrugged. "Probably better that we use a sophisticated instrument anyway. But we must use exceeding care in making the adjustments and reckoning the settings, for we'd but exacerbate matters were we to put them down say two hours early and ten yards out in the river. And we must make certain that they all are in one place, one small spot, with their instruments, when we activate our projector."

"They are all together in one suite of rooms on the archepiscopal estate now being used by Webster Buddy. I have carefully plotted the coordinates of the building, the rooms, and the elevation, elder one. When shall we do it?"

The elder shrugged again. "Why not now? I assume you brought the projector with you, as usual?"

Evelyn Mangold awakened to complete darkness and the familiar sensation of being in a moving vehicle. Her wrists were handcuffed and her ankles were tied. Her mouth was filled with some kind of cloth, and she could feel tape pulling painfully at her lips, chin, and cheeks. Movement of her eyebrows made it clear that more tape had been used to secure pads over her eyes. She decided after a while that she was lying on the floor of a truck or a station wagon, traveling at speed over a smooth, paved road, and she felt as if she were wrapped in canvas or something like it.

From somewhere up ahead she could hear a soft rumble of men's voices, but they were not speaking English and she could understand not a single word of the three-way conversation. A woman's voice once said a few words in the same strange tongue, but it was not Millicent's or any other she could recall having heard.

Abruptly, she felt the vehicle slow, then make a turn that sent her body sliding over to her right to slam against the side of the compartment in which she lay. This new road was not at all smooth, and her flesh and bone recorded each bump and rut and wrinkle and pothole of the ill-kept surface. Another turn propelled her over to the opposite side, and the following stretch of road seemed to be no better than the preceding one.

"Christ Almighty, Kogh," said Mariya, in Armenian, "why don't you or Papa hire a scraper to make these roads at least passable for something more modern than a Model T or a jeep?"

"What for, big sister? We only come out here to visit the graves, anymore, and then we come by chopper," replied Kogh Ademian. "Besides, we'd have to buy a damned scraper, bad as this drainage has gotten out here, and keep a permanent operator for it. You recall how smooth these roads were when we buried Marge?"

"Have you decided where best to keep her?" asked Boghos.

"Yeah, we got a place all ready for her nibs," affirmed Bagrat Ademian. "The old smokehouse is as solid as it was the day that whoever built it built it, and it must be a hundred years old if it's a day. Me and Kogh, we put a chemical toilet in there last weekend and a steel army cot, chained to a staple in the wall, too. We can put a bucket of water in there with her. There's no lights, of course, it don't smell too good, and there may be a few rats living under the floor, too. But she'll

never get out of there, and nobody that did get clear back i▮
here would hear her with the door shut. And if she shoulᵈ
happen to croak on us . . . well, the river's not far awaʸ
down the back road.''

"Don't even joke about such a thing, Bagrat," snappeᵈ
Boghos. "She looks to be a tough, resilient woman, anᵈ
she's survived at least one total drug withdrawal recently,
while she was serving her jail time; there's no reason why she
shouldn't survive another under my supervision. The only
thing that might kill her is plain, outright abuse. And that wilᶫ
not happen, you hear me? I'll not condone torture of any sort.
Besides, it would not achieve our purposes, as it might welᶫ
leave traceable scars.''

At long last, the bumping ceased as the vehicle came to a
halt. Doors opened and then slammed, feet crunched gravel,
a lock clicked, and a tailgate came down with a shrill squeal
of metal on metal. Hands grasped the sack and dragged it anᵈ
its living contents out to thump upon the ground, bringing a
moan from within the sack.

Evelyn Mangold felt herself pulled onto her numb, bound
feet, felt the top of the canvas sack loosened, gaped wide,
then pulled down the length of her. Still bound and manacled
as she was, she was afraid to try to move lest she fall again to
the hard, stony ground. She heard another car drive up and
come to a stop nearby, the subsequent opening and closing of
doors, muted conversations. Her captors seemed to number
five, six, maybe seven, at least one of them a woman, all of
them probably foreigners, since she had heard not a single
word of English since she had regained consciousness. She
felt herself trembling all over, inside and out, she knew that
she needed a fix . . . *bad*.

Then she began to tremble in earnest when a horrifyingly
familiar bass rumble of a voice spoke close beside her. "Now
we can do this the easy way or the hard way, cooze. I can
take off them cuffs and cut your feet loose, then strip you
nekkid, then take you into where you gonna stay for a while
and take out the gag and uncover your eyes. Do what you
told and won't nothing be done to you; you won't be raped or

nothing. Ain't any man here is low enough to stick his wang in no ugly slab of meat and bone like you.

"Or," he continued, now with a note of keen anticipation in his voice, "you can give me some trouble, try to, anyhow. Then I can leave you chained up and tied and I can cut your clothes off before I do anything else . . . 'course, I'll prob'ly take some of your horny hide, too. Then I can do what I done to you back in Richmond, by the Duck Lake. That was fun, for me. How'd you like it?"

Even blinded as she was, Evelyn still could see in her mind's eye those cold, black, reptilian eyes. Tears of terror soaking into the gauze eye patches, she shook her head violently from side to side, her body's crying need for the drugs to which it had become reaccustomed completely forgotten in her frenzy of fear of this terrible man and the agonies his huge hands could so easily inflict on her quivering flesh.

Meekly as any lamb, she allowed herself to be divested of every shred of clothing, not even moving to lay the goose flesh raised on her skin by the chill, night air. Then one of those big hands took her arm and led her barefoot over the coarse gravel, through a swath of cold-leaved, knee-high grass or weeds, up two icy stone or brick or concrete steps, and pushed her through a low doorway into a place with a wooden floor.

After six or seven short steps across the floor, Evelyn was pushed down to sit on what felt like a bunk and admonished not to move. When a cold, metallic something had been fastened around one of her ankles, the gag and the eye patches were removed, and she found herself sitting on a war-surplus steel bunk and bare mattress, with a GI blanket folded at one end.

The walls of the hut or whatever it was were constructed of thick, old-looking logs and, like the broad floorboards underfoot, were greasy to the touch. Into one of the nearby logs, two three-inch steel staples had been hammered. The bunk was chained to one of them. A much longer chain and a flat steel ring secured her right ankle to the other.

Across the width of the long, narrow space was a chemical

toilet of sheet metal with a roll of toilet paper sitting atop its closed lid. Just beyond the foot of the bunk a small galvanized bucket sat on the floor with a chipped enamel dipper submerged in the water that almost filled it to the brim.

Two men, their faces unidentifiable under the nylon stockings they had pulled over their heads, were up in the rafters, just finishing tacking down an electric wire at one end of which was dangling a bare bulb of at least a hundred and fifty watts. The yellow-white glare hurt her eyes after so long in her blindfolded darkness.

Then another man in a stocking mask came in. This one had a stethoscope hanging from his neck and a black physician's bag in one hand. At sight of the bag and the thought of all the blissful pharmaceuticals she could imagine it to contain, her need for drugs briefly overrode her fear of the man who sat beside her and the pain he had proved capable of inflicting on her.

"Doctor?" She spoke fast, frantically. "Doctor, you gotta do suthin to help me! I got this terrible condition, see, an' I need—*I gotta have*—suthin *soon*! Some Demerol or suthin like that an'—"

The newcomer just laughed coldly. "We all know precisely what your 'condition' is, you murdering bitch. You're a drug addict. I may eventually give you injections of drugs, but whether or not I do will be entirely dependent on how cooperative you are with us. Right now, I'm here to give you a physical examination; we wouldn't want you to die on us, you know. You three get out of here. I don't conduct physicals in public."

The man beside Evelyn arose, saying, "I sure hopes you gives the doctor some troubles. You're fun to hurt."

Some ten minutes later, Boghos opened the door clumsily. A blood-soaked handkerchief was wrapped around one of his hands. "I suppose we're going to need the gentleman's service again, in here. She snatched the bag, someway. There're no drugs in it, of course, but there are some instruments, one of which she just used on me."

Seraphino "Sara the Snake" Mineo was well named, for

despite his squat, broad muscularity, he was every bit as fast as one. In a trice, he had disarmed Evelyn Mangold and had her writhing on her knees, screaming in agony and abject terror of him. Much as he hated the woman, Rupen Ademian felt a sick disgust to see how much the short, powerful Sicilian relished the infliction of pain on her.

"Enough! Let her go, man!" He spoke Sicilian Italian this time, his command voice snapping like a whip.

Sara the Snake recognized the voice of a leader of men at once. He released Evelyn Mangold and spun to face Rupen. Speaking in a deferential tone in the same dialect in which he had received the order, he asked, "You speak my language, then, honored sir?"

"Only a little," replied Rupen, shrugging and flapping his spread hands slowly. "Just the small amount I learned while fighting the Nazis in Sicily, during the war."

Rupen saw the very first of Mineo's excessively rare smiles. "I, too, fought the *tedesci* and the *fascisti* before them, honored sir. All of my brave family, we fought them. Many, they killed, but many more of them did we kill until none of them would dare to come into our lands and hills without *carri armati* and many lorries full of troops and *velivoli* flying overhead to guard them, and still we attacked them and fought them and killed them, except for those few we took alive for information or for ransom or for . . . sport."

"We will leave the woman here until morning," Rupen announced, in English, this time. "She can swap notes with the rats tonight."

"R . . . r . . . *rats*?" quavered Evelyn from where she had crawled to huddle on the bunk.

"Sure, rats, great big brown ones, a whole damn family of them," said Bagrat, with a merry grin. "This is an old smokehouse here, and they live under the floor. That's why we just put in the light, so's you can see them coming for you. Heh, heh, heh."

Evelyn really began to scream then, piercingly, without pause, for longer than it took to breathe in enough air to scream yet again. She was still screaming as they closed and locked the heavy old door.

"Are there really rats in there, Bagrat?" Boghos asked.

"I sorta doubt it, Doc," replied the youngest Ademian brother. "We found where a weasel or a skunk had been denning up in there when we first got the idea of cleaning it out and using it, and if it's critters that rats won't stay anywhere around, it's skunks and weasels. That's one of the biggest reasons it smells so bad in there, you know; there's just no way to get that skunk-weasel smell out quick. But that bitch in there, *she* thinks it's rats in there, and I guarantee you she'll get damn few winks of sleep this night."

"She'd not sleep anyway, you know," said Boghos. "Not in this stage of drug withdrawal. By the time our friends get down here on Friday night, she should be malleable enough to tell us anything and everything about her past misdeeds."

Krystal Foster was in seventh heaven for the first few days she spent in company with the five young women who had been projected into this world with the Ademian band—Jenny Bostwick, Ilsa Peters, Kitty Hutchinson, Helen Pappas, and Rose Yacubian. She had done her level best to explain to them just what had happened to them and the men of the band, reciting her own similar experience of years back and trying to give the impression of an assurance that she did not truly feel that everything would be all right for them all when once they had adapted to this strange, primitive world and its people and the incomprehensible language they called English.

But then the exposure began to pall. Two of the women had had husbands and children in the other world, one had been a new bride of less than six months, and all three were worried, terribly homesick, and skating perilously close to mental derangement, in Krystal's professional opinion. The other two just might make it, she thought, though she could not say she liked either of them, nor did she admire the "talents" that bettered their chances of survival.

As for the men, Arsen Ademian spent half of his time brooding and the other half drinking copious quantities of ale along with any other alcohol he could lay his hands upon. Greg Sinclair and Mike Vranian did their best to match him gallon for gallon, which meant that all three were nearly comatose much of the time.

John Othondoyatros, since being granted access to the estate library was usually nosed into one quarto and surrounded by any number of others, as he could read both Greek and Latin. The other Mike, Mike Sikeena, a young man of Lebanese extraction and a onetime United States Marine, could usually be found in company with Buddy Webster, who also had served in that branch of the services. Al and Haigh Ademian, too, were well occupied, all day, every day. They had found and had had borne up to the suite an immense chess set—the board a yard square and fashioned of squares of semiprecious stones framed in gilded silver, the pieces each an exquisite little marble or alabaster statuette, the kings and the queens wearing real golden crowns with tiny gemstones inset, the knights all armored and grasping perfect little swords of real steel, the bishops equipped with steel maces, the rooks complete to the last detail and including infinitesimally small bombards of brass mounted on the towertops. The pawns were all pikemen, each of them wearing a steel cap and a scaleshirt and bearing a pike. The chess game had been going on ever since the set had been brought upstairs, and as both men were good players and evenly matched, no end was in sight.

Krystal would have liked to talk with the oldest man, Rupen Ademian, but he seemed to always be closeted with Hal.

Then, of a day, completely unexpected and unannounced, his grace, Sir Sebastian Foster, Duke of Norfolk, Markgraf von Velegrad, Earl of Rutland, Baron of Strathtyne, Lord Commander of the Royal Horse, and Krystal's husband, came riding into the forecourt followed by his gentlemen, staff, and entourage. He was traveling light this time; only some hundred and fifty horsemen accompanied him onto the archepiscopal estate.

Krystal's cup then ranneth over, for only a fortnight earlier,

the archbishop had arrived; a week later Reichsherzog Wolfgang and his troop of Kalmyks, then, two days ahead of her
noble husband, Pete Fairley and the hulking Dan Smith.

The breaking of Evelyn Mangold was accomplished rather
more quickly than had been anticipated, after only a few days
of a multipronged attack. Early in the morning that followed
her first night-long vigil against the dreaded rats, a woman
and an old man brought her food and coffee. Although she
could not see their faces well because of the nylon stockings—
the only face she ever was allowed to see unmasked was that
of Mineo—they were both soft-voiced, gentle with her, and
considerate of her, doing what little they could to make her
comfortable. They admitted to having no real power in the
group that held her captive, admitted to a shared fear of
Mineo and the other men, and urged Evelyn, for her own
good, to be cooperative with her cruel, merciless, murderous
captors.

Evelyn's next visitor was the doctor, fresh, neat sutures
showing on the back of the hand she had gashed with one of
his instruments. For a long while he stood just out of her
reach, verbally abusing her and tormenting her drug craving
with a three-gram vial and a hypodermic syringe, demanding
that she confess to the murder of Marge Ademian.

When he had driven her to a frenzy, when she began to
scream invectives and deadly threats and lunge against the
ankle chain that restrained her, the doctor opened the door
behind him to admit Sara the Snake Mineo, smiling in a way
that turned Evelyn's legs to rubber, her bowels to water.

Mineo would never allow her to actually lose consciousness,
stopping the torment just long enough to restore her to full
sensibility before he again went to work on her nerve centers
with skilled fingers, a knowing touch, and no more mercy
than a graven image of some centuries-dead Roman. By the
time she had finished cleaning up the mess of vomitus, feces,
and urine which her suffering body had voided under his
ungentle ministrations, and he had promised, in a soft tone
that chilled her very soul, to soon return, it was nearly noon.

They took turns at her thus for nearly three days before she began to talk about things they wanted to hear, at which point Bagrat and Kogh brought in, loaded, and wired up a tape recorder with seven-inch reels. By the time the two attorneys came out to the old farm—one from Richmond, one from upper New York State—there was a goodly amount of tape for them to hear before they themselves actually questioned the multiple murderess.

By Sunday night, the conspirators had amassed miles of recording tape on which were detailed confessions of criminal acts spanning fifteen years and nine states, including no less than four cold-blooded murders and one infanticide. For the five homicides and certain of the other crimes, they had typed, signed, attested, and properly witnessed confessions, several copies of each. This time, the legal net would be drawn tight-shut and there would be no way in which Evelyn Mangold could wriggle out and away from the punishments she had so fully earned over the years.

Rupen did not remarry, and most of his family and friends erroneously thought that it was because he was mourning Marge. In actuality, his period of mourning had ended on the day that Evelyn Mangold, Marge's murderess, had been convicted of another, earlier murder in Troy, New York. He simply could see no point, since he never would be able to sire children, in taking unto himself another wife.

He tried going back to college, stuck it out for a year, then quietly withdrew, deciding he was now just too old. Succumbing to the blandishments of his father and brother, Kogh, he moved up to Fredericksburg and tried working in the executive offices of the Ademian Corporation. That was a bust, too, so Kogh and Bagrat took him out to the farm one weekend to fish, and outlined to him another proposition, one that needs must be detailed out of the hearing of Vasil Ademian.

"Rupen, Bagrat and me, we mean to start up a new sideline for Ademian Corp., but we need another body and we think you'd be the ideal man for the job. You can put up money and buy in if you want to or you can just work for us as a salaried employee—salary and commissions and expenses. It's up to you, and I don't give a shit one way or the other, because we've got enough backing to start, anyhow.'' Kogh snapped his wrist and sent his lure flashing into a clump of weeds, then blasphemed in Armenian as he tried to reel in and snapped the monofilament line just above the leader.

"I tell you, I'm never gonna learn how to use one these damn spin-casting reels right!''

Handling his old-fashioned open reel expertly, Rupen sent the lure far, far down the slough toward the river, then reeled it back in a fast, jerky manner, hoping that it looked like the swimming of a small, injured fish. Apparently it did, at least enough for a black bass to rise to it. The conversation was not again taken up until the catch was boated and feebly flopping its last on a bed of ice in the bottom of the big Coleman cooler.

"We, me and Kogh,'' said Bagrat, "we've already got the right licensing and all to buy guns at wholesale and import 'em and sell 'em in this country at wholesale or retail. Rupen, it's millions of guns just laying around and rusting away all over the world left over from World War II, ammo, too, billions and billions of rounds of it. A man could come close to naming the price he was willing to pay for most of it, 'cause ain't nobody in their right mind getting ready to fight a war today is gonna try and do it with no bolt-action rifles; they're gonna want semiautos or submachine guns. I figger was we to offer the govermints that is stuck with all these old guns and ammo just a little over what a scrap dealer'd give 'em for the steel and brass and lead and all, they'd plumb jump at the offer.''

Of course, as Rupen quickly discovered in Europe, Asia, Latin America, and Africa, it was not anywhere near as simple as his brothers had thought. But he made out and the new enterprise made good, selling by mail out of their warehouse on the banks of the Rappahannock River, shipping out via freight. Rupen often reflected in later years that had his father known that the first major transaction of Souvenirs, Incorporated, had been the purchase of some thousands of stands of arms from the Turkish government arsenal, he would probably have immediately shot all three of his sons with one of those fine, if venerable, Mauser rifles.

More Mausers came from Ireland, from Spain, from Argentina, from Germany. From France came captured Mausers, along with Lebels; Italy sold Carcanos, Austria sold Steyr-Mannlichers, and Belgium offered tens of thousands of contract Mausers. Then, as Great Britain belatedly rearmed her army with semiautomatic shoulder arms, she made available at rock-bottom prices a veritable flood of Enfield rifles and carbines.

As the reputation of the firm and of Rupen himself became established, he found himself being offered and sometimes actually buying and shipping back to Virginia some rather esoteric items in the way of military arms, ammunitions, and related equipment. Also, well-heeled collectors in the United States and elsewhere took to placing name-your-own-price-but-get-it-for-me orders with the firm. The filling of these orders sometimes took Rupen to some strange and deadly backwaters of the world, but he usually came out with that for which he had gone in.

Despite all that had occurred since he'd first marched off to war in 1943, the Rupen Ademian who had come home from Korea still had been a rather insular, small-town American, speaking the languages of his youth—Armenian and English—plus smatterings of Italian, Japanese, and Korean, hardly aware of how much to tip a *maître d' hôtel* and very often cheated while on R&Rs in Tokyo because of his difficulty with rates of exchange.

But the Rupen Ademian of 1960 was certainly not the Major Rupen Ademian, USA, of 1953. He had learned that he had an ear for languages and he now was fluent in enough tongues and dialects to make himself understood in almost any part of the globe that his nearly constant travels criss-crossed via airplane, ship, and all manner of other land and water conveyances. He had learned well the lesson that so few men and women ever learn—human nature is human nature, regardless of race, nationality, politics, or sex. He

now knew just how much to tip a *maître* . . . and how much
to offer as bribe to a government minister, who often came
more cheaply than anyone would have suspected.

While he continued to make purchases from hither and yon
for the still-brisk mail-order business originally established, a
good deal of his and the firm's business of late had been more
that of middleman between countries with goods to sell and
countries with an urgent desire to buy them, despite alliances,
treaties, or a political climate that would have rendered open
negotiations either risky or impossible.

Presently, he was savoring a cup of strong tea with dark
rum, having just seen off a large shipment of assorted hand-
guns and ammo gathered from all over Europe and shipped
from Hamburg for the Chesapeake Bay and the Rappahannock warehouse. The nucleus of the shipment had been a real
find at this late date—cases of late-production but brand
spanking new Lugers and Walther P-38s. His agents had also
scoured up French MABs and Rubys, some Norwegian
11.25mm Colts, Swedish 7.65mm Brownings and 9mm Lahtis,
Polish Radoms, Italian Berretta autos, and Glisenti revolvers,
a few dozen Russian Nagant revolvers in poor shape, three
different configurations of Spanish Astra pistols, some practi-
cally new 7.65mm pistols made by Femaru-Gegyver es
Gepgyar of Hungary and stashed away God knew where in
the sixteen or seventeen years since their manufacture, some
broomhandle Mausers, and a thousand or so assorted flare
pistols.

With the ship slowly moving out toward the North Sea,
Rupen had telephoned his local message service and had been
informed that a Herr Kobra wished most urgently to arrange
a meeting at his, Rupen's, convenience. Was Herr Kobra in
Hamburg, by chance? No, but he was in Hanover and could
come soon to Hamburg, could Herr Ademain make time and
name a place, preferably a public place, to meet with him. So
now Rupen sat sipping the rum-spiked tea and wondering just
what nationality this Herr Kobra might be to choose such a
nom-de-guerre.

"Cobra" was a Portuguese word, of course, but that would

be too simple. Besides, Portugal had no trouble getting modern arms from the West and had long ago sold him and other arms dealers its antiquated Mausers and Lugers. Indian or Pakistani? Maybe; there always was some variety of trouble brewing somewhere on the subcontinent with its unhomogenizable mixture of races, creeds, tribes, and politics. But then cobras were indigenous to Africa, too, and all hell was going to kick off in various parts of that continent, and that damned soon, or Rupen Ademian had learned nothing in his almost forty years of life.

Southeast Asia, too, the whole damned peninsula, not to mention the multiple rebellions set to break out against the government of Indonesia. So Cobra was a good cover name. The man who had chosen to bear it could conceivably be from almost anywhere.

Then a waiter approached his table, diffidently. "Mein Herr Ademian, a Herr Kobra has telephoned and leaves word that he will be unable to keep his appointment with you. He says that he at your hotel will be in one hour."

In his car, Rupen drew his cunningly concealed PPK and checked it carefully. Pulling up coat and shirt sleeves on his left arm, he examined the little razor-edged knife and the mechanism that would spring it into his hand. Finally, he very carefully checked out the custom-made "fountain pen" nestled among the others; this one fired a single 4mm explosive bullet and had saved his life on at least two sticky occasions in the past.

CHAPTER ————————————————
THE TWELFTH

The elder of the two men who had met in a Northumberland graveyard on a recent dark night moved about the suite of rooms assigned to the men and women brought out from York by Archbishop Harold. In his guise of a humble, unspeaking servant, none of the occupants really took notice of him. There were so very many servants, after all, in the sprawling, multistoried, palatial country residence, and still more of them arriving with each new party of guests.

The pretended servant was worried. The projector hidden in the graveyard many miles from here had been carefully set and painstakingly calibrated and would perform that act of projection of all living persons within the bounds of the suite upon his activation of the remote-control device secreted on his person. But it needs must be done soon, very soon, else he must travel back down to that graveyard and reset the projector.

At no time when he had been able to get away from his mundane duties and come up to this suite had the elder one been able to find all twelve of the occupants within its confines. Even now, as he puttered about, giving the appearance of being busily employed at lighting tapers and lamps against the encroaching dusk, there still were two missing— one man and one woman.

But still, this was the largest number he ever before had found within the rooms at once, and so, pressed as he was for time, he decided to act. Perhaps he and the younger one could find a way and a time and a place to project the missing two back. For now, however, he could be certain that these ten, at least, would shortly be back when and where they belonged. Smiling, he bowed his way out of the suite, took a few paces down the hallway, and activated the projector.

Simon Delahayle was of gentle birth, though a younger son of a younger son. He had been as well reared as his family's modest means had allowed, had fostered for a few years at the hall of a more prosperous distant, but noble, relative, then had gone overseas with a scion of that noble house and soldiered a few years in foreign lands. The scion he had helped to attend had been slain, but Simon had lucked onto a wealthy knight, and the proceeds from that ransom had seen him back home in Sussexshire with a fine small farm, a wife, children, a couple of good horses to ride, a decent sword, and the respect of all his neighbors, both great and small.

Because of his long-ago but still unforgotten foreign military exploits and experiences, it had seemed but natural that the earl should have sent a galloper directly to his door, urging him to raise a troop of horse and join with the earl's own force to go to the aid of the young king and the regent in London.

Captain Delahayle's troop had become a part of Monteleone's Horse and, with that elite unit, had raided deep into lands loyal to the Usurper, Arthur Tudor, harrying the rebel army, burning standing crops and painfully gathered supplies, running off horses and cattle, slaughtering swine and sheep, and otherwise creating havoc until that fateful day when they had ridden into the jaws of a trap set and sprung by the wily, Satan-tutored Arthur.

Stripped of his arms, armor, boots, and everything else of any value, Simon had been left for dead on the stricken field whereon Monteleone's Horse had been virtually exterminated and brave Monteleone himself had been slain.

Somehow, Simon must have staggered off that field and into a place of hiding, but he could not remember doing so. Indeed, he could recall nothing until a good three years after

that battle, when he regained his memories of his previous
life. That he had neither starved nor frozen, betimes, could be
attributed to the fact that he had been delivered in a very poor
condition by the folk who found him to a small country
monastery. The monks had nursed him and cared for him and
shared their own frugal sustenance with him for years, while
the civil war and crusades raged all about them and their tiny
haven of refuge.

With the cessation of general fighting, last year, Simon had
left the monastery and had tramped the roads as a sturdy
beggar and itinerant farmhand, slowly working his way back
east and south, bound for Sussex and home. On a particular
rainy, windy night in southern Yorkshire, in need of shelter
from the elements, he chanced across an ancient, untended,
unkempt graveyard.

Being of a bent unusual for his time, Simon had no fear of
the dead or of the ground wherein they moldered. He had
right often slept in graveyards, and the only time he had been
in fear in one was when an elderly sexton had loosed a
crossbow at him, then set his dog at him. The quarrel had
scored a clean miss, and though the hound had bitten Simon,
he had strangled the beast and borne the body with him,
dressed it when at a safe distance and feasted well for a
couple of days on fat dog. He'd also rough-dressed the skin
and sold it to a tanner in a nearby town. He still wore the
dog's upper and lower fangs strung about his neck and impressed those who asked by asserting them the fangs of
wolves—one from each one he had slain with his stout cudgel
and his long, heavy-bladed all-purpose knife.

Pushing through the high weeds and the brambles, cursing
under his breath at the profusion of briers that pulled at his
foot wrappings and tattered breeches, Simon made his way
through the outer ranks of weathered headstones and cracked
crosses—some of them so old as to be of Danish or even
Celtic design—until he came to what he thought to have
glimpsed in the dimness, a stone-built tomb wherein he might
spend this coming night dry and safe from biting winds.

Once there had been a grille to protect the door—the

rust-stained rectangles left by the hinges still marred the stonework—but grill and hinges were long since gone, probably stripped off in daylight by roving ironmongers. But the arms of a noble house still were carven over the door, though so far gone in erosion as to be indecipherable to Simon's eyes. The iron bolts, too, had been torn from off the doors, and those doors now were held closed by only a half-dozen head-sized chunks of rock, which Simon shoved or lifted aside.

The odors which came to him when he gaped open those doors were not those associated with death and decay, but those of caves, of places long denied sunlight. Surely this was a very old tomb indeed, he thought, as he paused with his head inside, waiting for his vision to adjust to the darkness of the interior.

The inside dimensions of the aged tomb were about what he had had reason to expect—twelve broad, stone steps led downward into a flagged chamber some eight feet across and ten or twelve long. Each side wall was pierced by four tiers of four openings, each wide and high enough to slide in a coffin, and a few of the coffins still were in place, but all that were were of wood and scattered bits and pieces of ancient bones littered the flags.

It was an old story. In these lawless years, with no lord about to periodically inspect the tomb of his ancestors or place men to guard it, it had of course been stripped and plundered, probably many times over. The grave goods had gone first, of course, then the leaden coffins and the metal fittings from the wooden ones. None of the loot was of any use to the long dead. Living men and women must eat to stay alive, and scrap metal brought money. Simon had himself sold bronze hinges and nails and decorations torn from off a coffin in a tomb where he had slept up north.

Gathering up a handful of splintered wood, mostly by feel, he took flint, steel, and tinder from his beltpouch and soon had a small, cheery fire ablaze on the steps. By its light, he found bigger pieces of wood to feed it and propped himself against the lowest step warming his back and wishing he had

something to eat and drink in this comfortable nighttime
bivouac.

In an effort to take his mind off the ferocious growling of
his empty stomach, Simon got up and began to explore. He
would, in any case, need more pieces of coffin wood to keep
the fire going throughout the night, and mayhap the looters
who had come before him had missed a bauble or two in the
evident haste of their depredations. Leaving his cudgel on the
steps below the fire, he took hold of a coffin at about head
level and began to worry it out of its deep niche in the wall of
the tomb.

As he struggled with the weight and bulk of the box, he
thought to himself that it seemed very sound for a coffin of
the venerable age it gave the appearance of being. He might
well have to go out and fetch back a heavy chunk of stone to
help him break up this one for fire fuel. Finally, he had
pulled the entire length—only about five feet, so probably the
last couch of a woman or a good-sized child—out of the
niche, deliberately allowing the far end to slam hard upon the
floor in hopes of weakening the fabric. To his very great
surprise, there was a metallic clanging when the coffin end
hit the flagstones, and a flaming splinter brought over from
the fire for closer examination showed no slightest damage to
any portion of the casket.

There was no catch nor handles nor even visible hinges to
the thing. An intricately rendered set of arms done in what
looked to be a bronze with a very high tin content was affixed
to the lid, but the arms told him nothing as to the patronymic
of the corpse within. He could not recall ever having seen
their like.

After a solid half hour of beating on the top of the coffin
with one of the big stones that had been used to hold shut the
door of this tomb, he had a quantity of stone dust and shards,
but the wood—whatever devilish kind it was, the grain and
color were completely unfamiliar to him—had only been
scuffed here and there. When he had replenished the fire with
pieces of those coffins smashed by his predecessors, he sat on
a step below it to think out the matter.

A heavy stone powered by all his strength did no visible damage to that supposedly ancient wooden coffin, when it should have quickly been smashed to splinters by such abuse. Why? The point of his knife would not penetrate the seam at any point on either end or either side. Again, why? There were no handles, no catch, no hinges to be seen, and he, who had seen full many a coffin, had never seen one so constructed no matter how highborn the personage it had been made to hold. Why and why and why?

There were far too many unanswered and unanswerable questions to be housed in some simple ancient tomb crouched amongst the briers and brambles of a country graveyard. *Could it be. . . ?*

Everyone knew how kings and high noblemen sometimes hid away treasures in odd places, sometimes marking them with a seal that it would have been death to break, if you were unlucky enough to get caught at it or apprehended soon afterward. Could this strange, unnaturally strong coffin be such a repository? Was that bronze design affixed to the lid actually the seal of some royal house, ancient or modern? No way but to examine it with greater care.

Maneuvering the long box about, he dragged it to the foot of the steps, as close to the firelight as he could get it. He knelt on the far side of the thing, so as not to get into his own light, his cudgel close to hand giving him a small measure of peace of mind. When he had scraped off the worst of the oxidation from the lid decoration or whatever it was, he sheathed his big knife and began to rub at the arms with a wetted sleeve. With the encrusted dust off, the arms, while still unfamiliar to him, were clearly not those of any royal house that had reigned in England for the last century or more.

Peering very closely, he noted what seemed to be a staggered line or regular pattern of depressions, each some inch or less across; scraping at one of these with a filthy fingernail, Simon shattered and dislodged a plug of dusty dirt, beneath which a something glittered in the firelight. He immediately thought of inset gemstones, and the air hissed between his teeth. Feverishly, he cleared out every one of the depressions he could discern, ten in all, it developed.

But when he took a splinter from the fire and bent far over to gaze, his hopes were partially dashed, for no gems were at the bottoms of the shallow holes, rather disks of silver that looked to be roughly a little smaller than the tips of his thick fingers. Absently, he fitted all eight fingers and two thumbs into the holes and began to feel and press to see if there existed an easy way to get the silver disks out, for he had already ascertained that any attempt to pry up the bronze decoration would most likely give him only a broken knifeblade to show for his troubles.

Simon experienced a brief moment of atavistic terror when, with no sound of warning, the lid of the coffin began to slowly rise toward him. Scooting backward on his knees, he grasped his oaken cudgel and prepared to fight whatever demon he had chanced to loose. But when once the lid had risen to the perpendicular, it and the coffin simply sat there, and, gingerly, he edged around to where he could gaze within it.

"*God's Holy Blood*!" Simon swore, gaspingly.

"No, indeed, Bass," said the archbishop, "I did not send word for you to ride up here, nor do I employ any Father John atte Nash. Who accompanied him?"

Bass wrinkled his forehead, "Why, some half-dozen of your own horse guards, Hal. None that I knew by sight, but they were all wearing your livery and seemed to know me of old."

The old man regarded the square of vellum unrolled on the table before him. "It's my signature, all right, but that's not to be wondered at, for I sign scores of documents for my secretary and scribes, sometimes just blank sheets even. As for the seals, they're kept in the escriborium, ready to hand when needed. I think I detect the stench of Roman rottenness in this matter. But why, in God's name, would they want you up here? Can you think of a good reason to go to such lengths as this must have entailed, Bass? I can't, just of the minute.

Have you perchance been in recent attendance upon the king?''

"No, Hal." Bass shook his head slowly. "I've not seen Arthur or even been up the Thames since before the fleet set sail for Gijón-port. Why? You think there's some bearing on this phony message business?''

The archbishop shrugged. "Who's to say what strange schemes move through the convoluted minds of madmen. And I am every day more firmly convinced that old Abdul is either mad or fast becoming so; many of his actions over the last few years have simply not been those of a rational man.''

"Well, be that as it may, you're here now. You don't intend to ride back south immediately, do you?''

"Why, yes, I had thought that I would, Hal. There's still a lot to do getting my squadron and ships and all ready for the trip to Ireland, you know. Why?'' Then a sudden thought struck him and he grimaced and demanded, "Oh, no, Hal, you don't want me to ride up to Strathtyne again, so soon, do you?''

Chuckling, the old man reached across the breadth of the table and patted Bass's hand. "No, no, my friend, nothing so traumatic as that, this time around. There's nothing now left at Whyffler Hall, save memories of the long, long ago . . . I hope. Though what Dr. Stone told you as she lay dying still worries me from time to time. But there is nothing to be done that I have not done already.

"No, I wanted you to stay here for a few days to meet and talk with a most remarkable man, one of those who was projected here at Hexham. I think he will be most valuable to me, and he might just prove helpful to you, as well, in Ireland. His name is Rupen Ademian. He is a twentieth-century American of Armenian antecedents and Syrian birth. He fought as an officer in two of the midcentury wars, worked in an artillery-ammunition factory, dealt for many years in armaments of war, is a natural and gifted linguist, and owns a true host of other, widely varied talents.

"Besides, if you stay up here for a few days, you might be able to persuade Krystal to accompany you on back down to

Norwich, or at least talk her around to giving over this feud with Captain Webster. She is most wroth at him since he seduced one of her ladies."

"*Wer ist da*?" demanded Rupen, standing well back from the door, grasping a cocked Welrod pistol leveled at the center of that door. He had more modern weapons of heavier caliber and larger magazine capacity, but the OSS assassination piece had the advantage of being completely silenced and the custom 7.65mm loads he had in this one were far more deadly than the off-the-shelf variety of such ammunition.

"*Ich bin Herr Kobra, mein Herr Ademian,*" came the reply in an accented German.

Standing well to the side, Rupen unlocked the door, then took three rapid steps back before saying, "*Herein, Herr Kobra, langsamer, bitte.*"

Slowly, the door swung inward to disclose not one but two men, both neatly attired in business suits of American cut, one bearing an attaché case of flashy ostrich hide. Seeing their hands to be empty of weapons and none of the four anywhere near to the flat bulges that his trained eye could identify as concealed pistols, Rupen looked up at the faces . . . and almost discharged the light-triggered Welrod in pure shock!

"As I live and breathe," gasped Rupen in consternation, "it's Seraphino Mineo! What the hell are you doing in Hamburg?"

With one of his fleeting near-smiles, the stocky man switched to Sicilian Italian to say, "Mostly, following you, honored sir. That and selecting a convenient place to set up a meeting between you and this gentleman. He wishes to conduct some business with you."

Willing to at least listen to the proposal of almost anyone, Rupen waved his guests to seats, but remained cautiously standing himself. The strange man presently produced some documents which identified him as one Karl Olwen Torgeson, an employee of the Department of Defense of the United States of America.

"Okay," said Rupen casually, "what does DOD want with me, this time? Or do you really represent DOD, Mr. Torgeson? If I'm wrong, I'm sorry, but I've been at this game a long time and I think I sniff something very spooky about you and this whole setup. If General Macey or whoever had wanted to see me, he would have simply contacted my firm and they would have had a coded message to that effect in my hands far quicker and easier than the shenanigans you went through took.

"So until you convince me you do represent who you say you do, I consider this meeting to be at an end, and if you don't get out of this suite damned quick, I'll shoot your ass!"

Torgeson sat stock-still, stunned, his mouth open and moving but no sounds issuing from it. Mineo, his own face its usual blank, just nodded slowly.

"I told you all," he said in English. "I told you you couldn't put nothing over on Mr. Ademian here—he's sharp as a shiv, he is! You damn CIA boys with all your college degrees make me sick sometimes, honest to God you do. Youse seems to think ain't nobody but you got brains or knows how to use 'em. Well, you learned this time!"

Torgeson's mouth snapped shut and he paled, a tic starting up under one eye. "Dammit, Mineo, you had no right to reveal . . . to speak of the . . . be warned, our superiors will assuredly hear of this unforgivable breach of security!"

Mineo shrugged. "I'll get piles on my piles and lay awake every night worryin' 'bout it, you shithead. Besides, Mr. Ademian knowed what you really was without me tellin' him. Cain't you see that, or are you really as fuckin' dumb as you act and look? I hadn't thought that was possible."

"The Central Intelligence Agency?" queried Rupen, a little doubtfully. "But Mr. Mineo, I had thought . . . at least we were told years back when we . . . ahhh, employed you briefly, that you were a . . . that you were connected to another, entirely different group, a civilian organization, shall we say."

"Oh sure, Mr Ademian," said Mineo. "I'm mobbed up,

have been mosta my life, even before I come to the States. But my family, they's working with thesehere boys on some things for two-three years, now. That's how I come inta thishere. And when I told 'em I knows you personal, like, they flew me over here to interduce Torgeson here to you.

"Look, at least hear the stupid little fucker out, huh? He may have shit for brains, but then he's just the front man and the fellas wants to talk to you is back in Paris, see. They got damn serious problems and need help real bad."

No gold or jewels were visible at first glance in the opened coffin, but nonetheless, what was there appeared a true treasure trove to Simon Delahayle's astonished eyes. A *sword* lay in its sheath—from its hilt, a modern sword, too, no relic from ages past. There was a long dirk, too, of a peculiar pattern, several daggers and knives and a wheellock pistol, but apprently no balls or powder for it. There were also some bags and leathern pouches, but the thing that really caught and held Simon's gaze was a big, egg-shaped thing of a silvery sheen.

The thing was about a foot long and nearly as wide, and it shone as if but just polished; no trace of oxidation anywhere marred its surface. Simon reached out for the silver egg, then changed his mind and took up the sheathed sword instead. After so many years deprived of one, his hands fairly itched for the feel of the hilt.

He drew the blade and examined it before the firelight. It looked to be damascus steel, a wavy, colorful pattern irregularly reflecting back the flames down the length of steel, from quillions to point. The outer guard was of pierced sheet steel, padded inside with softened leather. Although completely lacking any gilding or silvering, it was nonetheless a splendid, beautifully made weapon, a gentleman's battlebrand, no question about it. And Simon felt more noble than he had in long years, just to be holding the weapon in his hand.

He laid aside the other edged weapons and the pistol, which last was simply an unhandy club without charges for it, and went next at the bags and pouches. One pouch contained some two dozens of strange, thin, flat pieces of an unusual glass with a fine wire of tin or silver protruding from each end and one side. It was beyond him what they might be good for, so he closed the pouch and laid it atop the pile of daggers and knives down at the end of the coffin.

The first bag that he picked up jingled, and, hardly daring to hope, Simon untied the drawstring and then poured his hand full to overflowing with minted silver shillings and sixpences. All of them were well worn, and not a few had been clipped to one degree or another. Most were of Arthur II, the grandfather of the Usurper and great-grandfather to the rightful king. A smaller bag contained about a troy pound of gold coins of equal age and condition.

Simon sat back and earnestly recited a prayer in thanks to God. No need now to tramp the roads like a runaway serf, doing manual labor for yeomen, or stealing at risk of his neck, or poaching game for his keep. Now he could buy decent clothing and a horse and return to his home in a few weeks instead of months or years. He could return looking like the gentleman who had ridden away so many years ago, too, not like some louse-infested beggar.

And there might be even more treasure yet to be found. Picking up the silvery egg, he found it to be heavy. He shook it by his ear, but nothing rattled, although there was a low-pitched buzzing and ticking coming from somewhere inside it. Could the silver egg house the works of some kind of clock? And was the metal skin truly of silver? It did have the appearance, but not the feel; it felt more like some kind of glass. Nor did there appear to be any way of opening the thing; there were no traces of a seam anywhere on it.

Simon sat back and thought. If he did manage to break into the ovoid by main force, he might well smash or at least damage whatever was inside buzzing and ticking. But then, he had more than enough gold and silver coins to take him back to his Sussexshire farm in style, so why worry about damaging some treasure so singular that he might not dare to try to sell it, anyway, for fear of his life, since he was still half convinced that his find was a royal treasure repository of some kind. Of course, he could merely take those objects he could easily use and leave the rest, perhaps even close up the coffin that was not a coffin and return it to its niche in the wall. He could do that, but then he never would know just what the silvery-glassy egg-shaped casket contained.

Simon's curiosity got the best of him. Lifting the smooth egg from out the coffin, he placed it on the stone step beside him and began to tap on it with his oaken cudgel, increasing the force of his blows only gradually, since he expected the thing to soon shatter. But it did no such thing, so he stood up, took a two-handed grip on the cudgel, and swung it down with all his might, as he might have swung a maul.

Arsen Ademian figured that the booze had finally done it; he must surely be hallucinating. At one moment, he had been stretched out on the deep carpet on his back, absently stroking his oud, his sole remaining grip on reality. At the next, he was slammed down on his back on hard ground, as if he had fallen several feet. Above him, the gilt-plaster decorations of the suite's ceiling had gone, to be replaced by the waving branches of what looked from the distinctive leaves to be a maple tree!

He lay stunned for a moment, hearing screams and shouts all about him, in voices he recognized . . . and in one that he did not. Then he sat up, the precious oud tumbling unnoticed from his lap . . . and decided immediately that he was not just hallucinating-drunk, he had lost his marbles completely and was probably sitting in truth in a padded cell somewhere, maybe in Eastern State Hospital for the Insane in Williamsburg, Virginia.

John the Greek stumbled up to Arsen, limping, still holding a huge leather-and-iron-bound volume. "What in hell is going on? Where are we, Arsen? What happened? Were we drugged and brought out here, do you think?"

Ignoring the man and the questions, Arsen looked around him. He and John were in a smallish clearing surrounded by brush and treeboles. He was sitting in a pile of half-rotted leaves, their sogginess soaking the seat of his pants with a cold moisture. A small stone building sat across from him at the other side of the clearing; it looked old and weather-worn and totally lacked windows or any other visible openings on the two sides he could see.

Somewhere off in the forest to his right, the girls were all screaming their silly heads off, and somewhere closer by, voices he could recognize as those of his cousins, Al and Haigh, were praying aloud and loudly in church Armenian.

Then, from out of the hidden side of the little stone building, a man emerged. He was shaggy and unkempt and dressed in tattered rags. He grasped a heavy-looking length of dark wood in one hand, but he looked around him with an expression every bit as dazed as Arsen felt. He needed a bath, too, badly. Arsen could smell him the full width of the clearing.

"Arsen . . ." began John the Greek, plaintively.

But Arsen interrupted him, knowing beforehand just what the plaint would be. "John, *I* don't know where we are or what happened or how we got here any better than you do, dammit! Maybe that guy does, though. Let's go ask him, huh?"

Arsen would have fallen back down when he stood up had the trunk of the maple tree not been close to hand. He felt dizzy for a minute, then a sharp pain commenced in his back, shoulders, and buttocks, as if somebody had beaten him across them with an ax handle. Nevertheless, he pushed away from the trunk and slowly hobbled toward the strange, shaggy, smelly man, John trailing after him.

Closer, he could detect wisps of pale smoke issuing up out of the little stone building to be borne away by an upper-air breeze that he could not feel.

At speaking distance, he said, "Mister, where in hell are we? Do you know why they brought us here? Do you work for whazizname, this archbishop fellow?"

By way of answer, the shaggy man shouted something Arsen could not understand and charged down upon him and John, his stick drawn back for an overhand blow. All pain forgotten, Arsen himself countercharged, running in under the crude weapon to grab the man's hard-muscled arm, take him on the hip, and throw him, very hard, to the ground. The violent stranger still managed to retain his grip on the stick, but when Arsen kicked him in the armpit, his next kick was able to send the stick spinning across the glade.

Seeing the man's left hand gliding toward his front midsection where Arsen thought he had spied a scabbarded knife of respectable size, he next kicked the man in the head. The stranger shuddered the entire length of his body, then became utterly limp.

"Jesus H. Christ!" exclaimed John the Greek. "Where in the devil did you learn to do *that*, Arsen? Did you kill him?"

"In the service, John, in Vietnam. I thought I'd forgot. I guess I got a better memory than I ever thought I had." He squatted and placed two fingers below the angle of his former opponent's jaw. "Naw, he's not dead. God, he stinks, though!"

Roughly, touching the man and his tatters only with his foot, he rolled the inert body over and disarmed it of the big knife. Then he walked on around the small building, but warily, the knife held ready for thrust or slash. There could well be another of the smelly man's kind inside.

THE THIRTEENTH

Only six or eight weeks were required to convince Timoteo di Bolgia that the only troops upon whom he and his employers could depend in any crisis were his own company, the Afriquan company, the fortress garrison, and, just possibly, King Tàmhas's personal bodyguards, the Fitzgerald Squadron. His attempts to impose real discipline—the firm foundation of which any army needs must be built—on the rascally *galloglaiches* and the unhung criminals who were known as *bonaghts* had resulted ultimately in mutinies, murders and attempted murders, and arson. These had of course been punished by hangings, floggings, and other corporal punishments, the impositions of which had bred large-scale desertions, with concomitant disappearances of weapons, equipment, and horses.

Therefore, Timoteo requested and almost immediately received an audience with the Papal legate, Giosuè di Rezzi, Archbishop of Munster. Di Bolgia had had a brief meeting with the frail, slender man shortly after his arrival in the Kingdom of Munster, but since then, Sir Ugo D'Orsini had been the condottiere's liaison with the representative of Rome and the Papacy. Sir Ugo accompanied di Bolgia to this second meeting.

The unnaturally pale little man greeted them both graciously enough, gave them and their purpose a quick blessing, saw them served with a decent wine and a tray of sweetmeats, then sat in silence, regarding them with pale gray eyes, his long, slender fingers steepled.

Thinking once again that this pitiful specimen of a man was even the more pitiful when compared to what he, Timoteo, recalled of the legate's illustrious elder brother, Captain Barone Mario di Rezzi, a now deceased Bolognese condottiere of some note in the last generation, rich in goods, honor, and victories won, di Bolgia went directly to the sore point of the matter.

"Your grace di Rezzi, the so-called army of King Tàmhas is no such thing. It would better be called what it is—a war band made up of the dregs of society, banditti, murderers, parricides, rapists, robbers, sneak thieves, and cutpurses, along with an unwholesome assortment of berserkers and out-and-out madmen. I have been a soldier, have lived mostly in camps and garrisons, for the most of my life, your grace, and I never have seen a worse aggregation of men than this Royal Munster Army. I have seen them do things in broad daylight that dumb beasts would be ashamed to do in the dark of a moonless night!

"They possessed no shred of order or discipline when I arrived here in Munster, and discipline is, as your grace assuredly knows, the keystone in the arch of victory. My attempts—mild ones, at that—to instill discipline upon them have resulted in mutiny, murder, arson, executions, and floggings, and now in a vast number of thefts and desertions.

"Naturally, the king is mightily displeased; any man would be to watch his war band dissipate like dew under a hot sun. Naturally, he blames me directly for everything. That too is to be expected, since I am both a foreigner and a stranger. But he had best not be too openly wroth at me, your grace, for I and my companies are now the only troops left that can be depended upon to defend him and whatever portion of his realm can be held.

"Which point, your grace, brings me to what I really sought audience with you to say. Your grace, should King Brian march south again this summer, Munster is his for the plucking. There simply is no way in which I can hold off an army of the size his is reputed to be with the force now available to me, not for any longer than it took King Brian's army to surround that Munster force and butcher it, and I have never been of a suicidal bent, your grace.

"Now, all things considered and weighed out, it is just possible that this capital city could be held, especially in light of the fact that *Impressionant* and the other ships give us the complete command of the river and we thus are guaranteed a means of resupply while under siege. But are we to contemplate even this, we must start to work, *now*, which means that your grace must have words with King Tàmhas, immediately."

"You have not then talked with his highness, my son?" asked the archbishop mildly. "You know far more of military matters than do I, alas. Surely your words would weigh much more heavily upon his decisions than would mine own."

"The royal ass won't listen to me!" Timoteo burst out. "Your grace, in spite of all I've told King Tàmhas, he still insists that he will meet King Brian on the field at his border and there defeat him in open battle. *With what*, pray tell, your grace? My company, the Afriquans, his fancy, combed, and curried bodyguard squadron, and the artillerists at the fortress are all the field troops he has left, by all that's holy! And the artillerists are standing rock-firm on the last jot and tittle of their damned contract and refusing to serve guns or to fight anyplace save in that fortress or on the city walls. By the four-and-twenty balls of the Twelve Apostles, now, I—"

"*Duce di Bolgia!*" The little man had come upright in his armchair, his pale eyes blazing with fire, his previously mild voice now cracking like a whiplash. "Soldiers are infamous blasphemers, but you will never do such again in my hearing! Do I make myself clear? You might also think of the good of your soul when you are out of my hearing.

"As regards the military situation, I can understand your predicament. King Tàmhas is not only stubborn and overly prideful, but stupid, as well, and that is a bad combination in any man of rank or station, but calamitous in a ruling monarch, as you have seen. Yes, I shall speak with him and his equally stubborn and stupid advisers—bad blood in all of the

Fitzgeralds; I think it comes from too much inbreeding—but I think my successes will be no more than were yours.

"Meanwhile, please order Sir Marc to ready his fastest vessel for sea. I shall send a message to his eminence D'Este urging that you and your force be withdrawn from Munster because the situation has become untenable. I and my staff and household will begin to make ready to depart with you, so please make allowances to carry us on one of your ships, my son.

"Also, knowing the king as I have come to know him, it might be wise to gather all of your force and the Afriquan horse back into the city, close to the ships and the fortress, lest King Tàmhas decide to make military slaves of you all."

Rupen's very first mission for the Central Intelligence Agency was also very nearly his last trip of any kind for anyone. In the end, he had to use the PPK, the spring knife, *and* the special pen, not to even mention several grenades and an ancient Thompson that almost literally fell into his hands. But what he fought and killed for was his own life and that of Mineo, not—as they all clearly believed—for the group of whom he had overseen delivery of the consignment of modern weapons. Those people left a very bad taste in his mouth, and he very much regretted that there had not been a way for him to allow the government troops to mete out to them the deaths that they so richly deserved. He, along with most Americans, had always considered that country and its government to be allies and friends of long standing, and he could not imagine why an American agency would be arming fanatics to destabilize or bring down that government. Questions along that line directed at the CIA types, however, brought invariably the same answers, which all boiled down to their contention that he had no need to know and would be best advised to keep his mouth shut if that was all he could think of to ask.

He went back to arms dealing and hoped to God that he never again would hear of the CIA or any other clandestine organization of his own or of anyone else's government, for it was far too easy to get killed playing the games that those types customarily played. Of course, the arms markets were not what they had been eight or nine years before, when he first had entered them. For one thing, those few World War II and earlier cartridge weapons that were still around and occasionally offered to him and other buyers were generally in sad shape or worse, having been through war after war after insurrection and uprising, mostly fought out in damp or dusty places by simple people whose idea of weapons maintenance most often came down to keeping the bayonet sharp, while trusting in God or Allah or Buddha or Krishna to keep the firearm functional, regardless of filthy actions, fouled bores, and total absence of lubrication.

It now was a red-letter day when Rupen received word that somewhere in some dark corner or sub-basement of an armory, in a forgotten warehouse or a deserted military depot, or in a long-sealed cave on a Pacific atoll. fine weapons in decent condition had been turned up and were for sale to the highest bidder.

Most of his work, these days, had to do with matching buyer with seller in complicated deals involving jet planes, tanks, artillery pieces, helicopters, military wheeled transport of all kinds, rockets, and even the occasional small warship. Rupen was tired unto death with trotting hither and yon all over the world. It was a young man's profession, and Rupen was forty-three years old.

He was vacationing in the ancient and beautiful city of Syracuse, Sicily, when he made his decision to wait a few weeks, tie up a few loose ends in Europe, then go back to Virginia for Christmas and announce his immediate resignation to Kogh and Bagrat.

The week or two here and there was just not enough, besides which, he rarely got all of those short respites from business; he was just too well known, and customers or their agents followed him and pestered him wherever he tried to hide for a few days. He was also tired unto death of spending his every waking or sleeping minute of life with a pistol either holstered on him or within easy reach, like some movie-version spy. Not that he had not at times had pressing need of his personal armaments, for not everyone liked him, not by any means. He was an American, after all, and Americans were becoming less and less popular around the world that their generosity had virtually rebuilt from the ruins of World War II. He moved and worked strictly as an apolitical businessman, which factor made him automatically suspect in the eyes of the more extreme factions of both left-wing and right-wing governments and movements. There were also the sore losers, sometime customers who had come out second best despite infusions of modern armaments and equipment and who found it much more satisfying to blame the arms and the persons who had gotten them those arms than to place the onus on bankrupt ideologies and ill-led or mutinous troops. A subgenre of this species was the ones who felt that they had lost because they had *not* been in receipt of arms either through lack of cash, lack of credit, or both, and who felt strongly that there must be one more death for their cause: Rupen Ademian's.

Which was one reason that Rupen vacationed so often in Sicily or Naples—he felt safe in those places. His original contacts with the Honored Society had been through Seraphino Mineo, back in 1960. Against the advice of many well-meaning people, he since had consistently refused to do any business with or for them and, oddly enough, thereby gained the sincere respect of the upper echelons. They had not only refused numerous contracts to kill him, but had seen to it that he received detailed information on those who had sought to employ them to assassinate him, often complete with color photos, make and color and year of auto, and passport numbers.

When he made his usual daily call to Virginia, a sobbing operator put him through directly to Kogh, rather than to Bagrat. "Kogh, what the hell are you doing up there? Has something happened I should know about?"

"Fucking-A-right, it has!" His brother's agitated voice crackled over the undersea cables. "About an hour ago, JFK was shot in Dallas, Texas. It was on TV, for Chrissakes. A sniper got him in the head—nobody knows whether he's dead or alive, now. Honest, Rupen, he was shot right on TV!''

"Who would—" began Rupen, but Kogh cut him off, brusquely.

"Hell, I don't know. There's all kinda rumors, though. Some say the Cubans, some say the Russkis or hide-out SS or American Nazis or beatniks or the John Birch Society, even. Anyhow, I was thinking it might be a damn good idea for you to get back here as fast as you can get on a plane. If you can't get on a commercial flight, hire a plane of your own. We'll pay for it. Just get back Stateside, Rupen. God alone knows what's gonna happen next.''

Six months after the demise of President John F. Kennedy, Rupen Ademian was back in Italy, but in an entirely different capacity, this time around. The American Civil War Centennial had bred a thriving market for shooting reproductions of nineteenth-century caplock weapons—ranging up from Philadelphia derringers to full-size field cannon—and his firm had sent him over to try to strike a deal with certain of his contacts in the Italian arms manufactories involving production of these reproduction weapons at a cost less than that charged to them by American arms companies, with their millstones of higher overheads and production costs, and grasping, predatory unions.

Rupen was authorized to place orders for revolving pistols of .36 and .44 caliber, a revolving, fixed-stock carbine of .44 caliber, and a .58 caliber rifled musket in two barrel lengths, to start; he also was to keep eyes and ears peeled for anyone with a good idea for faster, cheaper, and safer production of musket and pistol percussion caps.

Bagrat Ademian had become a fanatic enthusiast of blackpowder, muzzle-loading shooting, driving or flying off weekend after weekend to meets and shoots and encampments all over the country. His had been the idea—and a very profitable one it had been—to develop a sideline of reproduction bayonets, powder flasks, bullet molds, cap boxes, and other accessories which were sold through the old mail-order retail outlet.

Now, Bagrat wanted his own line of firearms, but the bids he had solicited from American manufacturers had slammed right through the ceiling, and he had strongly doubted that he could have unloaded them even had he sold them at a hefty loss. That had been when he had started to chivvy Rupen into accompanying him to black-powder shooting exhibitions.

At the first, his elder brother had been very skeptical of an involvement of the firm. "Look Bagrat, in another year, this whole Civil War thing will be just a memory, and there we'll be, stuck with a carload or two of cheap reproduction charcoal burners that won't even have any collector value. Unless you were thinking of doctoring them to look like originals? Is that what you have on your devious, Yankee-Armenian mind, little brother? Or were you of a mind to convert them all to floor lamps and bookends, huh?"

But gradually, Bagrat had won him over. "Look, Rupen, what you've seen is just the tip of the iceberg, man! Its thousands of black-powder buffs don't belong to clubs or teams or anything, and others—lots of 'em—that collect repros and never shoot 'em, because they're priced out of collecting the originals. Then there's rich collectors who buy repros so they won't be tempted to try and shoot their real ones and blow them up, like as not. There's *real* moneybags, even, pays an outfit down in Tennessee to cast *cannons* for 'em—shooting-type cannons."

"What, pray tell, do these nuts use for ammunition?" asked Rupen dryly, "Old bowling balls?"

"Aw, naw," replied Bagrat, dead serious. "The cannons ain't *that* big. Mosta 'em shoots frozen orange juice cans fulla concrete; the bigger ones uses beer cans."

"So you want me to stump all over Europe looking up bellfounders, eh? Listen, Bagrat, there are people over there who do not like me at all, but at least they all consider me to be sane, as of now. If I start soliciting bids on casting bronze muzzle-loading cannon, the next thing you're likely to hear is that I'm in a soft room in Switzerland, courtesy of my European friends.''

"No, no, Rupen, I don't want bids on cannons . . . well, not yet. anyhow," Bagrat assured him. Then he told him exactly what he did want to start, queried the vastly experienced Rupen as to the best possible bets for reproducing the weapons, and, after some lengthy and detailed discussion, agreed with him that Italian firms might be what was needed in this instance.

Despite Rupen's misgivings, despite fierce competition for the American market from subsidiaries of massive Interarmco, up in Alexandria, Virginia, and a veritable host of others, the first shipments of Italian-made reproductions sold like the proverbial hotcakes, and the newest branch of the Ademian Enterprises tree, Confederate States Armaments, was off with flying colors.

The eldest Ademian brother had managed to acquire only about twelve percent of the Rappahannock operations in the ten years he had worked for it, but most all of his traveling had been paid by the firm or reimbursed to him later; the vast purchasing power of the U.S. dollar worldwide in the fifties and early sixties had always assured him of first-class accommodations at very reasonable dollar rates on those things he had himself paid, and what with salary, commissions, dividends on his little block of stock, and a few gifts that various customers had pressed on him over the years, he had managed over the decade past to sock away a fair chunk of money, which, as it turned out, was a damned good thing.

For Kogh Ademian, president and chairman of the board of Ademian Enterprises, Incorporated, was dead-set against CSA from the very outset. "Look, fellas, we're doing damn good on the damn international arms deals, so it's no need at all for us to keep peddling old guns or new ones, either, by mail around the damn country. Just remember that damn crazy Commie bastard Oswald shot poor John Kennedy with a fuckin' Carcano 6.5mm carbine—thank God it wasn't one *I* imported! Though for all any of us know, it was our ammo the murderin' lunatic used—and you can bet your sweet tootsie that the damn liberals in Congress aren't gonna rest til they've got it made illegal to sell imported guns to anybody 'cept cops and the military. Then, I'll give you odds these damn socialist one-worlder bastards keeps on pushing to where it'll be illegal for most Americans to even own a gun of any kind.

"So if you wanta do this crazy thing, Bagrat, you better figger on doin' it without one cent of Ademian Enterprises backing, you hear me?"

Thus, Rupen cleaned out his various accounts of all save a bit under fifty-seven thousand dollars, but he came into Confederate States Armaments, Inc., as a full partner and the executive vice-president of the new firm. He it was who persuaded a not unwilling Bagrat that, as they now were in no way, shape, or form connected to Ademian Enterprises, it might be to their best business interests to move the operation to another part of the state, and what better location for a firm playing upon the Confederate States theme than a location or at least a mailing address in the city that had been the capital of the Confederate States of America: Richmond.

Boghos—now grown chubby and jowly—and Mariya—still slim and toothsome as a girl, despite four children and a regimen of truly epicurean meals—would not hear of his staying at a hotel while looking for a location for Confederate States Armaments in Richmond or its environs. Rupen accepted the hositality with not a little trepidation. It had been around fifteen years since he had lived in a stable, home-type environment with relatives, and he was not at all certain that he could readapt, or sure that he wanted to do so.

Not that he thought he would be in any way cramped in the home of his sister and brother-in-law, for Boghos's lucrative medical practice, his astute investments, and the goodly chunk of Ademian Enterprises stock willed to Mariya by her mother had combined to give the family a current net worth of between three and five million dollars, and their present house reflected it.

The house sat on a bluff above the James River. There were two master suites and six bedrooms, each with a private bath. The eight other rooms in the main house included a spacious parlor and formal dining room with a butler's pantry connecting it to the huge kitchen, a family room, a library, a music room, Boghos's study, and a sprawling, tile-floored Florida room for Mariya's legions of plants. Pantry, freezer lockers, and wine cellar were in the basement and connected to the kitchen by both stairs and a dumbwaiter. The basement also housed the laundry room and Boghos's big-game trophies and guns and cameras.

When Boghos had finished showing him through the two-and-a-half-story brick mansion, Rupen's first comment was, "Talk about flaunting what you got, Brother Boghos, you live in a testament to visible affluence, you know that? I know you've got a chef, but how many other servants does it take to keep this museum shipshape? I know Mariya couldn't possibly do it all alone."

"Stephanie, the housekeeper, is the wife of Etienne, the chef you just met," replied Boghos. "We had them before this place was even built, but now they live here, on the grounds, in that brick bungalow you passed as you drove in; they're Algerian-French and more old friends than mere employees. Stephanie has a couple of nigra girls to help her five days a week.

"At Mariya's insistence, we employ a gardener, fellow name of Lemuel Steptoe and his son, who live up the road in Manakin. And then there's my chauffeur cum bodyguard cum the best goddamned automotive mechanic anybody has ever had . . . but hell, Rupen, you know him! Seraphino Mineo, the hard man my attorney got to help us with that Evelyn Mangold business, years ago, though for some reason I never pried into, that's not the name he's using now."

"What does he call himself these days, Boghos? Mr. Cobra?"

Boghos shook his head. "No, all his IDs are in the name of Anonimo Beccacciniero. Maybe that was his real name all along, huh?"

"Not hardly," said Rupen. "The literal translation of that name comes out as 'Nameless Sniper.' He's a deeper man than you think he is, Boghos. The last time I saw him was in 1960, and he then was working for the . . . well, let's just say he was with an American intelligence group. How long has he been with you?"

"About two and a half years, off and on, Rupen."

"Off and on, Boghos? What do you mean?" asked Rupen.

"Well, there have been two or three times when he's had to leave for Italy to visit his mother, who seems to be in very poor health. Those trips usually take him about a month. Also, he has relatives in New York City and he drives up there every so often, but he's never gone more than a week at a time on those trips."

Rupen just nodded. "And I'll bet he leaves when he leaves at the drop of a hat, with little or no prior warning, eh, Boghos?"

"Why, yes . . . usually, Rupen. How did you know?"

Rupen did not answer the question, just asked another. "And why do you put up with an employee who disappears from time to time with no notice?"

"Because when he is around he's invaluable, Rupen. I told you, he's a fantastic mechanic, and with our nine cars, plus a pickup and two jeeps, he earns what I pay him and more. And if that were not enough, Anonimo saved my life last year, in Alaska.

"It was this brute here, Rupen." The doctor gestured toward the mounted head of what must have been a near-record brown bear. "I'd dropped him from a stand at about a hundred yards with my Westley-Richards .425, then the guide and I trotted over and he put a soft-nose .30-06 into him at close range, while I was setting up my Leica on a folding tripod for a remote shot.

"All of a sudden, that 'dead' bear roared and jumped up, coughing blood, and knocked that guide ass over biscuit and started shuffling toward me. Rupen, the only weapon of any kind that I had on me was a belt knife. The Westley-Richards was back at my stand, the guide had rolled to the bottom of a gully, and the bear was between me and his rifle."

"What did you do, Boghos?" asked Rupen.

"I wet my pants, for one thing," admitted the physician, without shame. "And I think I started to pray. The stand that Anonimo was on was more than two hundred yards away, you see. We'd been communicating by walkie-talkie. Mine was back with my rifle and the guide's was on him at the bottom of the gully.

"The bear was only ten feet away from me—we measured that distance, later—when he squalled and reared up on his hind legs. Then, just about the time I heard the first shot, the second one sent the fur and tissue flying, blew out a section of his spine at the very base of his skull. He dropped like he'd been poleaxed, almost at my feet."

"And it was Cobr . . . Anonimo who shot him, at two hundred yards?" queried Rupen.

Boghos nodded. "He apologized, later, for making me wait so long, Rupen. His scope wasn't working right and it had taken him a couple of minutes to get the thing off and flip the open sights up, then make the shot. Two hundred yards, Rupen, a downhill shot at a moving target, with open, iron sights; the first shot smashed the bear's left shoulder, the second one killed him outright! Rupen, even should I find out that that man is actually Adolf Hitler's bastard son, he still would have that apartment over the garage, a decent income, and work when he wants it, those things, plus my friendship and deep respect."

"And where is this paragon of virtue now?" asked Rupen. The shoe was on the other foot with him and Mineo-Cobra-Beccacciniero. He'd shot and likely killed several men to save the mysterious Italian's life on that CIA business years back, not the other way about.

"He took the pickup into Richmond to bring back some parts for the Jag. God, but those Limeys are slow—six months ago those parts were ordered!"

"Mere imported sports cars and luxury sedans, Boghos?" mocked Rupen. "Tch, tch, tch! Don't you know that one is not truly of the landed gentry until one's holdings include a stable of real thoroughbred horses, usually horses with pedigrees longer than one's own?"

*   *   *

The search for the ten missing guests—Arsen and his
group—went on for three days. Horsemen, dismounted men
with keen-nosed hounds, all worked out from the center of
the archbishop's estate in ever-widening circles. But no single
trace of the six men and four women was turned up.

Neither Rupen nor red-haired Jenny Bostwick could think
of any slightest reason why Arsen and Haigh and the rest
would have left without first contacting them.

"Der Hal," said Rupen earnestly, "I just don't think
they'd have taken off like this, not if they'd had a choice in
the matter. For one reason, the biggest and best reason, we
all of us have a lot of trouble even understanding the dialect
you folks speak, much less trying to speak it ourselves. Even
to my ear, the language you all call English sounds more to
me like a bastard concoction of Plattdeutsch, Old French, and
Lowland Gaelic; I think I'm finally getting the hang of speaking it fairly fluently, but neither Arsen nor any of the rest are
blessed with my linguistic abilities. So could it be possible
that they were taken away by force?"

"Now it is just barely possible," Archbishop Harold told
Bass Foster an hour or so later, in private, "that they snapped
back to where they were projected from the same way your
house eventually did. But I sincerely doubt that that is what
happened to them, for if it is, why then Rupen and the other
woman would have snapped back as well.

"No, Bass, I think that the threats of a dying woman are
being carried out. I think that Gamebird has gotten a second
projector into Whyffler Hall, that they have used it—possibly,
unknowingly—to project this latest batch of unfortunates God
alone knows where, for as I told you long ago, even to the
projector staff at Gamebird, this project is still in only an
advanced experimental stage.

"I also think that you had best inform your host to be
ready to ride out for Strathtyne on tomorrow's dawn. This
time, I shall be accompanying you, along with my own
guards and servants and staff. I think we'll take along Rupen
Ademian, too, if you don't mind—who knows but what his

lifetime of experiences so different from our own and his flexible mind will be of value to us."

"Hal," began Bass, "the king expects me to—"

"Yes, yes, that Irish business. Don't worry, I'll send a galloper to his majesty immediately, telling him that I have preempted you and your services for a few more weeks on matters every bit as urgent as the earlier ones. There'll then be no difficulty, you'll see."

What with the archbishop's horse litter and coach and wagons, the shorter, faster, but far more rugged cross-country route used by Bass and the *galloglaiches* on their last trip up to Whyffler Hall was out of the question this time around. Perforce, the long, slow column had to make its way up the Pennines "road" down which Bass had traveled on a winter trek that had removed the then-vital, then-endangered Royal Gunpowder Works from Whyffler Hall to the relative safety of York. The road which the Scots army had used both on its march to and its retreat from the Battle of Hexham.

The weather turned foul only a single day out of York and so remained for all save the last two days of the trip, with rain, mist, fog, and unseasonably cold, biting winds to add to their wet discomfort in the higher elevations of the mountain chain.

Twice during the protracted journey, they were attacked by robber bands who, what with the poor visibility and the cloaked and hooded manner in which everyone was riding, did not until it was far too late realize just what manner of beasts they were awakening. The cold, wet, miserable *galloglaiches* proved themselves ever more than willing to impart to these intemperate Sassenach amateur banditti lessons that were almost invariably fatal in nature.

Bass's order that some few of the would-be ambushers from the second attack be allowed to escape was fruitful, in that there were no more attacks of any nature for the remainder of the trip, much to the disgust of Sir Calum, Sir Liam, and the rest of the *galloglaiches*, who all had relished the occasional light amusement.

Sight of the distant, ancient tower of Whyffler Hall on the

horizon was very welcome to each and every member of the
weary, dreary, saturated, and wind-burned column. Welcome,
despite the fact that it meant for most of them only a pallet of
straw in some unheated outbuilding or a tent or, at best, leave
to sleep in the great hall on a bench or under a table. At least
the straw would be dry and the roof would keep it so and
their cloaks would provide warmth with the icy-toothed winds
kept at bay by the walls.

But the *galloglaiches*, other troops, and servants were
allotted scant time to rest after their long, difficult ride.
Hardly were they dismounted when the duke and the archbishop had them in the old tower keep, hacking once more at
that same wall to the ensorcelled chamber that many of them
had but so lately walled up.

Clearance of the walls this time brought the same pulsing
pale-greenish glow. But it brought something else, as well,
on this second occasion, something discomforting for all its
common familiarity—the strong reek of a battlefield, the
stench of corporeal corruption, of corpses left too long unburied.

"I thought you said that you and your men buried the body
of Colonel Dr. Jane Stone," said the archbishop, who had
once been Dr. Harold Kenmore, wrinkling his nose against
the assault of the stink from below.

"And so we did, Hal. We buried her out beyond the hall
privies, where the dead rievers of Laird David Scott's force
lie."

"Then who," demanded the archbishop, "in the name of
all that's holy is rotting down there below us, Bass?"

The Duke of Norfolk meticulously checked the primings of
his pistols, then grasped a torch and moved into the archway.
"I don't know, Hal, not now, but I sure as hell mean to find
out."

"Can you not think of any reason why the ground level, below us here, would have suddenly flooded, Geoff?" said Sir Bass Foster, Duke of Norfolk, Earl of Rutland, and Baron of Strathtyne, to his seneschal and castellan for his barony, Sir Geoffrey Musgrave. "Clearly, it's not been prone to flooding ere this, else rats would not have tunneled under that dirt floor in such numbers. Why, when I was down there on my last trip, that floor was pocked with dozens of burrow openings."

Musgrave scratched at his scar-furrowed, balding scalp. "Well, your grace, as your grace may have noted when he rode in yesterday, Henny Turnbull and me, we had decided that rainwater had commenced a-pooling up too much in the rear court, so we had set some lads a-digging aside the old tower keep for to put in a gravel sump, but then this last month it's been near steady rain and nae work could be done on't."

"That could well be our answer," said Bass. "And none of you thought that channeling a new drainage pattern in the rear court might flood the ground floor of the tower, Geoff?"

"Why, o' course not, your grace. Ever mon aboot knows that the foundations of the auld tower keep goes clear doon tae bedrock." In his agitation, Musgrave was occasionally slipping back into his Northumbrian country brogue. "In the hunnerts of years it's stood, ne'er could ony thrice-domned Scot dig deep enough for tae undermine't!"

"Maybe so, maybe not, Geoff; and even if so, the shifting of but a single foundation stone could leave more than enough of an opening for a flood of water to enter and percolate up through that dirt floor.

"All right, Geoff, forget about what's past. It's damned good for you and everyone else hereabouts that it happened as it did. Those three men were evil men and far better dead than alive."

"But your grace, please . . . what kilt them? I watched the three of their rotten corpses stripped and nae single mark was on them."

With a hand signal to Bass, the archbishop took over. "Look you, Sir Geoffrey, suffice it to say that great power, deadly power, lay in the square metal device and in the silver plate on which it rested. They put that deadly power into the water in which they were partially submerged, and when those three men were transported near knee-deep into that water, the power stopped their hearts and so killed them.

"You may call the power alchemy or sorcery or witchcraft, to yourself, but you are never to make mention of this incident to anyone else—man or woman or child—save those of us here at this table. For the remainder of your life, on your honor, you are to maintain your silence. Do you understand me, Sir Geoffrey?"

"Aye, your grace," answered Musgrave humbly. " 'pon me oath as a belted knicht, 'twill be."

"Now, Geoff," began Bass, "whence came the slate with which the newer portions of Whyffler Hall are roofed over?"

"From a auld quarry, your grace, once in the lands o' the Heron family, it lay; but noo it be a part o' your grace's own Barony o' Strathtyne."

"Then find quarrymen quickly, Geoff, and see it reopened. You're to have loads of quarried slate delivered here to Whyffler Hall until his grace, Harold of York, indicates that there is enough. He will need stonemasons, too, all of them that you can locate and hire on.

"That matter aside, now, Geoff, answer me this: Is there a good source of really good potter's clay about?"

Musgrave wrinkled his brow, then said, "The best what I knows of is the claypits on the lands of Laird Michael Scott, fu' brother tae the late and unlamented Sir David Scott, but a gude mon, for a' that."

"Allright, Geoff, contact Laird Michael and tell him that I'll be wanting to buy more than a few wagonloads of his potter's clay. I'll leave you enough gold for the job."

"Your Grace's pardon," said Musgrave, with a worried frown, "as I said, Laird Michael be a gude mon and honest, but neither he nor I can speak for a' his relatives and retainers. Far better tae pay him for the clay in honest siller and let nae single Scott, Scott's man, or Scot suspect that there might be gold at Whyffler Hall."

Bass shrugged. "Very well, Geoff, you know this border far better than I do. You handle it your way. I'll not be here but a day or so more. I have king's business in the south.

"But his grace, the archbishop here, will be remaining for an indefinite period, he and Master Rupen Ademian. Try to do whatever they ask, unusual as the requests may be. I'm leaving a Spanish knight, Don Diego, from my staff to help you out here; he has managed his own estates, so he should have no difficulty in assuming some of your more mundane responsibilities, subject always to your approval, of course.

"When the archbishop and Master Ademian have completed that which they are remaining here to do, Don Diego and your lances will escort his grace back down the long road to York."

Sir Geoffrey nodded and essayed to finger the forelock that had moved far back on his head, now out of easy reach, "Aye, your grace, a' will be as your grace has ordered't."

As Bass Foster led his staff and *galloglaiches* down the long, cursive roadway toward the gate that pierced the wall circumscribing the old outer bailey of Whyffler Hall, the taste of the good brown ale that had filled the stirrup cup still on his lips and the adrenaline rising at the thought of the cross-country hellride that would put them all back in York considerably faster than they had proceeded from that city's environs, his musings lay with all that had gone before, as well as all that loomed on the near horizon.

"The first time that I rode out of here bound for York, it was behind Sir Francis Whyffler and his banner, with Buddy Webster on my one side and Professor William Collier on the other. That was not so long ago, either, but now I'm the only one of that leading party left. His grace of Northumberland, Duke Sir Francis Whyffler, is now his majesty's voice at the court of Egon, the Holy Roman Emperor and husband to Arabella Whyffler, Sir Francis's only daughter; Buddy was hurt so badly at the Battle of Hexham that he no longer can sit a horse in comfort; while Bill Collier, after turning on me, his wife, the king, and England is now howling away his life in some Scottish monastery's madhouse.

"And then there was the last time I rode out of here to war for the king against those Crusaders still left on English soil, in the south. I was already Lord Commander of the Royal Horse by then, though the only titles I held were both Empire titles, *Freiherr* and *Markgraf*. That was when a part of my following was Sir Andrew, Laird Eliott's wild pack of Scot rievers. Little did I then think or even suspect that there existed troops that could frighten those devils incarnate, much less that I would one day be the chosen war leader of those troops. Yet here I ride at the head of half the squadron of the Royal Tara *Gallowglasses*, the selfsame squadron that smashed, rolled up the vaunted Spanish heavy horse at the Battle of Bloody Rye.

"Every damned way I turn in this savage world, titles and allegiances and honors keep falling on me, binding me more and ever more tightly into a mold that I don't feel fitted for, not really, deep down. I guess that, deep down, that old, peace-loving Bass Foster, who lived in a house by the side of the Potomac River with a splendid woman named Carol— Carol, dear Carol, ever loved, never really forgotten—and sometimes let her talk him into driving to D.C. to take part in protests against a war that seemed to be unwinnable, is still down there somewhere deep yelling and screaming his head off every time that this surface Bass Foster gets another title or whatnot for being an accomplished killer of men.

"What would've happened if Carol had lived, I wonder? Well, I never would've been projected here, for one thing. She would've had us two and the cats all packed up and on the road in the jeep headed for higher ground long before the floodcrest got within twenty miles of the house. Her obsessive need to work for the betterment of the suffering masses did not at any time include any slightest wish to risk her own life or health or comforts."

In her own particular way, Carol had been easy to love, and he had dearly loved her for the too-brief time that God had given them together, but that was not to say that he had not recognized her faults. She had been a left liberal of the born-to-wealth, Brie-and-chablis crowd, and she had been every bit as hypocritical as any of them in her often-spouted and completely unworkable socialistic-Utopian schemes.

Carol would not have lasted for long in this world. Herself born to old money and all that went with a distinguished patronymic in Tidewater Virginia, she had nothing more than a scathing contempt for anyone bearing a title of nobility. Elective titles impressed her even less, unless the bearers were of a similar background and of views similar to her own fuzzy theories of egalitarianism, justice, and the need for social change.

Krystal was like Carol in some ways, which was probably a large part of the reason that she and Bass meshed so quickly upon that traumatic arrival in this world. But also because of those ways in which she was like Carol, plus a few ways in which she was most uniquely herself, he knew that he was losing her through his frequent and long-term absences in the king's service.

"Maybe," he thought, while the long legs of the hunter he was astride today ate up the ground and distance, "I should accede to her frequent demands that I pack her along with me wherever I have to go, whenever I'm ordered there. As she's said often enough, a good many noble officers do just that, taking wives and mistresses—ammunition-wives, they're called by the troopers and gun men—along on campaigns.

"What she just can't seem to realize is that the field camp of an army in this world is in no way, shape, or form like any army camps she probably recalls from our world . . . that is, the world we came from. Any camp here, no matter how good the location chosen, no matter how good the weather, has inevitably become nothing less than a pesthole within less than two weeks' time, breeding farms of dysentery, cholera, typhus, typhoid, tetanus, lung infections, poxes, internal parasites, noxious insects, and God alone knows what else. Only the very toughest men and women survive long in this world's armies, not because of combat, but because of the conditions under which most of them live when they're not in battle, that is, most of the time. And I can't see exposing Krystal to it.

"Of course, it can be changed. I've already effected some of those changes in my own cavalry camps. I did it first with the *galloglaiches* and then I let them enforce compliance on the rest of the troopers, most of whom are rightly scared shitless of the *galloglaiches*, to start out.

"Every ranking personage who chances by remarks on how very clean and sweet-smelling my permanent cavalry camp is, and there's damn good reason that it is, too. Two six-foot straddle trenches for each sixty troopers and harsh punishments of those caught relieving themselves elsewhere; pits adjacent to the horse lines for collection of shoveled-up horsebiscuits; and other pits to be filled with offal, wastewater, food scraps, and the like. On my strict orders, stray swine are chivvied out of camp whenever they wander in. I allow dogs and cats around because they tend to go after rats and mice and also because the men like to have them about, but each unit is under standing orders to keep its areas clean of canine and feline droppings, trash, and discarded clothing.

"And it's *working*, dammit, it's working for me and my command. Illness and common camp diseases are way down in the reports I receive. Few of the minor injuries that troopers suffer in the course of drill or in handling spirited horses wind up in lockjaw or worse, these days. And since I made them start boiling their water for a quarter hour before they ingested it, dysentery has become infrequent in camp.

"My next project, once I can get this Irish business, whatever it turns out to be, behind me, is to try to get my troopers and my officers, too, for that matter, into the habit of bathing a little more often. Then, maybe, into changing their linens and washing them, rather than wearing them until they rot off, and then just throwing the filthy rags away. But even just the bathing—if I can get it started—should cut down the incidences of boils and festered sores and skin rashes that the troopers all suffer now to greater and lesser degrees in their crotches and their armpits.

"Now, if the Welsh and English and Scots troopers who've been indoctrinated in my cavalry camp carry these new-fangled ways back home with them, deaths and permanent crippling from disease can be significantly lowered throughout this kingdom and parts of Scotland, as well, and maybe then I'll feel like I've done a bit more for the world in which my little son will grow up and live out his life than simply introduce some more effective ways of making war and killing."

During the course of the three weeks of slow, ox-pace journey following the supposed madman's revealing of his true, noble identity and his tragic ensorcellment, Abbot Fergus spent more and more of his time in converse with the English earl, riding beside the cart that bore the bear cage during the days and sitting near to it and its occupant in the night camps.

A younger son of very minor nobility—his elder brother was a knight as their father had been before him, holding a few, poor acres in feoff from the Earl of Ayr in return for service—Fergus had earned elevation to abbot by his administrative abilities, not by his family's wealth or his own erudition, of which latter he owned painfully little. Therefore, being treated and bespoken as almost an equal by this wellborn, noble, obviously highly educated and widely traveled Sassenach lord was a singular and most exciting experience for the humble man.

Day after day, night after cold, firelit night, he sat as one enthralled to hear the tales of Earl Uilleam's travels to and exploits in distant lands and seas and cities of fable. And the very fact that his lordship insisted that he remain confined within the locked cage lest a fit of the sorcery-induced madness suddenly come upon him, that during emergences to wash his body and clothes in nearby burns and tiny lochs he be close guarded by sharp-eyed monks and brawny gillies, reassured Abbot Fergus enough of the poor, unfortunate, put-upon and gravely suffering man's good intentions that, upon request, he loaned his charge his razor and his precious bronze scissors that the earl might trim his beard and hair and filthy, cracked, and clawlike toe and fingernails. The man that emerged from beneath the gray-white hair looked indeed very noble to Abbot Fergus and even more so to the other monks, who began to treat their mad prisoner more like a captive nobleman and less like a dangerous wild beast.

Which treatment was a deadly error, for one night, while all of the men slept deeply after a heavier-than-usual meal, the mad earl slipped the single ankle fetter, exited the cage—apparently by picking the huge iron lock—and silently strangled Abbot Fergus where he slept. Armed then with the too-trusting abbot's razor, the madman slit the throat of a sleeping gillie and robbed his victim of all his effects—broadsword, targe, dirk, knives, tartan, shirt, rawhide brogues, wallet, and bonnet. Somehow avoiding notice of the drowsy, nodding horseguard, the madman saddled and bridled the dead abbot's big mule and stole out of camp, not mounting until he was well out of hearing distance. Then, taking a heading from the twinkling stars above, he put the mule to his best gait, riding southeastward, in the direction of the port of Glascow.

Professor William Collier vowed to himself as he rode the dead abbot's mule, dressed in the dead gillie's clothes, that there would be no bringing him to bay like some beast of the chase and dragging him, naked and beaten and chained, to be caged and ill treated, this time. No, now he was armed with substantially more than a rude club of a broken branch and a shard of sharp flint. If they came after him this time, he would either win free with sword and dirk or force them to kill him on the spot.

If he could win free, however, sell the mule and its gear for enough to provide himself with some better clothing and a passage to Ireland, he could find there the Papal legate, spin some tale that could not be checked out, then find a way to get his deserved revenge on that damned thankless usurper, Arthur III Tudor, and on the bastard who had been at the root of all his troubles and woes, Bass Foster.

"I am, after all," he thought as he rode, "the most intelligent and most highly educated man in this entire world. When once I've placed my innumerable talents at the service of the Roman Church, England and Wales will fall to Church armies armed with the weapons I'll show them how to make and use properly almost overnight. I'll not ask much in return, only a duchy or two, for my real reward will be watching Arthur and Foster slowly tortured almost to death, then crammed full of gunpowder and burned at the stake."

In far-southern Munster, most of King Brian's siege train and a portion of his army lay entrenched before the landward walls of Tàmhas'burh, the *ard-righ* himself being off on other pursuits with the rest of his army. He realized that the siege was really a standoff when his first and only, to date, assault on the city was bloodily repulsed by a deadly combination of impressive gunnery by the wall batteries and a two-pronged sally by hard-fighting mercenaries—horse backed up by foot—that took his assault force in both flanks and routed them to race pell-mell back down the hill to safety beyond the range of the wall guns.

Brian knew that the city could be supplied *ad infinitum* as long as King Tàmhas retained control of the river, but Brian's present fleet included only two galleons, neither of them as big, well found, and heavily armed as the aptly named *Impressionant*, and he was not about to risk them against the Papal fleet that now served the interests of his old enemy. He just thanked God on high that the topographical layout was such that the batteries of the ships could not be used to menace his land forces.

He comforted himself with the thought that, after all, he

had attempted to do it all peacefully. Shortly after his army's arrival before the city, he had sent in a sacred herald with an offer to withdraw from out all of Munster—save only the border lands that were never really a part of Munster to begin with and were the basic reason for the generations-long bad blood and feuding between Meath and Munster—did King Tàmhas but cede to the safekeeping of the cathederal vaults at Tara the Star of Munster.

King Tàmhas's answer had been to return the herald's body in bloody chunks, by way of an old-fashioned trebuchet, which action, to Brian's way of thinking, demonstrated the utter barbarity and complete lack of imagination in his enemy.

And so he had marched away about other business with the best, more mobile elements of the army of the *ard-righ*. Should he have need of the siege train elsewhere, he could always send for them. Meanwhile, why not let them squat before Tàmhas'burh, bottling the ever-troublesome Fitzger-alds safely up and living well off what their foragers could strip from the lands of Munster at no cost to Brian? He had forbidden them to fight against those within the walls unless first attacked, had left them a plenitude of gunpowder and a brace of priests who knew how to fabricate more, so they should be able to make it reasonably unpleasant for the folk of the city and their king with enough fighting men available to protect them from sallies, entrenchments that could be defended adequately from either side, and a ditched, ramparted, and well-fortified camp to house administration and supply functions.

At the age of five and thirty years, Ard-Righ Brian VIII had been engaged in war for two and twenty years in all parts of the island called Eire. Though mostly victorious, he had suffered a few defeats, but he had never lost an army or any substantial portion of one, or any single one of the precious and difficult-of-replacement bombards or siege cannon, and he had no slightest intention of now breaking that sterling practice through leaving his siege train undefended.

He marched off to attempt to overawe the smaller king-doms and kings, gain their Jewels of Sovereignty, allegiances, and the loan of the their armies, then redescend on Munster with more force than even the stubborn Fitzgeralds would dare to oppose. He knew that he had scant time to assemble the Seven Magical Jewels of Eire and could but wish that he had a second army.

For many a long week after the Duke of Norfolk had ridden off southward with his *galloglaiches* and personal staff, Archbishop Harold of York and Rupen Ademian took turns supervising the three master stonemasons—two of them Northumbrians, one a Lowland Scot found for Sir Geoffrey by Laird Michael Scott—and the dozen or so journeymen and apprentices bringing in the inch-or-more-thick slabs of slate, marking and chipping and carving and smoothing them, before carefully laying them end to end and edge to edge in the handspan-deep bed of mortar that covered the old earthern floor of the tower keep's ground level. The masons and other workmen, the oxmen and quarrymen, none of them questioned this project or even thought to so do. It had been ordered by a mighty lord, and they were one and all more than happy to take his silver and thank God for the unexpected largesse that the work brought to them and their families. They all could be assured, now, of enough food to bear them through the coming winter, good harvest or ill.

Wain after wain trundled down from Scotland, behind spans of sturdy, slow-plodding red-and-white oxen, each loaded to near overflowing with fine-quality potter's clay from the claypits on Laird Scott's demesne. At Whyffler Hall, the clay was shoveled into sacks and baskets to be stored in various outbuildings until needed, safe there from rains and mists.

Laird Michael Scott did not question just what the Sassenachs at Whyffler Hall intended to do with so much clay. It was none of his business, for one thing; for another, Laird Michael was more than happy to get the silver that Sir Geoffrey Musgrave promptly paid him or his agents. Silver was hard to come by in Lowland Scotland by legal means, and the new-crowned King James had offered dire consequences to any borderer clan or family so rash as to go a-rieving into England sans his royal say-so. And Laird Michael had two sons who must shortly be fitted out as became young Scots gentlemen, as well as a daughter who one day soon would be in need of a suitable dowry.

He was, however, of an inquiring mind and a consistently curious nature, so when he met with Sir Geoffrey on a day, he asked, half-jokingly, if the denizens of Whyffler Hall had the intent of cornering the chamberpot market for all of England, Wales, and Scotland.

But Musgrave had not risen to the joke. Dead-serious had been his answer. "I dinnae ken what a' the clay be for, Laird Michael. Belike, some project o' his grace o' York. A' I ken be that my o'erlord, his grace of Norfolk, has ordered it so, and so it shall be, 'pon my sacred oath."

The archbishop had insisted that Master Rupen Ademian, though untitled as yet, was as wellborn in his own land as any present and must therefore he seated at the high table for meat. Central place at that elevated board went, of course, to the archbishop, whose rank was in most all ways the equivalent of that of a duke. Unless Laird Michael Scott was present for meat—his rank being the rough equivalent of an English baron—the archbishop was flanked by Sir Geoffrey and Don Diego. In addition to Rupen, two noble clerics of the archbishop's staff were usually present with them.

Don Diego's command of English was improving. Nonetheless, he and the archbishop usually conversed in Latin, while Rupen exercised his twentieth-century Spanish on this seventeeth-century Spaniard, quickly discovering that there were significant differences between the two tongues. For one thing, the famous Castilian lisp did not exist in Don Diego's version of Castilian Spanish.

Of a day, while the pages, squires, and other servants were briskly clearing away the remnants of the fish and carving the poultry for serving, Archbishop Harold asked, "Tell me, Don Diego, have you any relatives, distant or near, living in this Kingdom of England and Wales, perchance?"

"No," replied the Castilian knight, "that I do not, your grace. I own a few distant cousins in Valencia—outcome of

the marriage of my grandsire's half sister to one Conde
Ernesto of that realm—and one of my younger brothers is
secretary to his eminence, Cardinal de los Llanos Luviosos
de España, who presently is in Rome. . . . May one inquire
why your grace asks?''

''No thing of much import, Don Diego. It is simply that
you chance to bear a truly startling resemblance to one of my
scribes back in York, but he is of West Country English
antecedents.'' The archbishop leaned forward and bespoke
his secretary, ''Brother Hugh, see you not a resemblance
between this noble knight and one of our scribes?''

''Why, yes, now that your grace mentions it,'' replied that
worthy, setting down his cup. ''Don Diego looks the very
spit and image of young Brother Matthew Olson. They two
might be father and son or elder brother and younger, so very
similar are they.''

But then the geese were served and there was no more talk
for the while.

Arrived at the archepiscopal estate southwest of York City,
Bass proceeded with doing all that was necessary for getting
the *galloglaiches* accustomed to the pairs of new flintlock
horsepistols delivered in their absence by Pete Fairley. Those
now with him would have the job of teaching those left in
Norwich. Several pack-mule loads of the new arms and their
accessories were ready and waiting at the manufactory in
York.

Bass had intended to send Nugai—who was an old friend
of Pete Fairley's—over to York to arrange a rendezvous point
for the loaded mules along his line of march, but surprisingly
was unable to find the usually faithful little yellow-brown
man. Nor did he come across him, not for more than two
days. So he ended by sending Sir Ali ibn Hussain.

When the missing Kalmyk finally did turn up, it was with
abject apologies. He recounted that he had been herb-hunting
around the countryide, seeking out ingredients for the various
salves and medicines he concocted, remarking that he had
come to know the plants of England better than he was likely

to know those of the land where they so shortly would be bound and where, was there fighting, they surely would have need of some of his nostrums.

For his own part, Bass was so plesed to have back the little nomad with his quick, intuitive mind, his amazing level of intelligence, and his easy adaptability to all the circumstances that they had encountered, to date, that he forgot his brief flash of anger at the unannounced and protracted absence and got back to his own duties, leaving Nugai alone to sort and prepare his sacks of ingredients. For, with the dawn, they all would depart for Norwich.

The elder and the younger met but briefly, once more by night, once more in a graveyard, though not the same graveyard.

"We have a problem" said the elder. "You set the controls and I sent all save two of them a-journeying, barely within the set time period. But I have just visited the point from which they all were snatched at the proper reference points. They are not there. Through manipulations, I jockeyed back and forth, and while I could witness their disappearances, I could find no trace of any reappearances. So where has your bungling inexperience sent these projectees? Riddle me that."

The younger hung his head in contrition, while the elder went on. "Nor is that all, or even the worst of the problem. When I journeyed down to check the settings on the journey device, I found it and the entire repository gone, torn from out the earth like a rotten tooth, leaving only a hole wherein the foundations had been so long set."

The younger gulped. "Then I am trapped here, with no way to journey in either distance or time or between the universes."

"Just so." The elder man nodded again. "And I'll be far too busy on this level to journey to where I can secure you another device for some months. So lie low in York and live the part of your present persona until I return; it is all that you can do. Let this serve as a lesson to you. Our work here is vital to our people; moreover, the price of failure in performance of assigned tasks is usually suffering of some nature, sometimes personal extinction. Let us hope that your eventual price be not so steep.''

State Police Lieutenant Martin Gear sat behind his office desk, chewing at the knuckle of his thumb until the two FBI agents were done. Then he could hold it back no longer.

He grinned maliciously as he said, ''Well, you damn federal hotshots come up just as dry as me and mine did, didn't you? I never knew just why yawl were called in on this case anyhow. It all fell within my state, and ain't nothing to make anybody think it might be kidnapping.''

One of the agents looked quizzically at the other, briefly, and the other said, ''Hell, Larry, it won't hurt to tell him, now.''

''Lieutenant Gear,'' began the agent called Larry, ''the missing men, the ones to whom you have been referring in press interviews as 'cheap A-rab musicians,' are neither Arabs nor cheap, not by any means. Their band was a hobby to them. One was a Greek, one was a Syrian-American, but most of them were Armenian-Americans, all but one American-born. Two of them are very wealthy men in their own right, the rest are the sons of wealthy, well-connected businessmen.

''Surely you are familiar with Ademian Enterprises, Incorporated, and its subsidiary, Souvenirs, Incorporated?''

Lieutenant Gear nodded. ''So?''

''All save a couple of the missing men are connected to those firms either by birth or employment or both, and one of the out-of-state Ademian plants is producing some very sensitive material under federal contract.''

''I'll take over, Larry,'' said the senior agent. ''So sensitive is this material, Lieutenant Gear, that certain foreign powers have already gone to a great deal of trouble and expense to try to get samples and plans. So far their schemes have all been foiled.

''Now consider these facts, Lieutenant: All of the audience that night on that secluded estate far from the main roads were foreign-born—Iranians and a few assorted Arabs—and Iran shares a long border with the Soviet Union; Mr. Kogh Ademian is the chairman of the board of Ademian Enterprises, Incorporated, and the missing band leader, Arsen Ademian, is his son.

"Are you beginning to grasp an inkling of just why we were called in on this case, Lieutenant Gear? Why we intend to continue that investigation, however long it takes, until we turn up firm evidence of just what happened out there that night?"

Gear looked bewildered. "Well, what the hell can I do, boys? My department couldn't turn up any more than yours could on it, and we all flat-out worked, too, till that fellow Asissi got a court order to keep us off his estate, anyway."

"That's 'Azizi,' Lieutenant Gear," put in Larry informatively.

The senior agent, Jerry, grinned. "Well, the distinguished Ameer Azizi knows better than to try that kind of garbage with us—he'd find his green card lifted so fast it would make his self-important head swim! He and his fellow oil million-aires may *think* that they've bought this country lock, stock, and barrel, but they haven't, not yet, not by a long shot.

"No, what we'll be needing from you, Lieutenant Gear, is the full cooperation of you and your department—willing cooperation, this time, not the grudging cooperation we had to pressure your governor into ordering you to give us. With that kind of help and with any kind of luck, we should be able to get to the bottom of these strange disappearances within the time that I've promised the director we can have the case solved."

Martin Gear shook his head again, sorrowfully. "Boys, you got it. Whatever me and mine can do for you, give you, is yours. But I can't help feeling this feeling that it ain't nothing in this old world is going to help you one damn bit in finding them people. Nothing in this world."

ABOUT THE AUTHOR

ROBERT ADAMS lives in Seminole County, Florida. Like the characters in his books, he is partial to fencing and fancy swordplay, hunting and riding, good food and drink. At one time Robert could be found slaving over a hot forge, making a new sword or busily reconstructing a historically accurate military costume, but, unfortunately, he no longer has time for this as he's far too busy writing.

Ⓢ

Great Science Fiction from SIGNET